Sword Art Online Alternative

Sword Art Online Alternative
Gun Gale Online
III

2nd Squad Jam: Finish

Keiichi Sigsawa

ILLUSTRATION BY
Kouhaku Kuroboshi

SUPERVISED BY
Reki Kawahara

CONTENTS

DESIGN: BEE-PEE

Sword Art Online Alternative

GUN GALE ONLINE III

2nd Squad Jam: Finish

Keiichi Sigsawa

ILLUSTRATION BY
Kouhaku Kuroboshi

SUPERVISED BY
Reki Kawahara

YEN ON

NEW YORK

SWORD ART ONLINE Alternative Gun Gale Online, Vol. 3
KEIICHI SIGSAWA

Translation by Stephen Paul
Cover art by Kouhaku Kuroboshi

SWORD ART ONLINE Alternative Gun Gale Online Vol. III
©KEIICHI SIGSAWA / REKI KAWAHARA 2015
First published in Japan in 2015 by KADOKAWA CORPORATION, Tokyo.
English translation rights arranged with KADOKAWA CORPORATION, Tokyo,
through TUTTLE-MORI AGENCY, INC., Tokyo.

English translation © 2019 by Yen Press, LLC

Yen On
1290 Avenue of the Americas
New York, NY 10104

Visit us at yenpress.com
facebook.com/yenpress
twitter.com/yenpress
yenpress.tumblr.com
instagram.com/yenpress

First Yen On Edition: February 2019

Yen On is an imprint of Yen Press, LLC.
The Yen On name and logo are trademarks of Yen Press, LLC.

Library of Congress Cataloging-in-Publication Data
Names: Sigsawa, Keiichi, 1972– author. | Kuroboshi, Kouhaku, illustrator. |
    Paul, Stephen (Translator), translator.
Title: Second Squad Jam : finish / Keiichi Sigsawa ; illustration by Kouhaku Kuroboshi ;
    translation by Stephen Paul.
Description: First Yen On edition. | New York, NY : Yen On, February 2019. |
    Series: Sword art online alternative gun gale online ; Volume 3
Identifiers: LCCN 2018057016 | ISBN 9781975353858 (pbk.)
Subjects: CYAC: Fantasy games—Fiction. | Virtual reality—Fiction. |
    Role playing—Fiction.
Classification: LCC PZ7.1.S537 Sas 2018 | DDC [Fic]—dc23
LC record available at https://lccn.loc.gov/2018057016

ISBNs: 978-1-9753-5385-8 (paperback)
          978-1-9753-5391-9 (ebook)

10 9 8 7 6 5 4 3 2 1

LSC-C

Printed in the United States of America

THE 2nd SQUAD JAM FIELD MAP

Sword Art Online Alternative
GUN GALE ONLINE

Playback
of
2nd SQUAD JAM

After the first Squad Jam, Karen got to be good friends with Saki and her team of high schoolers. Having them over at her apartment to hang out and drink tea was a level of sociability that had seemed impossible to Karen not long ago. In the meantime, she wasn't as deep into *GGO* as she used to be.

During this period, a second Squad Jam was abruptly announced. Karen wasn't enthusiastic about participating, but M's real-life player, Goushi, who somehow knew her real identity and address, spurred her on.

"On the night of the second Squad Jam, someone is going to die."

Apparently, Pitohui was intending to take part in the tournament, and if she died during the event, she would die in real life, too. Goushi

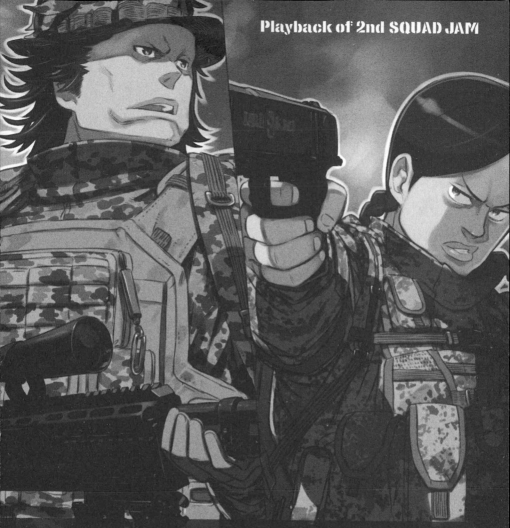

begged Karen to help save her… After much agonizing, Karen decided to enter SJ2 to complete her mission: kill Pitohui in Squad Jam, the only way to avoid the worst-case scenario…

At last, the event arrived.

In order to reach Pitohui as quickly as possible, Llenn teamed up with her hometown friend Miyu, who converted her character over from *ALfheim Online*. Miyu's avatar, Fukaziroh, dual-equipped powerful grenade launchers to blow their enemy obstacles to smithereens.

Meanwhile, Pitohui and M's team utterly brutalized an enemy team that was foolish enough to attack them.

Can Llenn triumph over Pitohui's power and madness—and save her erstwhile friend?

CHAPTER 10

Ten-Minute Massacre II (Start)

SECT.10

CHAPTER 10
Ten-Minute Massacre II (Start)

Ten minutes earlier, at 1:40 PM...

The same moment that Pitohui's group had successfully lured their foes into the ravine trap and begun counting down to massacre, in fact.

"Let's check the scan!" said Llenn, a tiny shrimp dressed in pink who was all dusty from falling down.

"You got it!" replied Fukaziroh, the other shrimp, dressed in a MultiCam camo shirt, matching shorts, and a green vest, with a huge grenade launcher in either hand, as they stood at the edge of a giant dome.

The dome, which was a mile and a quarter across and several hundred yards high, was just like any other mountain up close. Its walls were made of some mysterious white material with no seams whatsoever. They curved gently toward the reddish-brown sky.

There was what appeared to be a door every three hundred feet or so that would provide entry. They had to pray that as long as you could get in, you could also get out.

The girls had watched the one-thirty scan at the train station and taken the next ten minutes to travel to the dome. They hadn't encountered any enemies along the way.

The area surrounding the dome was soft, empty earth that once supported grass but was now dried and dead. The visibility was good, and while there were no enemies in eyeshot, Llenn and

Fukaziroh were staying vigilant. They were on their bellies, facing away from the dome. Llenn placed her Satellite Scan terminal on the ground in front of her and turned it on.

The fourth scan of SJ2 began.

This one started from the north and pushed its way south.

They tapped the lit dots for the surviving teams to check their names. The fearsome members of MMTM were still alive in the mountainous region to the northeast of the dome. The championship contenders were living up to their reputation.

Once the scan passed the dome, Llenn grunted. "Ugh..."

They were northwest of the dome's circle on the map, right at the ten-o'clock position with north being up. But directly to the south, at the six-o'clock position, was Boss's team: SHINC.

"But why are there so many...?"

And right under the dome, practically in the middle, were three more teams.

Llenn tapped them, but she didn't recognize any of the names. They were about one or two thousand feet apart. By Squad Jam standards, that was very close, so they could well have been in combat, but it was impossible to tell from atop the dome.

"Gaaah! Stay out of our way!" she yelled. The quickest route to Pitohui was through this dome. Why did there have to be three whole teams inside?

"Guess I'm not the 'lucky girl' this time around," she grumbled.

"Now, now," Fukaziroh lectured. "You should know that we Japanese have a superstition about infusing spoken words with the power to make them come true."

The seven dots in the southeast region of the map were in exactly the same locations as ten minutes ago. Pitohui's team didn't seem to have budged at all, either.

It wasn't too much of a stretch to imagine the other teams leaving their leaders together and sneaking up the mountain in one big group.

Pito, M, good luck! Llenn prayed. *Please don't die until I can kill you.*

"No new disqualified teams. Seventeen still left. There are a few in the west and the northeast, but aside from the squads in the dome, nobody seems likely to run into us!" Fukaziroh announced as soon as the scan was finished.

"Oh...thanks." Llenn had been so distracted by Pitohui that she'd forgotten to count the dots. It was a good thing her partner was paying attention.

"..."

Llenn stayed on all fours, considering what to do for their next move. To help her organize her thoughts, she spoke them out loud to Fukaziroh. "In order to reach Pito, going through the dome is by far the quickest route, but there are three squads inside..."

"That's right."

"If we go around the dome, it'll take longer. Plus, if we go around to the north, it's likely we'll run into MMTM, a tough enemy. On the south side, we'll collide with SHINC."

"That's right."

"Fuka... Could you grow some wings on your back right now? Then you could carry me and fly over the dome, right?"

"Sadly, that's not possible. I'm not a fairy anymore."

"So we'll have to pick one of those three routes..."

"Not so fast. It's too early to decide that, Llenn. Regardless of the final choice, we ought to see what's going on inside this dome. We can still pick after that," Fukaziroh advised.

Llenn's face shot up. "Oh... Good point. Thanks," she said, leaping to her feet and trotting to the door.

"It's the women who get their men to say 'If you didn't have me around, you'd be helpless' that get the most romantic attention," Fukaziroh murmured, skipping after her.

They weren't the only ones who weren't sure what to do next after the 1:40 scan.

"Hrmm..."

Saki's character, named Eva, aka Boss, was in the same boat.

Her team was on the south end of the massive dome, right outside one of the entrances, watching for hostiles as they waited.

"So what do we do now...?" grumbled the woman with the stern features and braids, her wide rear end planted in the dirt and thick arms folded.

"It's so strange to see you worrying, Boss," said Anna, the blond beauty checking the surrounding area through her Dragunov sniper rifle's scope, about twenty yards away.

"But she looks cool. Like she should have a big bottle of sake next to her! Like a samurai!" said Tohma, her black-haired sniping partner, who was glancing sidelong, away from her binoculars.

"Well, whatever she chooses, we'll follow!" exclaimed Tanya, the silver-haired, foxy-eyed woman with her Bizon held at the ready on the opposite side of their defensive circle.

"Okay, let's be honest. She's trying to figure out whether to go into the dome or not."

"Meaning?" asked Sophie the dwarf, the shortest and squattest of the members. She and Rosa, the tough mama in prone firing position with her PKM machine gun, were on support at the moment.

Then they heard Boss's voice through the communication items they all wore.

"If we go into the dome, we might end up facing the three teams loitering inside all at once."

"Uh-huh," murmured Sophie.

When the team captain (Saki, aka Boss) and vice-captain (Kana, aka Sophie) had a serious discussion, the other members had to be quiet and listen. That was the rule, both in real life and in the virtual world.

"If Llenn's team or MMTM or possibly both go into the dome, it's going to be total chaos for the next ten or twenty minutes. We'd win, of course, but we might suffer more than a little damage as a result."

"Good point. Llenn and those guys are pretty tough."

2ND SQUAD JAM: FINISH

"But it's not my style to run away from a fight. We haven't fired a shot in over twenty minutes."

"True. I'm stiffening up over here."

"But there's one concern on my mind. What if Llenn's team goes around, rather than through, the dome? Around the north, we won't contact them, and our fight will have to wait. If they go south, we'll have the clash we've been waiting for..."

"But if we go into the dome, we won't be able to come into contact for the next ten minutes."

"That's right. Especially since the inside of that dome is all—," Boss started to gripe, then caught herself. "Argh! It's a waste of time just going back and forth! We're warriors! We're going inside in search of combat!"

After most of a minute of deliberation, Boss decided to fight.

"Let's go, ladies! It's our first jungle battle!"

While the Amazons were busy roaring a big "Urrraaahh!" on the opposite side of the dome, Llenn and Fukaziroh were screaming on their own.

"Wh-what is thaaaat?!"

"Hya-eeeeee!!"

They were shrill and loud and probably overheard by any potential enemies in earshot.

Inside the dome, they headed through the sliding door, which opened quite easily, and proceeded down a long tunnel through the exterior structure of the dome to find...a southern paradise.

"It's a jungle...!"

"It's a jungle...!"

Unlike the cold, colorless world they'd been in moments before, this place was green and lush. Grass grew everywhere, as tall as a human being, and the ground was nearly invisible. Here and there were giant gnarled trees seventy feet tall, their trunks coated in moss. Their branches exploded with leaves, forming a canopy that blocked out the sky.

Which was, in fact, totally blue.

Since this was inside the dome, it was really just the ceiling and undoubtedly designed to look that way, but it was indistinguishable from the real thing. Llenn had spent dozens of hours in *GGO* by this point, and this was the very first time she'd ever seen blue sky here. The lost environment of Earth was still alive under this roof.

"Wow...," Llenn marveled.

"This is incredible! It's a completely different world under this dome! How awesome! It's a greenhouse, right? Or maybe a nature park? What's the deal?" Fukaziroh jabbered. She seemed to be feeling nostalgic for her old haunt of *ALO*, which was famous for its lush, natural setting.

It was fun just to drink in the sight, but they couldn't allow themselves to be distracted. Llenn had to make up her mind right away. Were they going to charge through the mile or so of the dome, which housed three enemy squads, or would they take the detour around it?

The longer she pondered, the more valuable time trickled away. She wasn't going to waste any more of it or suffer additional mistakes.

"I've decided!"

"Huh? Decided what?" asked Fukaziroh. She was the type of girl who suggested something and then, moments later, asked what they were talking about.

"Dargh! You were the one who said we should peek into the dome, then decide whether to charge through it or go around!"

"Oh! Yeah, that's important!"

"So we're gonna go through the jungle! Yeah, there are three teams in there, but the chances of getting one-hit killed are lower here than outside, where the visibility is good," Llenn said, opening her game window. She pulled out a green camo poncho from her item storage.

It materialized out of thin air, and she wriggled her head through the collar. It enveloped her body all the way down to the ankles, so the only part of her that was pink now was her shoes.

"Llenn just disappeared! Wh-where did she go?" Fukaziroh joked, peering around from just ten feet away.

"Don't worry," Llenn said helpfully. "I'm right here."

"Oh, there you are. But seriously, don't go too far away, because I might lose sight of you, and that'd be kinda scary, okay?"

"Sure. But the same goes for the enemy. If they split off from one another, they could have a hard time connecting again."

If the entire dome was jungle like this, visibility might be five yards at the worst and maybe fifty at best. That was unbelievably poor compared to anywhere outside. That meant that, for one thing, you couldn't do teamwork like support fire with machine guns or sniper rifles while others charged up close. All three teams inside must have been struggling with this.

"But the bullets will still come, even if you can't see," Llenn warned. And it was true; thick grass was no match for the piercing power of a bullet. The unique part about fighting in a jungle was that it offered plenty of places to hide but very little protection from actual gunfire.

"I see. So if they just spray machine-gun fire horizontally, you're still vulnerable? That's scary. But at least you can see the lines."

"Well, I've thought of a plan for us to get through this battlefield without getting split up—and one that will allow us to fight if we need to. If it all goes well… No, I'm sure it will!"

"Oh? What kind of plan?" asked Fukaziroh, leaning in closer despite the presence of their comm units. Llenn reacted in kind, putting her mouth next to Fuka's ear.

When the plan had been relayed, Fukaziroh's eyes went wide and blinked.

"Hya-hoo! I love it! It sounds fun!" she exclaimed, like a kid receiving an allowance. "But…won't that be dangerous for you?" she followed up, switching to play the role of the parent concerned for her child.

And Llenn was the kid going off to live on her own for the very first time.

"I know."

*   *   *

Three minutes earlier, back at the moment prior to the 1:40 scan, a man inside the dome's jungle screamed.

"Shit! I hate this horrible place!"

He belonged to one of the three teams inside the dome. His camo was in a gray gradient pattern, both fatigues and helmet, and he wore a thick-looking protection vest around the torso. It was the team's uniform style, designed to blend in well with the concrete jungle, but it was having the opposite effect in the regular old jungle.

The man was crouching amid the thick, tall grass, clutching a ZB-26 in his hands. It was a Czechoslovakian machine gun designed in 1926, as the name implied. Despite being a century old, it was known for having good stats and hardly ever breaking down; it was right at the top of the list of "recommended machine guns that are cheap and totally acceptable quality" in *GGO*.

"Where are you guys? Are you actually nearby?" he asked through the comm.

"Sure we are. Just stand up, and you'll see. Don't worry about it," came the immediate answer. But crouched down where he was, all he could see were stalks of green grass. It was scary, feeling like you really were all alone in the overgrowth.

"This is a fresh green hell…"

From the moment they walked into the dome, it had been jungle, jungle, jungle.

It was completely flat and unchanging, hard to traverse, and had no good visual features for gauging distance traveled. At this point, they had no idea where they were anymore.

Without visibility or a grasp on their location, the team came to a stop, determining that it was dangerous just to wander around.

Each member spread out to reduce the danger of being taken out by random bursts of fire, and from there, they awaited the next scan.

At last, the time had arrived. The leader said, "Scan's coming up. All of you, check your screens."

The man followed this order, pulling the Satellite Scan terminal out of his thigh pocket and turning it on. He watched the results from the scan come in.

Then he went pale. "E...e-e-en-en-en..."

He could see his position on the device's screen—almost in the middle of the dome. They had traveled halfway through the jungle. Mentally, it felt like much farther, so maybe it was more accurate to say they'd *wandered* that far.

And he saw the enemy's location. Frighteningly enough, their dot was just a few hundred yards from his own squad's. Two of them, in fact, on either side.

"E-enemies! They're close!"

"Don't shout, dumbass!" shouted one of his teammates.

"What should we do, Leader?"

"Crap, I dunno, man... Dammit, they're so close! Holy crap!" stammered their squad leader. He was not taking it well.

Oh boy... We might be screwed, thought the man with the ZB-26, feeling resignation sink in.

The regrets were numerous.

They shouldn't have gone into the dome just because it looked interesting. They shouldn't have headed into the jungle just because it was rare in a setting like *GGO*'s. They shouldn't have determined the squad leader by a game of rock-paper-scissors, just because nobody wanted to nominate themselves for the job.

"Don't shoot! Don't shoot! Do not shoot!"

He was starting to hear things at last. This wasn't through the comm but was a faint, actual voice. No enemy would say such a thing, so this was obviously just his ears playing a trick on him.

"Hear me out! You guys over there! I want to talk! Please don't shoot!" continued the hallucination, getting louder and clearer. "Got that? Don't shoot me! I've unequipped my guns! Please!"

The voice was close enough to sound fairly ordinary now. "Guys, I think I'm done. I'm hearing things. I've done too much gaming. I need to log off."

The man waved his left hand to call up the window and looked for the LOGOUT button.

A warning said THE SECOND SQUAD JAM EVENT IS CURRENTLY ACTIVE. IF YOU LOG OUT OF *GGO* NOW, YOU WILL NOT BE ABLE TO REENTER THE EVENT. ARE YOU SURE YOU WANT TO LOG OUT?

"No, you idiot!"

He was about an inch away from pressing the YES button when one of his teammates rushed over and grabbed his arm to pull it away.

There were eighteen people gathered into one place in the jungle.

"This is the worst battleground I can imagine for a fight. I think we're all in agreement that it was a mistake to come in here," said one man while the other seventeen listened.

The eighteen were split into three groups.

One team wore gray camo. Another wore a pattern of red and brown, a rusty mix that would help them only in an autumn setting. The last team shared no clothing in common; their appearances were all over the place.

The man in rust-red camo carrying an AC-556F assault rifle continued his speech:

"At the last scan, we learned that the previous champion, LF; the runner-up team, SHINC; and third-place MMTM are all in the vicinity of the dome. They're going to come in here—mark my words. That's the way battle royale works: You attack the closest threat."

He had no idea what exactly had brought Llenn to participate this time, so he was speaking only of the general strategy for the event. "We should team up and hit them back! There are seven teams in the southeast corner of the map, working together. Who says we can't do the same thing? My team managed to take out another one last time by cleaning up the scraps, and then someone else did us in the same way. So it occurred to me—you ought to team up with other groups to survive in Squad Jam! In fact, one of the great aspects of this format is wondering how you should approach another squad to work together!"

The man who got blown up by the team consisting of Air Self-Defense Force members last time was passionate in his delivery. "There must be some cosmic reason that we got so close without firing and met up without any kind of combat first! Let's work together! Let's take down all those heavy hitters on our own!"

"Question for you, teacher!"

Two seconds after his plea was over, a character dressed in a black top and bottoms with a number of long, narrow pouches across his front raised his hand.

"Yeah, you! The handsome guy! What is it?" asked the leader of the rust-red team affably.

Indeed, the question-asker had a tremendously handsome avatar. "Don't call me handsome. My name is Clarence. But everyone calls me Clay," he protested. Even his voice was handsome, though.

He was the kind of character you would expect to do gangbusters in a VR game where the player is a male singer who gets to perform in front of screaming women all day long. Of course, there was no guarantee he would get the same avatar if he converted his character to such a game.

"Your question, Clay! Go right ahead!"

Clarence continued. "Let's say that everything you just said works out, and we beat all the major contenders right here and now. Shall we assume that from the moment they're out of the picture, our bloody battle resumes? Or to be blunt, is that when you turn and stick the barrel of your gun straight up the ass of the guy next to you?"

Geez, why did he have to put it that way? wondered everyone else. They didn't say it out loud, but it was clear from their body language.

Whether in *GGO* or another VR game, there were certainly plenty of players who derived pleasure from killing their opponents in gruesome ways. A game is a game, of course, and if you were tough enough, you could do what you wanted.

But it was still a fact that people could think, *What's wrong with you as a person?* and avoid you accordingly. Even Clarence's own teammates in their random outfits didn't seem to want anything to do with him.

Of course, the leader of the red-camo team had no choice but to answer the question posed to him. "You know, you might be handsome, but you've got issues… Anyway, it's a good question. I bet everyone wants to know the answer."

"And? Are we pro or anti shooting up the ass?"

"I want to say no. So I propose a gentleman's agreement that if we eliminate all enemies outside our alliance, we wait until the next scan to aggress against one another. And if that scan happens to be close—say, within three minutes—we'll wait until the scan after the next one. What do you say to that?"

The gentlemen replied, "Very well."

"No objections here."

"I agree. That's for the best."

"Three minutes seems appropriate. If we run without a second glance, we should be able to get out of firing range in that time."

Each member had his thoughts, but none argued against it.

"What do you say, Clay?"

Clarence simply shrugged and said, "Roger that. I'm not a gentleman, but I can get my killing on at any time, so I'm fine with it. Thank you for the answer."

"Great! Then the eighteen of us are partners! Let's do what we can to survive this jungle! We'll defeat our hardy foes with the power of numbers!" the leader shouted.

"But…what exactly is our plan? We've all been practicing teamwork within our own squads, but how are we supposed to do that with other groups?" said someone on the gray-camo team. The others nodded and murmured in agreement with the sentiment.

Within a team, each member had a clear role: who lays down covering fire with a machine gun, who sneaks around the side in the meantime, and so on. It would be very difficult to effectively work that way with a character you just met moments ago.

Another person raised his hand. "And the visibility is atrocious. We can barely work as individual teams. Did you consider that before you suggested a unified regiment?"

This, too, was a reasonable question. All eyes turned back to the leader of the red team. He grinned, as if this was what he'd been waiting for the entire time.

"Yes! I have an idea. I think we should use the trick that beat our team last Squad Jam. Listen closely, gang..."

When their undivided attention was on him, he said, "What do you think is the best way to know what another person is doing when visibility is bad?"

*   *   *

1:43 PM.

A little green gremlin crawled through the thick of the jungle.

It was Llenn in her camo poncho. When she moved in a crouched position, she was entirely hidden in the grass, and with the help of her camo, she was essentially invisible. The only hint of her presence was the faint sound of rustling grass.

Like the movement of an insect that shall not be named, crawling on the floor of a messy room.

"I've gone a hundred yards. No sign of hostiles," she said, her voice traveling to Fukaziroh's ear.

"Roger that. I'll catch up now. Just guide me in the right direction," replied her teammate.

Then Llenn engaged in something different. She turned back the way she came, readied her P90 at her shoulder underneath the poncho, placed her finger on the trigger—and aimed it at Fukaziroh.

It almost looked like she was aiming at her enemy through the jungle. Llenn saw the bullet circle it produced.

"Okay, I see it!" cried Fukaziroh. A few dozen seconds later, she came charging through the jungle, straight along the line, until she reached a spot where Llenn could see her.

"Good. Me next." Llenn lowered her P90 and turned on her heel. This time, it was Fukaziroh who aimed her weapon. She pointed the MGL-140 barrel toward Llenn and brushed her finger against the trigger. It produced a red spray of a bullet line that stretched forward over the jungle grass.

"I see it," Llenn said, looking up at the line reaching over her back, and started running.

As long as a bullet could maintain its velocity and keep flying, the bullet line would continue through obstacles. So Llenn's idea was this: "A jungle's just tall grass, so the bullet will keep going, and so will the line. If we use our bullet lines to shine at each other, we should be able to keep moving straight forward without losing track of each other!"

It was dangerous for her to be the lead person pushing ahead, but that was utterly familiar to her by this point. They tested out her idea and found that it was actually even more effective than she thought it would be.

They repeated this pattern, back and forth, and pushed through the jungle with impressive speed.

Then, at 1:44, Fukaziroh caught up to Llenn and was preparing to shine her bullet line forward at a distance of thirty feet, when they heard a gunshot.

"Get down!"

"Got it!"

Llenn and Fukaziroh hit the soft dirt of the jungle, listening to raw gunfire.

There was a quick drumroll of 5.56 mm automatic fire, *ta-ta-ta-ta-ta-ta-ta-tam*, and the heavier fire of a 7.62 mm gun, *do-do-do-do-do-do-doom*. On top of that was the woodpecker-fast rhythm of what sounded like a submachine gun with pistol rounds, *ta-ra-ra-ra-ra-ra*.

They couldn't see any muzzle flashes, due to the thick jungle overgrowth, but Llenn could tell by the sound.

"Ahead to the left. About two or three hundred yards off. Not quite the direction we're heading." She looked upward, watching carefully. "Can't see any bullet lines. The gunfire isn't coming this way."

"Okay! It must be those three teams! They're all fighting! I hope they eliminate one another! Make it easier on us!" Fuka-ziroh said, not bothering to hide how she really felt.

Llenn agreed with her. She listened to the sounds of continuous battle for another five seconds. "Something's…strange."

It just wasn't quite right. There was something about the way the guns were firing. She couldn't tell what it was yet, though.

"It's weird… Something's weird, Fuka!"

"What is?"

"The guns I'm hearing—," she started to say, right as she figured out the answer.

And with it, the enemy's strategy.

"Oh, I get it! I know what it is! It's a trap!"

Right at that moment, most of the audience in the pub was watching Pitohui's battle.

"I wanna see more of Llenn kicking ass."

"Yeah. I hope she shows up soon," said a pair of creeps obsessed with young girls—or perhaps just some fellows who enjoyed watching cute little girls. Apparently, their wish came true, because one of the screens abruptly cut to a scene full of greenery.

"Yes! Here we go! Is it gonna be Llenn?" they cheered. Others nearby began to murmur to their friends, noting that the previous champion was about to get into the thick of things.

On the screen, a number of people were shooting in the midst of a dense jungle setting.

There were two members each from three different teams, six

in all, lined up in a row. They were all firing right into the jungle undergrowth. Dozens of leaves and blades of grass flew into the air from the bullets, the muzzle exhaust hanging thick in the air.

The audience already knew that the three teams were working together, because they'd seen the footage of them talking it out. So it was clear that they must have made contact with some other squad by now. However, usually a battle prompted images from both sides of the combat, and it was just the one source at the moment.

The only things in the four frames caught by four cameras were alternate angles of the six shooting into the greenery. That meant they were firing one-sided at an unseen enemy, and yet, it didn't look like they were wasting ammo out of fear.

"Wait… Who the hell are they fighting?" the audience started to wonder.

"Oh, I bet I know. One of those invisible aliens who came to Earth to hunt humans and prove their worth as heroes."

"You mean like that old movie?!"

"Who knows—maybe it was just a normal monster? Wasn't there a boss monster that had optical camo or something?"

"Have you ever heard of a monster spawning in the middle of a battle royale tournament?"

"I just mean inside this dome! It's not like there's ever been a jungle in *GGO* before—it could happen! Maybe it's a message saying, 'Hey, watch out—this area has traps!'"

"Actually, now that you mention it…"

While most of the audience prattled on about nonsense, there was one sharp-eyed observer in their midst who figured out the trick.

"No, it's not that… No monsters. They're not fighting anyone. They're just shooting."

"Huh? Why? Target practice…?"

"Nope. They're creating the false impression that they're currently engaged in battle."

"Oh!" "I get it!" "Of course!"

It all clicked into place. The three teams were working together to fight off Llenn's team, or Boss's team, or MMTM, whichever one entered the jungle. Any of those three would be a fearsome foe, so even with the advantage of numbers, the teamed-up group had to be cautious.

Therefore, they laid a trap.

If they continually fired into empty space, they could create the appearance of a firefight in progress. That way, a third party might think they should sneak up and join in, picking off one of the weakened combatants.

The leader of the rust-red camo team understood this well, as his squad had been eliminated before with just such a trick. So he was determined to turn the tables and use it himself this time.

"Ah, I get it… That's clever. You can't see anything in the jungle, but you can still hear the gunshots from a distance."

"And Llenn and the other teams don't know that the three squads are working together yet, right? It just makes sense that you'd assume they ran across one another and started fighting."

"Then you wander in, hoping to take advantage…only to get ambushed by the other members."

"Exactly. So the other twelve from that group are probably scattered around the area, lying in wait."

"If we get too close, hoping to take advantage of them, the other members around the area will get us."

"Ohhhh… But how did you figure that out, Llenn?"

Llenn and Fukaziroh were having a strategy meeting in the midst of the jungle. The gunfire was still audible now and then.

"The shots are coming from the same direction and distance. It's too unnatural. It can only mean that they're lined up in the same spot, shooting in the same direction."

"My, what excellent ears you have. What kind of skill is that?"

"It's the 'got combat training from M' skill," Llenn replied, all the while thinking, *I'm so glad he trained me in this stuff before the last Squad Jam.* She'd had no idea how useful that kind of information could be before he taught her.

"So what's our plan? Do we circle around and catch them from behind?"

"If I didn't have a more important goal, I would probably do that," Llenn admitted. "But instead, we'll quietly and slowly escape from their net. I wouldn't want to waste valuable ammo on this."

"Roger. That sounds best, I guess."

"We're going to swing around to the right a bit. Make a line for me again."

"Okay. I'll place it about a hundred yards ahead."

Fukaziroh used the MGL-140 to light the way with another bullet line. Llenn ducked beneath it and rustled through the jungle, scuttling like the afore-unnamed insect. Once she had gone about fifty yards, she suddenly called out, "Fuka! Lower the range about thirty yards and shoot!"

Is all the luck I had last time getting canceled out this time? Llenn wondered, cursing her misfortune.

There were four enemies before her, just barely over thirty feet ahead through the jungle. They were crouched beside an especially thick patch of grass, watching alertly. One particularly attentive soldier spotted Llenn leaping from the grass and pointed his HK33 assault rifle at her. "Enemy! Right!"

Llenn hit the deck and prayed, *Please let Fukaziroh do exactly what I told her to do, right now.*

They did not know where Fukaziroh was.

Thus, the first shot was treated as a sniping bullet from an unknown hostile, and it did not display a bullet line. Her grenade burst right near the line of four combatants, all pointing their guns at Llenn. It didn't kill any of them immediately, but one suffered light shrapnel damage.

"Aaah!" "Aaah!" "Dah!" "Wha—?!"

But more importantly, it completely stunned them. The attempt to keep them from shooting their target was a success.

Thank you, Goddess Fukaziroh!

She upped her gear to full speed and started firing the P90 through her poncho. There was no conservation at this point; time for maximum firepower.

She placed her bullet circle over the nearest person and unloaded a hailstorm of bullets into him. As he died, riddled with bullets, the second target was already in her sights. She shot him right in the face. After her second kill, she had the third target lined up. Her bullets for him were merciless and many.

The fourth fired wildly with an MP5K compact SMG. One of the 9 mm bullets pierced her left arm, but Llenn kept charging, firing back as she ducked under his line.

Glowing bullet effects peppered his legs and body, and he died right as she had finished firing a full fifty bullets from the P90's magazine. Right as the DEAD tag appeared over his head, she heard a voice say, "Llenn, are you okay?"

She hesitated for a moment, considering what to say, then replied with "Fine but not ideal spotted by baddies thanks for backup used one magazine beat four guys!" in one breath.

At this rate, they should've just taken the long way around the dome. But hindsight was always twenty-twenty.

"Well, that's good! But you got shot, too!"

Llenn checked her hit points—she had lost 20 percent. That was a very inconvenient amount of damage to take. If she had lost at least one-third of her health, she would have been able to use a healing kit at full efficiency.

She exchanged her P90's magazine under the poncho and dropped the empty one on the spot. It didn't matter where you discarded items in the tournament, because at the end of the com-petition, they were all back in your possession.

This left Llenn with seven hundred bullets to use in the event.

"I'm still fine. Can you get over here?"

"I'm coming now— Aieee!" Fukaziroh suddenly screamed. Llenn heard the fierce rhythm of gunfire. "Hya-hya-hya-eee! I'm gettin' shot at! Hya-hohhh!" It was hard to tell if Fukaziroh was scared or enjoying herself.

Llenn couldn't see the situation, but she could imagine it. About fifty yards away through the jungle, Fukaziroh was under heavy fire. After they'd taken out four hostiles, the rest of the group was surely closing in fast, firing at full strength.

"Fuka! Get away from there!"

"I can't, I can't! If I look up, I'll get shot! The lines are thick and furious! Whoa! It grazed me! Yikes!"

Llenn could tell from the sound that the gunfire was coming slowly closer.

"The end is nigh for me, young Llenn... You must go on!"

A number of words floated through Llenn's mind: Abandonment. Tactics. Valuable sacrifice. Main objective. Strategic retreat. Friendship between women.

"Fuka! Can you switch out your grenades on the spot?" she asked, opening her inventory with her free hand. A window appeared and showed her item list, from which she selected one backup magazine.

"Um, yes? I'm faceup in a little hollow in the ground!"

Llenn selected another item, then hit the ok button to materialize the two things into actual space. "Then do as I say! First, shoot five shots, all in a row! Empty your ammo!"

"Um, okay! Yaaah!"

The cuter sound of Fukaziroh's grenades joined the bright and noisy gunfire. In the distance, there were explosions.

"Reload! I'll use the you-know-what over here! Tell me when you're ready!"

"Y-yeah! Got it! Hang on!"

Llenn stuck the fresh magazine into an empty pouch, then stuck the other item she produced into the barrel of the P90.

It was a metal tube over an inch and a half wide and seven inches long: the P90's silencer.

With the credits she'd earned practicing with Fukaziroh, she was finally able to find and buy this extremely rare and expensive item. The gun's high-pitched rattle was significantly quieter with it on, but because it made the gun longer, it made handling it a little inconvenient.

Ten seconds later, Fukaziroh announced, "Reloading complete! I'm ready!"

Llenn ripped off the camo poncho with her left hand and shouted, "Now shoot straight up!"

"Oh, that poor grenadier is a goner."

On the video feed, Fukaziroh's situation was dire.

Llenn's speed, combined with the shock of the grenade blast, had helped her take down four enemies, but now their entire group knew where to find them, and thus, the other fourteen were closing in.

As they moved, they formed a single row, keeping their heads low, and fired in turns. This pattern of movement with constant rotating fire kept their targets from firing back or escaping. For a brand-new group of strangers, this was an impressive strategy. Fukaziroh was completely trapped in place on the monitor.

She escaped damage because she fell into a little dip in the ground by chance, but it was clear from the tracers that their gunfire was whipping right over her head. The leaves around her were getting blasted off their branches and falling onto her.

Once they were closer, they could toss a few grenades into the hollow, and that would be the end of it.

"If she goes down, Llenn's in trouble, too, yeah?"

"At this point, with her speed, she could leave her partner behind, right? You can't handle that many guys at once. If I were Llenn, that's what I'd do..."

"But then that leaves her at a huge disadvantage. Remember how much that girl helped with the covering fire at the train station battle?"

Some of the people in the audience were carefully discussing the strategic benefits of various options.

"You keep calling them girls, but what if they're both in their thirties and just have young-looking avatars? You want that?" said one man, throwing cold water on their excitement.

"Thirty-year-old ladies? Well, I'm an eighteen-year-old virgin, and that sounds pretty awesome, if you ask me," said one brave young hero, unsolicited.

"Hey, you wanna go play one of those VR porn games sometime? If you're actually eighteen or older, I'll take you. You need someone to vouch for you to get in, though."

"Wow, really?"

"A man never goes back on his word."

"Please, sir! I'll follow you forever!"

"Sure thing! Just don't fall for *me*, got it? I only swing one way."

"Can you idiots do this somewhere else?!"

On the screen, the actually nineteen-year-old Fukaziroh shot five grenades in a row.

"Ooh!" This counterattack signal got the audience to lean forward, but the projectiles all landed off to the side. They didn't defeat any foes or stop their advance or even force them to get off their feet. "Aww…"

Fukaziroh reached around to her backpack to reload her grenades, but the audience was already cooling on her.

"Even an awesome weapon can't help in this situation."

"If she can't even get up to aim, it's kind of pointless to fire them."

On another screen, Llenn was attaching a silencer to her P90.

"Hey, Llenn's getting ready to rumble!"

"I didn't know she had one of those."

"Even the silencer's pink. That's dedication."

One of the two monitors hanging from the ceiling made it clear that Fukaziroh's reloading was done, and she had the MGL-140 ready to fire again. On the next monitor, Llenn ripped off her camo poncho, revealing her all-pink outfit. She would certainly stand out in the jungle like this.

"Huh…? Is Llenn going out in a blaze of glory?" someone wondered.

Then Fukaziroh pointed the MGL-140 straight up into the air to shoot.

"Huh…? Is she doing the same thing, too?"

The six grenades Fukaziroh shot rose into the air as a black mass, approaching the blue sky above—then lost their battle against gravity, and, in the order that she shot them, plunged to the ground around her.

It changed the color of the world.

"Whaaat?!" shouted a man in rust-red camo, firing and advancing on his target.

"What was that?!" screamed the men who were watching the battle on the TV screens. Suddenly, the jungle was completely pink.

"It worked, Llenn!"

"Okay! I see it!"

Beyond the grass in front of her, Llenn could see a world of pink. The air itself was infused with the color, and it spread like some kind of living creature. With her poncho off and pink outfit exposed, she raced at top speed for the matching color hanging in the air.

"It's smoke! Don't fire at random! Spread orders to the other teams!" shouted the man in rust-red camo, just as he was enveloped in the pink substance.

Fukaziroh had fired special smoke grenades that spread the powdery stuff around. It also happened to be a dull pink—the same color as Llenn's clothes and weapon.

There were no smoke grenades of this particular color, but thanks to Llenn's dexterity and Ballistic Customization skill, she was able to mix the exact shade of pink. Unlike similar gas attacks from monsters, this one was not poisonous. It didn't cause pain to the eyes or nose, nor did it affect breathing in any way.

The one thing it did, which was terrifying in its own way, was limit one's field of vision.

One grenade alone had a significant enough effect, but six of them? And in a cramped jungle with limited visibility to begin with and little cross breeze to clear it out?

"I can't see a damn thing…"

The fourteen survivors of the enemy conglomerate were finding out what that would be like.

"I can't see a damn thing…"

The men in the pub were in the same boat. The camera was supposedly capturing the action, but the only thing on the screen was the color pink.

It might as well have been technical difficulties on a TV station.

"Stay calm! The smoke will dissipate in moments! Don't shoot until then, or you *will* hit a friendly target! Tell your people!" came calm orders through the pink haze.

There was less than fifteen feet of visibility. The grass at their feet was clear, but as they looked ahead and around, everything had less clarity as the pink became thicker and thicker. The sky was bright and less choked with color, but there was little point in looking up if your foe wasn't a bird.

"What's going on? Why is their smoke screen pink?" someone asked, with good reason.

"Pink…? Oh. Pink…" Someone else came to a terrible understanding. "It's…her. She's coming…"

"Who?"

"Dumbass! I'm talking about the defending champion! Everyone be on guard! A pink demon is bearing down on us!" the man shouted, right as the readout for one of his squadmates' HP in the upper left corner of his vision dropped precipitously.

"That's another one!" Llenn said.

"Nice! Keep going!" Fukaziroh cheered as she hurriedly reloaded in the middle of the pink cloud. Naturally, it was another special pink smoke grenade she was packing into the MGL-140.

There were more in the backpack still. Once she was done, she'd fire off another wave of them to make sure the smoke wouldn't clear.

"I can't see now, so make sure you don't raise your head, Fuka!"

"Don't take it personally if I hit you by accident!"

Fukaziroh's firepower ensured that the entire vicinity was blasted with pink grenades, setting up a smoke screen. Then Llenn ran through the smoke, firing her P90 like crazy, which was kept quiet with her silencer.

Where would she shoot? Anywhere she could.

If she saw anything that resembled a person, she shot. If it turned out to be a tree or rock, fine—as long as she shot first. A minimum of five automatic shots.

She shot on the move. She didn't stop if she could help it. She shot as she ran and reloaded as she ran. If she ran into something and fell over, she wouldn't complain about it.

This was the kind of plan that Llenn and Fukaziroh could set up, thanks to being a team of two; the danger of friendly fire was minimized. And it was a tactic they had meant to use on Pitohui.

A last resort for use against a very fearsome enemy. Yet, here they were, using it already.

Llenn was angry—at her own overlapping ill fortune.

At her poor judgment in choosing to go into the dome.

And also at the trio of teams that chose to ally with one another and set this trap.

The last one wasn't a fair complaint to make, but that didn't stop her.

"I'm going to kill every last one of you."

Llenn tore through the cloud of pink smoke.

"What the hell is happening?!"

"I can't tell!"

With the view on every screen clouded by pink, the audience in the pub had nothing else to do but yell at one another. They understood the intent of Llenn's plan, but what was the point if they couldn't actually see what she was doing?

"I can't see my darling Llenn!"

The next moment, the screen abruptly shifted, like the famous satirical cartoon of the nouveau riche burning a bill of money to provide light to find a pair of missing shoes in the dark. *How's that? Can you see better now?*

Someone on the developer's side had mercy on the viewing audience and switched the footage to a monochrome view in which a person would show up white against a gray-and-black background.

"That's thermal vision," said a smarty-pants in the crowd, referring to the imaging technology that detected infrared signals instead. It was a type of night vision, but rather than simply amplifying light signals, it could display heat signatures, even through smoke.

As a result, any objects that were (designated by the game system to be) emitting heat would show up white on the screen. Of course, anything you actually saw in *GGO* was computer graphics, or to be even more accurate, just an imitation visual signal sent to the player's brain.

The group of people lined up in the middle of the screen had to be the trio of squads working as a team. Since they had just been firing their weapons, the barrels were white hot on the image.

There was also a small white shape sneaking up, unbeknownst to them.

It moved quickly, darting here and there so fast it left trails, and when it came close to another white shape, the gun in its hand shone brightly, and the person there would fall over, dead.

"Yahoooo! It's Llenn!"

"One of our guys is down! They should be to the left!" shouted a man in gray camo when he noticed one of his teammates' HP bar expire.

The area was still fully pink. Someone said it was going to clear up momentarily, but it had been over thirty seconds, and it was as thick as ever.

This was because Fukaziroh had reloaded and shot more smoke grenades, but the man couldn't even see that happening and had no idea what was going on.

There is a limit to how much stress a human being can endure. Surrounded by a cloud of pink, not being able to detect anything, but knowing that one's teammates are going down one after the other had to be mentally taxing.

"Damn it all!" The man in gray camo heard a shuffling noise and turned his ZB-26 machine gun in that direction and fired at full auto. "Eat this!"

"Gfhk!" he heard someone yelp amid the gunfire.

"Got 'em!" he declared triumphantly as he stopped shooting.

The next moment, a bullet came roaring back at him from the same direction, striking his machine gun and throwing up sparks.

"Gyak!" he yelped. "I'm hit!" The bullet ricocheted off his face and left a glowing mark as he toppled backward and fell onto his butt.

"Wha—?! Wait, is that *you*?" shouted one of his teammates.

When one hears loud gunfire nearby, the first instinct is to shoot back. A number of gunshots at full volume echoed through the pink smoke, mixed with the occasional scream.

"Oh, geez…"

The people in the bar understood exactly what was happening now.

The teams were shooting one another. Their comms allowed them to talk to their own squadmates, but with three different squads in the same place, coordination was nearly impossible, and the jumpier members were shooting on reflex when they heard nearby shots.

As for Llenn, once the shooting started, she hit the ground and froze. Let them shoot one another. There was just one person who passed in front of her, looking frightened, and she pumped him full of lead from below.

After a while, the chaotic, unintentional infighting trickled away, and the gunshots stopped. Llenn got to her feet and raced through the smoke, mercilessly unloading on the closest prey.

"There's a little pink one zipping around! Our guys are getting shot! You won't be able to see her!" shouted a man just as something jabbed into his right cheek from below.

"Tell your friends, 'I beat the enemy in pink; stop shooting now,'" said a menacing woman.

He didn't have to look her way to know she was not a friendly character. "A-and if I r-refuse…?" he asked.

On the screen in the pub, a small white shape pressing its P90 silencer barrel against a larger white shape opened fire.

The man shot through the cheek toppled to his left, along with his AC-556F.

"That's five!" the bar cheered.

"Eee! Ah!"

A man in gray camo within the cloud of pink swung the muzzle of the M4A1 assault rifle back and forth. Every two seconds, he would glance to his right, then to his left—to no avail in the smoke. But he kept his finger on the trigger, so he could shoot right away, just in case he saw something in the murk.

"Hya-eee!" he yelped, turning to the left. Just then, a pink ghost appeared behind his right side. The man never noticed.

A man in rust-red camo was flat on the jungle dirt. He had an AC-556F propped up and ready to fire, the bullet circle visible directly ahead.

"Here we go… Come at me, any direction…"

If the circle touched anything moving in the midst of the pink cloud, he was going to shoot. Friend or foe.

A red line split the smoke just to the side of his circle. Before he could so much as move, a swarm of 5.7 mm bullets descended on his location and riddled his body.

"Grfk!"

The audience watched as Llenn dispatched the enemy hiding over thirty feet away.

"Wait, what was that? She aimed that shot, right?"

"Yeah, she's been rushing them all, one after the other. Is she the only one who can see through the cloud?"

They were reasonable questions. The screens were all tuned to thermal vision, so the only terrain they could see was smoke. It wasn't possible to see as far as thirty feet in these conditions.

"It's the lines," someone declared. "That bullet line's gotta show up bright and clear in the smoke for it to help, right? She's just following the lines all those guys keep throwing out there—and shooting at the source."

"Oh! That makes sense!"

Argh! This is a waste of bullets! Llenn lamented as she aimed the P90 and held down the trigger for over a full second, aiming it at the root of the bullet line she just spotted. Her gun emitted a muffled burp and a stream of empty cartridges below it.

She didn't want to do all this shooting. She still had her main mission yet to come: defeating Pitohui. Waste not, want not!

She couldn't even see what her enemies looked like at the source of their bullet lines. They could be lying down or standing up. They could be completely covered in bulletproof armor, for all she knew.

So if she was going to ensure she killed them, anything less than twenty rounds felt insufficient. It was frustrating, because if she could just see their heads, three would do the trick.

She could tell she was beating them, because their lines vanished right away, but she was eating through her backup magazines quickly.

Then she saw another enemy line. She approached, evading its trajectory, and arrived at the figure casting it sooner than she'd expected. She knew he was there, but thanks to her pink outfit, the reverse did not hold true.

Llenn circled around her prey like a wildcat, placing her bullet circle over the side of the tall man's head and pressing a quick burst on the trigger.

"The next six are the last ones, Llenn!" said Fukaziroh through the communication device in Llenn's ear. She'd been regularly reloading and firing her smoke grenades.

They'd prepared twenty-four special grenades with the intention of using them against Pitohui. It was a shame that they'd already used up eighteen of them, even if they didn't have much of a choice, Llenn lamented.

"No, we're good! Save them!" she replied.

Slowly but surely, the pink smoke was growing thinner. But if Llenn's count was correct, she'd already taken out ten of their enemies.

"There are only three or four left, so I'll go around and pick them off! Take care of yourself, Fuka!"

"Gotcha!" came her response.

Llenn glanced at the P90's magazine. The clear plastic showed five rounds left. She decided to be bold and switched it out now.

With her left hand, she used the catch lever to unlock the magazine. As she lifted the muzzle to allow the magazine to fall out, she was already grabbing a new one with her other hand.

It was the sixth magazine she was now installing. That meant, including the single magazine still left in her pocket, she had 101 bullets on hand for prompt firing.

How could I use nearly two hundred bullets to take out ten people?! The waste was unthinkable. But it was necessary to ensure they survived this challenge. *Shit! Dammit! Dammit!*

Anger began to well up within her—anger at a variety of things.

"Hey! Let's get outta here!"

"Yeah! Forget fighting this monster!"

Theeere youuu aaaare. She swung her gun toward the sound of the voices.

"There! Two more dead! So…how many is that?"

"A dozen, I think. Only two left, at most."

"She won!"

"That's our Llenn!"

The footage being played to the pub audience switched away from thermal vision to the usual mode. Since Fukaziroh wasn't shooting more smoke grenades, the pink cloud was slowly dissipating. The green outline of grass was visible again, and so was a profusion of DEAD tags floating in the air.

It was a massacre.

Bodies littered the small patch of grass, some even stacked on top of one another.

CHAPTER 11   SECT.11
Ten-Minute Massacre II (Finish)

CHAPTER 11
Ten-Minute Massacre II (Finish)

"And up we go…"

Once the gunshots had died out for good, Fukaziroh raised herself out of the hollow in the ground. When she saw the jungle, the grass had been thrown far and wide with dead bodies right and left.

"Wowzers. This sure is something."

The space that had been cleared was maybe forty yards to a side—an extremely tight arena, all things considered. There were three bodies less than twenty feet from her position.

"Yaaaaah!"

And one of them got up and charged her. He'd just been pressed against the ground, not dead at all. The man was large and bald, dressed in green combat fatigues. He carried a SIG SG 510—a powerful 7.5 × 55 mm assault rifle commissioned by the Swiss Army. It was a very long gun at over forty inches, and the front end was as thin as a stick, with a heavy load at nearly thirteen pounds. All in all, a very rare gun in *GGO*.

The man charged Fukaziroh to make a body check. She noticed that there was no magazine in his SG 510. Apparently, he'd emptied one and removed it, but with Llenn's attack, he hadn't had the time to put in a new one.

"Whoo!" Fukaziroh hit the deck again.

"Aaah!" The man tripped over her and fell. The gun spilled from his hands, and he dropped a good ten feet.

"Heh! You wanna go?!" Fukaziroh growled menacingly, getting to her feet and dropping her shoulder-slung MGL-140s to the ground, as they wouldn't do any good at a distance of ten feet. There were buckles on the slings just for this occasion that would undo if you squeezed the sides.

The pair of MGL-140s sank into the soft jungle earth on either side of the man's SG 510, even as Fukaziroh's right hand was sneaking to the holster on her right thigh for her backup pistol.

"Ugh… Oh, dammit!" the man exclaimed when he realized he was no longer holding his weapon.

"Too bad! Make peace with your god!" said the little girl five yards away in striking fashion, pointing her pistol at him.

The M&P in Fukaziroh's hand spit fire.

Pa-pa-pa-pa-pa-pa-pa-pa-pa-pa-pa-pa-pa-pa-pa-pa-pow!

The gunfire was blazing fast. The slide retracted and spat out empties at a tremendous rate, springing forward to pull a fresh round back into the chamber each time, so that it was ready for the next pull of the trigger.

The golden casings danced and sparkled as they flew. After the last bullet was gone, the slide stayed back for good.

"Heh. How do you like that?" said Fukaziroh, jutting her chin proudly after that exhibition of wild one-handed firing.

"…"

The man had his hands in front of his face in a feeble attempt to block or hide himself from the onslaught. "Huh…?"

But then he realized that he hadn't actually been shot. He wasn't in pain, he wasn't glowing with shot-wound effects, and his hit points hadn't dropped.

"Wha—?" the bald man muttered.

"Wha—?" Fukaziroh muttered, in perfect synchronization.

"What the—? That was close enough to have hit him!" Fukaziroh fretted.

"Young lady… Are you really bad at shooting a pistol?" The man grinned.

He took a step forward, creeping closer to Fukaziroh.

"Heh, heh-heh… You know, in this tournament, dead bodies get treated like indestructible objects for ten minutes afterward…," he said with a creepy leer, taking another step with his left foot. Then, unbelievably enough, he continued, "Th-that means…I have that much time to touch a dead body w-without a harassment warning…"

In VR games like *GGO*, touching the body of a player of the opposite sex (or same, if they didn't consent) resulted in a harassment warning.

Penalties would be levied, or added upon, and if the player did not stop the activity, it could result in account termination. That ID would no longer be usable in any VR games, no matter how much time had been sunk into it. It meant starting over from the beginning—the worst possible outcome for any gamer.

But the exception was during battle. Otherwise, it wouldn't be possible to perform contact attacks with knives and fists and the like. Ordinarily, bodies turned into disintegrating polygons in *GGO*, but during the Bullet of Bullets event, they stayed in place until the end, while in Squad Jam, they lasted for ten minutes.

In other words, it was logically possible to feel up an opponent under the guise of attacking. And the camera wasn't going to follow a player unless they were in the midst of an actual battle, so there was no fear of being seen by the audience.

"Heh-heh-heh…"

Meaning that after this man killed Fukaziroh's cute little-girl avatar, he was planning on groping her dead body.

"Whaaa—?! Why, you repulsive low-down filthy knuckle-dragging spineless no-dick degenerate! I'll kill you, goddammit!" screeched Fukaziroh, the realization of what he intended to do prompting an impressive torrent of verbal abuse.

"Heh! How will you do that? You wanna blame anyone, blame

yourself for signing up for Squad Jam when you can barely play *GGO!*" he shouted, leaping toward Fukaziroh, hands raised. It had nothing to with *GGO* or SJ at this point; he was a sexual predator, plain and simple.

"Don't get ahead of yourself!" She hurled her empty M&P pistol at the man with all her strength.

"Guh!"

Despite her not being able to shoot him, her pistol throw nailed him perfectly in the forehead. But that alone was not enough to stop a man driven by red-hot libido.

Fukaziroh noticed the man's empty SG 510 at her feet. She stuck her left foot underneath one end and stomped on the stock with her right. "Hmph!"

Like a lever, it bounced the narrow stick-like barrel of the gun upward, where she caught it in both hands.

"And what are you gonna do with—?"

But before he could finish that question, Fukaziroh swung it upward and pulverized his chin from below.

"Yaaah!"

The audience in the bar saw this fight unfold as well.

When the man got up and rushed Fukaziroh only to fall, they cringed. "That was close!"

When Fukaziroh furiously unloaded her pistol on him, they assumed he was a goner, until—

"Wait, what?"

She had apparently missed every shot, and after a brief conversation, the man charged. *Oh, the poor girl. She doesn't stand a chance in a physical fight*, they all thought before the man's large body flopped backward from a vicious uppercut.

"What the—?"

"Gyah!"

The man fell directly onto his back, his chin glowing red with a bullet—er, nonbullet wound. He lost about a tenth of his HP.

"Wha...?" He looked up to see a little girl brandishing his weapon.

"Like I'd ever let you do that!" yelled Fukaziroh, holding the SG 510 by the barrel and brandishing the heavy hunk of metal like a greatsword.

"Huhhh?"

"Huhhh?" the audience said in perfect synchronization.

On the screen was a small girl holding a very long rifle backward.

"Uh, I know this fight is already kind of wild, but that's not going to work, right?"

"I dunno, that last shot hit him pretty clean, didn't it?"

"That was luck, right? *GGO* is a gun game."

"D-don't you humiliate me like this!"

The man with the shaved head got up and crouched for a tackle maneuver.

At this point, he was being driven by one simple desire: to knock over the little woman, strangle her to death, and then do something inappropriate after.

"Heh!" Fukaziroh slid her right foot out and turned in that direction, so her back faced him.

Nearly the entire audience assumed this was the start of an escape attempt. Of course, if she did so, he would catch her in moments and overpower her with the difference in size.

"Oh!"

Only one person noticed the truth behind the move.

She's played fantasy VR games before! he thought. *She knows how to use a long blade!*

Turning her back to him was only the initial motion to swing a long and heavy blunt weapon.

"Hrraaaaaah!" she bellowed, pulling her left leg back and

twisting in that direction, hurtling the SG 510 in a diagonal arc, up and over and down with ferocious speed.

"Huh?"

With perfect timing, it hit the man right across his left shoulder—a devastatingly powerful blow with the full benefit of momentum, strength, and velocity.

The upper half of the SG 510's stock literally shattered the man's collarbone to dust. Its impact continued to horrific effect on his ribs and sternum.

"Bwaaagh!" The man toppled over, a huge glowing gash of damage effects running from shoulder to belly. He stared up at the sky, wincing at his throbbing wounds, and saw a small shadow approach, its arms raised behind its head.

"Divine punishment to the enemies of womankind! Hi-yaah!"

"Huh?"

At a speed fast enough to leave an afterimage, she swung down her "sword."

"Fuka? Where are you? You okay?"

When the pink smoke had totally cleared, pink Llenn looked around for her partner, P90 in hand.

"Oh, over here! See the black gun?" came a voice, just as a black gun stock came rising up over the jungle grass.

Huh? It didn't look like Fukaziroh's MGL-140. Llenn made her way through the grass, cautious for a trap.

"Hiya!"

"Ngfh!"

It was truly a pathetic sight.

Fukaziroh had a long, unfamiliar rifle held by the barrel with both hands and was swinging it down on her opponent, a blubbering bald man lying faceup on the ground.

She smacked his right hand with the stock, then swung it back up and went for the left next. Then the right ankle, then the left ankle.

"—Agh! —Agh! —Agh! —Agh!"

The man seemed utterly helpless, but blows to the outer extremities did not cause much damage, so the visual effects could not accurately portray his suffering. He was losing hit points, but death was far off. But the parts she was hitting had to hurt a lot even with the numbing effects the game applied. It was practically torture.

"Hi, Llenn—glad you're all right," said Fukaziroh with another upward swing. Llenn, who had no idea what was going on other than that her partner was perfectly fine and cheery, asked, "Wh-what's up...?"

"Oh, I was just thinking, I could at least take one out myself!" Fukaziroh replied with a breezy smile. Then she glared at the man and said, "Go on! Just try to touch me and see what happens!"

She struck him again, bringing the rifle down onto the fingers of his left hand. There was an ugly cracking sound, and his fingers glowed red with the visual effect for damage. If this were real life, she would've shattered the bones in his fingers.

The shaved-head man looked up at Llenn and tearfully pleaded, "H-help me... I w-want to log out, but my left hand is...too numb... I can't open...my window... P-please, just k-kill me..."

You shut your mouth! A tormenter of women like you doesn't get to die easy!" Fukaziroh raged.

"I'm sorry, I'm sorry, I'm sorry, I won't do it, I won't do it, I won't do it!" he screamed at rapid speed, large tears falling from his eyes.

"..."

Llenn made eye contact with Fukaziroh.

"Okay, fine. You're off the hook now. Ahhh, that feels better!" she said, lowering the SG 510 and tossing it to the side. The heavy-looking rifle twirled away and vanished into the heavy jungle.

Llenn placed the tip of the P90's silencer against the man's temple.

"Ohhh... I'm saved... Thank you, God..."

And with a single bullet, she gave the praying man peace.

*   *   *

"Well, I think that's all of them, but let's count!" Llenn said, beginning to number the bodies around them. The smoke had cleared, and the jungle was green again. It was also much more open around here than before, thanks to the hundreds of bullets that had torn the grass and branches to shreds.

She trotted from body to body, counting the floating DEAD indicators. "Eight, nine, ten…"

By the time she got to thirteen, Fukaziroh had recovered her M&P and had both MGL-140s slung over her shoulders. "There you go. That's all of them, right?"

"You would think there'd be fourteen…," Llenn murmured. "Oh! That's it…"

She spun around, expression tense, and moved forward with her P90 at the ready. She was heading for the spot about ten yards ahead, where the dead bodies were overlapping in a pile.

"Hmm?" Fukaziroh followed her. Llenn stopped about four yards short, then started firing. Three shots at the dead body.

Corpses were indestructible, so the bullets wouldn't do anything. It was just a strange kind of magical wall that absorbed all the impact of the bullets.

But this body was different.

"Yeow!"

It leaped up with a shout when the bullets hit and landed on its backside. It was the handsome character dressed in black fatigues, Clarence.

"I knew it!"

"Ooh! The possum routine!" the girls shouted. He was lying facedown atop another body, hoping that the floating tag would look like it belonged to him.

Clarence held his glowing, damaged hands up from a seated position and said, "Fine, fine, you got me. I give up, I give up!"

A handsome smile adorned his face. "As you can see, I don't have a weapon. My main gun got shot in the battle, and I dropped it. I've got a pistol on my waist, but you'll just shoot me if I pull it, right?"

"Of course!" Llenn said, her bullet circle trained on Clarence's face. "I'm trying to save ammo, so I don't want to waste any. I'd prefer it if you resigned."

"Well, I'm in no place to argue. Actually, I was wondering if you wanted to talk for a bit? You girls are cute. And as it happens, I love-love-*looove* cute and powerful girls like you!" hc said, his beaming smile not even trying to hide the fact that he was hitting on them.

"Ugh." Llenn grimaced.

"Hey, he's pretty funny! You always want one of these guys at a singles' meetup," said Fukaziroh in contrast, delighted. "But we're not at one of those now, so it would be funnier just to shoot him."

Llenn sighed and started to say, "I'm going to shoot you now, so don't take it pers—" but she stopped.

"What's up?" asked Fuka.

"Hmm?" mumbled Clarence.

Llenn pointed at the stomach of his black outfit. "H-hey… That p-pouch…" There was a long and thin pouch there, also black. "What's inside?"

"Huh? Oh, this? May I move my hand?" he replied. Llenn nodded and tipped the muzzle of her P90, too.

"If you'll pardon me, then," he said, slowly lowering his right hand. When it got to the height of his shoulder, it suddenly sped toward the pistol holster on his waist to draw it.

Sh-pow!

Llenn's P90 shot first. The muffled gunshot was still piercing and high-pitched.

"Yeowwww!"

He was a quick draw, to be sure, but Llenn was obviously faster, given that she already had the gun pointed at him. The 5.7 mm bullet pierced Clarence's hand, causing him to drop the FN Five-Seven.

"Awww, fine! Go ahead! Just kill me already! Hmph!" Clarence pouted like a child, with his last means of resistance removed.

"The contents of the pouch! I'll shoot your ear next!"

"Geez, you're crazy… Here!" He used his other hand to lift the flap of the pouch and remove its contents.

It was a long, thin magazine made of plastic, with the bullets clearly visible inside. Aside from its color, it was exactly the same as the one loaded into Llenn's precious gun.

Her eyes flashed. "I knew it! You use a P90?"

"I don't. Do you know the AR-57? It's just the lower receiver of an M16 with the top the same as a P90, so they share the same magazines—," he said.

"Get them out!" she interrupted.

"Pardon?"

"Get 'em all out! Get out your magazines!"

"Whaaat? Oh, I get it! You shot a lot of your ammo in that battle, didn't you? And you're upset about how little you have left. So you want my magazines, as they're extra ammo for you."

Behind Llenn, Fukaziroh was nodding in sudden understanding.

"But I did plenty of shooting of my own back there," he explained. "I only have the one in the pouch here."

Clarence patted the various pouches around his midsection with the hand holding his magazine, and they all flattened, indicating they were empty inside.

"Wh-what about in your inventory?"

"Well, sure, I have some in there…"

"Get them out!"

"Wait, why should I?" he asked, handsome features twisted in annoyance. "Why do I have to serve the enemy who beat me in battle like this? I was just about to surrender."

That made sense to Fukaziroh. But Llenn, dead serious, said, "We'll win this thing! Using your magazine!"

"Bwa-ha! And what will that get me, huh? Bwa-ha-ha-ha-ha!" Clarence cackled.

Without turning her head, Llenn said, "Fuka… I'm going to shoot his fingers and toes, so you hold him down from behind while he's in pain and move his left hand for me, okay?"

"Oh, sure thing. I can do that," Fukaziroh said, understanding her meaning. Since the way to open the game window was with a specific movement with the left hand, it could happen even when you didn't mean to do it. That was one of the scary things about VR games.

You could be peacefully sleeping and have someone move your arms and fingers to materialize items that they could steal. You could bc in a safe place like a town and accidentally accept a duel from another player—these things did happen. It wasn't safe to enjoy a simple midday nap.

"H-hang on! Hang on!" yelled Clarence, who was finally starting to panic a bit. "For looking so cute, you two sure are ruthless! What will people say if they see you doing that? We're being broadcast, remember? They don't hear the conversation, but they'll see what you actually do! You'll go down in *GGO* infamy as a pair of real low-down, dirty sons of…well, daughters of bitches. You want that? You sure?"

"Was that all you wanted to say?" said Llenn in a deadpan.

"…Yeesh! Fine, fine. I will provide them to you. What do I care anyway; they'll all come back to me after the event is over."

Clarence opened his hand and dropped the magazine. But before he made the gesture to open his window, he smirked. "Y'know, I think this kind of magnanimity deserves some thanks, don't you?"

What kind of nonsense was he going on about now? "Forget it, Llenn. Why don't you just shoot him? This is a waste of time," Fukaziroh suggested.

Llenn ignored her and asked, "Like what?"

"Well, it's no big deal, but… How about a kiss?"

"Whaaaa—?" "Hwhut?" The girls gawked simultaneously.

"A kiss. A smooch. *Beso.* First base. Both of you, if possible, but at least the one in pink. I want a thank-you kiss. On the cheek is fine!"

"…"

Llenn couldn't believe what she was hearing.

"How dare you try to take advantage of us! Is this game populated entirely by pervs?! Llenn, I'm going to knock him loopy with a grenade, so you can move his left hand to do what you need to do," Fukaziroh growled, taking aim with the MGL-140 in her left hand. Clarence yelped and writhed.

Then Llenn made up her mind. "All right. You've got a deal!"

"Uh, he does? Are you in your right mind, Llenn?"

"He might be crazy... But still... I'll do it to get his valuable ammo. And that's still better than stealing them from him..."

"Yahoooo!" cheered Clarence, like a little boy.

"Well, as long as you're okay with it. I kiss my friends, too, as long as it's inside a game," Fukaziroh said, more on the annoyed side. "However! You must materialize all of those magazines first!"

"You bet! Just keep your word, little lady!" said Clarence with a wink. He waved his hand to call up his item storage. A number of P90 magazines materialized in the air and gradually fell to the ground. There were over ten, in fact.

"Ooh! It's a pile of treasure. Can I shoot him now, Llenn?"

"No."

"Fine, you want to shoot him instead. Be my guest."

"No, I'm not shooting. I'll keep my word," Llenn said, pointing the P90 away (but not letting it out of her grasp) as she approached the sitting Clarence.

"You're scaring me. You won't pull the trigger, will you?"

She crouched on Clarence's right side, readying the gun so she could shoot him through the heart at a moment's notice. "I hate you...but I keep my word!"

And despite the fierce look on her face, Llenn put her left hand on Clarence's right ear and gave him a light peck on the far side of his cheek. It was only for an instant, but the amount of time her mouth was close to the skin felt unnaturally long.

"Ooh, very smart. Now the people who watched this will think you were just whispering something," said Fukaziroh, impressed with Llenn's solution.

"Well? Are you satisfied now?" Llenn asked, pulling back with an expression of equal parts anger, embarrassment, and scorn.

Clarence turned his head to look at Llenn, beaming from ear to ear. Even though he was clearly getting dopey and lovesick about it, the frustrating part was that even *that* made him look handsome.

"I'm so satisfied! Whoo-hoo! That was thrilling! Hee-hee! Beautiful!" he said, suddenly in more effeminate tones.

"Wha—?"

"Huh?"

Llenn and Fukaziroh were both struck by this unexpected shift in behavior—in a bad way.

"Mmm, yes, girls give the best kisses! I just hate how rough and sloppy guys kiss!" Clarence giggled to himself. He was really enjoying this.

"…"

Kissing…guys?

It went so far over Llenn's head that she just froze in place, like a little pink statue with a gun.

With her typical country charm, Fukaziroh said, "Wait, what does that mean? You usually kiss guys…? Does that mean what I assume it does? Like, homogenized milk without the genes? A tomato short of a BLT?"

But now it was Clarence's turn to look confused. "Huh?" He looked between the alternately frozen and confused Llenn and Fukaziroh. "Oh! Oh, I get it now—sorry, sorry! I didn't explain that part. Of course!"

"Explain what?"

"I'm a woman. My avatar's pretty masculine, so I settled into talking like a guy to match it. I'm pretty flat, but I can show you my boobs. Oh, actually, this way is faster."

Wha-wha-whaaaat?

As the stunned girls watched, Clarence produced an electronic name-card display, the VR equivalent of a business card.

It said it right there. CHARACTER NAME: CLARENCE. SEX: FEMALE.

"But in real life, I like both boys and girls," Clarence said, unprompted.

At last, Llenn recovered her wits. "Er… Please don't talk about real life here," she pleaded.

"What?! Why not? Why don't the three of us get some tea sometime soon? A virtual girls' day out! There aren't enough girls in *GGO*! C'mon, be my friend!"

"Y-you don't know what we're like in real life! We could be fifty-year-old grannies. You might find us totally unrelatable."

"Oh, I don't care! I'm a humanist—I just love people! Please! Since we're here, why don't we form a squadron of just girls? Let's do it!"

Would you just resign already? Fukaziroh grumbled to herself.

"W-well anyway, I'm just going to borrow these magazines…," said Llenn.

"Please, be my guest."

Llenn opened her own window. She turned it to her inventory and started to pick up the pile of magazines to transfer them over.

"Taaa!" Clarence suddenly shoved her over, interrupting the process. Llenn's small body was pushed close to Fukaziroh, who pointed her MGL-140 at Clarence.

"Get down!" he—no, she—shouted. Something in her expression convinced them to obey.

Llenn craned her neck to look up, while Fukaziroh was face-down in the dirt.

"Win this thing—you got that?" Clarence said in the end, her body covered in bullet effects as she died.

Then they heard the high-pitched gunfire.

It was the crisp automated fire of a 5.56 mm assault rifle. The sound came from the north, about fifty yards away. As soon as they were aware of it, a number of bullet lines appeared among them.

"Hyaaa!"

"Crap!"

Bullets screamed over Llenn and Fukaziroh as they lay back flat on the ground.

We talked for too long! Llenn thought, cursing her poor judgment again.

If a new enemy squad was coming from the north, it could be no one else but MMTM. They had approached silently through the jungle.

If Clarence hadn't noticed first and pushed her over, Llenn would have been killed just now, too.

Thank you! Thank you so much! she swore in her heart.

"The ammo magazines!"

Just ten feet away, next to Clarence's body, were the dozen or so magazines she hadn't been able to store in her inventory. If she didn't get them, she didn't think she could last in this event. But…

"Let's go, Llenn! We gotta retreat!"

Fukaziroh was right. When they could barely even look up without getting hit, the obvious move was to make use of the jungle to escape.

Fwip-fwip-fwip. Covering fire zipped over their heads. They could feel the breeze.

If their opponents moved even a little bit, they'd be able to get a clear shot on the girls. They needed to act now, or they'd lose out forever.

They had to escape.

But all that ammo…

After three seconds of indecision, a bullet line appeared right on Llenn's face. It was coming down at an angle—the shooter must have climbed a tree.

"Aaah…"

There was no way for her to dodge.

The line vanished at the same moment that they heard a distant, heavy thump.

This came from the opposite direction of MMTM's shooting, a deep animalistic boom from the right side that roared over their heads at supersonic speed.

"Wh-what...?"

"Just go, Llenn!"

Fukaziroh grabbed Llenn and dragged her away from the spot. The booming reverberated, joined by a faster, high-pitched semi-auto rattle.

"There!"

"Oomf!"

Fukaziroh with her superhuman strength dropped Llenn into a low rut in the jungle, where she could listen to the fierce battle going on over them in relative safety. At last, she regained a measure of calm.

She'd heard that booming sound before.

Quite a lot, in the last Squad Jam—and at very close range. Which meant...

"Fuka! Can you shoot normal grenades?"

"Sure thing! Should I go for a full six? Which enemy, left or right? Or both?"

"Left! They're fifty yards away. Spray 'em over a span about thirty yards wide!"

I've got her right where I want her, thought the leader of MMTM when he caught the hateful little pink one in the scope of his STM-556.

But right before he fired, the "man" with her had noticed and knocked her over, leaving him as the only kill. He should've just splurged and fired a grenade, but it was too late for regrets now.

Instead, he had his teammates provide covering fire while he monkeyed his way up a nearby tree for a better shot.

"Gotcha..."

He had her cute little face right in the middle of his scope—when an even worse foe appeared and started firing mercilessly on his location.

If he hadn't quickly jumped out of the tree the second he heard the first shot, it would have been him riddled with holes at this moment, rather than the tree trunk.

That deep sound could belong only to a Russian PKM machine gun. Based on the locations from the last scan, he could guess which team this was. That's right—the Amazons.

They were firing from less than a hundred yards away, but the jungle was so thick that the bullet lines were the only visual evidence of it.

"All-out withdrawal! Don't bother checking them back—just get away! Watch for the lines!" he commanded. His teammates responded immediately.

Facing the enemy, all six backed away, tightly dodging the lines when needed.

Boom, boom, boom, boom, boom, boom!

Several seconds later, a series of explosions happened right where they'd been shooting from, grass and trees exploding in a horizontal line. If they'd evacuated five seconds later, they would have suffered colossal damage.

"Yikes! That was a close one! What the hell?!" one of the squad members exclaimed.

"That's the Denel grenade six-shooter. The little one's partner had two of 'em. I wanted to get rid of her before she could shoot, but I failed," the leader said. "We can't handle both them and the Amazons. Sadly, we'll need to leave the dome."

He checked his watch as he ran. It was 1:49 and forty-five seconds.

A man in the pub who'd been watching this string of fierce, crowded battles in the jungle exclaimed, "Holy crap, this is awesome! I gotta go tell those idiots over there watching the other battle what they're missing!"

He raced over to the crowd observing Pitohui's battle and cockily stated, "Why didn't you watch Llenn fight?! She's incredible! If she keeps going like this, she's gonna win this thing by a mile!"

CHAPTER 12

Shirley

SECT.12

CHAPTER 12
Shirley

Just before 1:50, lying on the ground on her back, Llenn listened to a large woman with braided pigtails say, "We didn't do this to save you. We did it because it looked like the best chance to take down MMTM, a fearsome enemy. And then they got away. So I guess we'll call this a temporary cease-fire between us. It would be easy to kill you, but I want to do it right, in competition."

All that Llenn could say in response was "I owe you."

She took out the Satellite Scan terminal. Her watch had finished buzzing to warn her of the upcoming signal, and it was now exactly fifty minutes past the hour. She decided to stay down while she checked the scan, rather than sit up. It was a slow one, coming up from the southwest.

"Fly faster! You call yourself a satellite?! You don't have to deal with wind resistance!" she scolded it pointlessly. "There we go!"

It showed Team PM4 still alive in the southeast portion of the map. Nearby were seven gray dots.

"Oh… Thank goodness," she said, clutching the device to her chest like she'd just gotten a message from her sweetheart. The possibility remained that their only current survivor was M, the leader, but Llenn believed that Pitohui was still alive. She knew M and Pito could do it. They had defeated seven teams at once.

"That's…scary, though. Now I have to find a way to beat them…"

*   *   *

The boss of Team SHINC glared at her own device while her squadmates watched the jungle closely.

"That's a bunch down at once! Ten whole teams in the last ten minutes!" she announced happily.

Seven of those teams were the alliance that Pitohui's squad had eliminated. The other three were singlehandedly dispatched by Llenn, with the exception of MMTM's kill shot on Clarence.

That left seven surviving squads.

Llenn and SHINC were in the dome. MMTM had retreated quickly and were now moving at top speed on the north exterior. There was Pitohui's PM4, of course. And as for the other three…

There was a marker reading KKHC east of the dome, between the two mountains. She didn't recognize that name. In the northern hilly terrain was ZEMAL, the Machine-Gun Lovers, still alive. They were doing well this time.

The last one was named T-S, and they were located very far away in the northwest, practically against the wall of the map.

Fukaziroh reloaded both her grenade launchers with normal ammo and stood. She looked up at the very large woman with the Vintorez silenced sniper rifle. The little blond girl grinned and said, "Hey, you big lug! You must be the boss. I'm Fukaziroh, but you can call me Fuka out of affection. Nice to meet you!"

"Why, pardon me for not introducing myself earlier, you sassy little blond child. You can call me Eva or Boss, whichever you like. And thanks. Whatever the details are, Llenn wouldn't have been able to compete in SJ2 if it wasn't for you."

"No need to thank me. We can have a proper introduction after this whole thing is over."

Fukaziroh had heard all about the real identities of the other team from Karen, but she knew that mentioning that inside the game would just make things awkward. When Boss grunted and nodded, Fuka added, "Thank you so much for helping us out of that pinch! I'll make it up to you later with a direct delivery of lethal grenades."

Then she side-eyed Llenn, who was putting away the Satellite Scan terminal. "Hey, Llenn! I'm holding this she-beast back with my scintillating conversational skills! Now's your chance! Grab the ammo!"

"Thanks, I will!"

Llenn bounded to her feet with the strength of a grasshopper and raced over to Clarence's body. At last, she had the magazines she needed: fifty rounds each of P90/AR-57 ammunition.

"Eight, nine, ten..."

Twelve in all. Six hundred shots!

"Oh, yes... 'You got new ammo magazines'!"

She'd brought 800 rounds into the event, and she was down to 450 now. What a boost this would be. Llenn could practically cry, she was so happy. A triumphant little fanfare played in her mind.

Now she had 1,050 shots on hand. She was even better equipped than she'd been going into Squad Jam. Llenn happily stuck six of the magazines into her hip pouches and put the rest into her virtual inventory.

"Thank you... You really helped me out," she said to Clarence's dead body. He—no, she—was faceup with arms outstretched, face frozen in a blissful expression.

Llenn remembered that she'd lost 20 percent of her hit points. Deciding that it was better to take the excess healing in order to reduce the risk of an instant kill, she used the emergency medical kit on her wrist. Her body was briefly enveloped in light, then her HP bar flickered to indicate an ongoing state of healing. It would take 180 seconds, three full minutes, for the process to complete.

She walked back to Fukaziroh and Boss and looked up at the large woman. "Thanks for saving me, Boss," she said, with a bow.

"You're welcome," Boss replied happily. "Well, since it's been long enough, shall we have a real fight now? We could do it here or find another place. Anywhere we can be sure other teams won't interfere—"

"Sorry, now's not the best time," Llenn interrupted, to Boss's surprise.

"Huh? Why not? You said the next time we met, we'd compete for—"

"I'm sorry… I just…can't…tell you why…"

Llenn grimaced. She didn't want to get those poor high schoolers involved in some kind of ugly real-world situation.

But then Fukaziroh said, "Well, Llenn has to beat Pitohui, or something bad's gonna happen. If Pitohui dies without winning SJ2, she's gonna die in real life, too. And Llenn's the only one who can stop her."

"Wha—?!" Llenn yelped, her mouth as puckered as a fresh-boiled octopus.

"You're rivals, right?" Fukaziroh said. "C'mon, let's have some faith in them."

There was no other battle happening at this time, so the virtual cameras were following the conversation. The audience couldn't hear the words, but they could see Llenn and Fuka and the members of SHINC huddling up for a serious talk while there were no other enemies around.

"What's going on? They started talking out of coincidence—you think they're gonna team up next?"

"Well, Llenn was whispering something into the ear of the last person earlier."

"That was thanks for receiving his ammo, right?"

"I thought…Llenn might actually have kissed him on the cheek…"

"When you dedicate yourself to being that much of a perv, it's almost admirable…"

In the wake of all that blistering, white-knuckle combat, the bar was in a daze. Some were ordering fresh dishes to replenish their hunger. Following the ten-minute waiting period, more and more dead players from SJ2 were returning to the bar, too.

"Those stupid Amazons! If they don't win now, I'm gonna make sure they pay for it!" snarled a sniper with an SSG 69.

"You can do it, Llenn! I wanna see you win again!" cheered a guy from the team of optical-gun shooters from the train station who had fallen in battle to Llenn and Fukaziroh.

The carefree mood lasted for a good two minutes, and then Llenn bowed deeply on the screen. Was she thanking them for saving her team?

Then Boss reached out to Llenn. Big Boss and her big hand enveloped little Llenn's small one. They clasped them in a firm handshake. With the stark difference in their sizes, it made for an odd image.

"Oh, I guess they settled up. What's gonna happen now? Think they'll fight it out?"

But to that fellow's disappointment, there was no battle. The two teams waved and went their separate ways. The Amazons went south, and Llenn's duo went east through the jungle. Soon the screens were showing nothing but a scene of inert dead bodies lying in the chaotic midst of tamped-down grass.

"I thought they were gonna join up. Guess they're just going off to do their own things," said a man chugging a beer. "Not that *that* team would ever join forces with another," he added.

*   *   *

Back in time for the 1:50 scan, M reported, "Llenn's team is still alive. They're in the dome. Three dead teams around them. SHINC is nearby, so maybe they teamed up."

"That's my girl!" Pitohui beamed as the scan concluded.

"Seven surviving squads. MMTM went north of the dome. ZEMAL's in the hill area, T-S in the northwest. Closest to us now is the team in the valley. KKHC. We'll go down the slope and beat them," M said in his usual officious tone.

"Roger that. Off to take a hike, then," Pitohui drawled.

"..."

The other four men maintained their silence and descended the mountain, heading northwest—toward the area with all the blue.

Pitohui's team's next target, the squad named KKHC, was watching the fifth scan come in from a small patch of woods.

Like Shirley, the four men on the team had outfits that looked like real tree patterns—but their personal appearances were wildly different.

One was a cool-looking middle-aged man with a receding hairline. He was the team leader, just because he looked a bit older than the rest.

One was a black man, which was a fairly common sight in *GGO*.

One was a tall white man with golden hair.

And the last was small with black hair and looked just like a typical Japanese person.

The team of five (including Shirley) learned that just about all their nearby foes were gone. They used their comms to talk.

"This is wild. That contender team, PM4? They wiped out seven whole teams in ten minutes, with just the six of them... I can't even imagine how they did that," the leader marveled.

"What do we do now? If we keep running and hiding like this, we might not lose, but we're not gonna win, either."

"Agreed. Should we make our move, Leader? Just remember, the closest enemy is none other than PM4."

"I can't see us beating them...," remarked the other three men in turn. As usual, Shirley maintained her silence.

Suddenly, the squad leader said, "Hey, guys, I've got an idea. Just hear me out. I think we might be able to 'win' this thing."

＊   ＊   ＊

From 1:50 to 1:55, the mood in the bar continued to be muted and lackadaisical.

"No battles…"

"I'm fine with that. When it's just nonstop action, even I get tired out."

Some of the audience members were taking advantage of the lull to relax after the last ten minutes of absolute bedlam.

Without anything else to show, the camera followed teams on the move. Llenn and Fukaziroh had passed through the jungle and out of the dome. Now they were on the east end, at the three-o'clock position.

At the same time, SHINC was leaving the dome, watching their surroundings carefully. They were straight to the south, essentially in the same spot as where they entered.

Then the camera showed another team. It was four men and a woman, running through a farm field broken up by a little brook. Everyone watching noticed something was wrong. They couldn't help but notice.

"What the hell?" someone asked, speaking for the rest of the crowd. "Why aren't they carrying guns?"

"Hostiles. Five. One thousand yards. Running this way," said M as he looked through his binoculars. Crouched nearby were three masked men carrying their guns—and one man without anything in his hands.

Lastly, there was Pitohui, who joked, "Five peas in a pod. And what peashooters are our peas shooting?"

They had descended the mountain and were now in a varied area crowded with flat farmland and little bunches of woods and brush. The roof of the massive dome was visible in the distance.

M had his M14 EBR hanging around his neck on a sling and a huge backpack over his shoulders, watching through the binoculars apart from the rest of the team.

"They don't have anything," he replied.

"Huh?"

*   *   *

Three minutes later, the five had run at a full sprint to stand before Pitohui.

It was Team KKHC. Four men and one woman, all wearing the same boots and brown pants and jackets with a camo pattern that resembled realistic trees—yet with no weapons in their hands.

The live camera filmed the interaction, even though there was no fighting.

On one side were Pitohui, M, and the three masked men set up to fire their guns at the drop of a hat. On the other was a man from the five-man squad who appeared to be their leader, doing all the talking.

Though the contents of the conversation were unknown, the audience in the bar had an idea about it.

"Ahhh, I get it."

"They're making a proposal for the endgame."

They assumed that the five-man team was suggesting PM4 join forces with them.

"I'm surprised the chick with the ponytail didn't just waste them all when they approached."

"She was probably interested in hearing what they had to say."

"So even a demoness can understand words, huh? By the way, I just have to ask—do you really love jerky, or what?"

"Hmm. I don't think it's necessary to fight alongside one another for now. Plus, we're trying to win this event. If we join up with you, and we end up being the final two teams left, what then? Do we just start shooting at one another, right then and there?" Pitohui asked the five, and in particular, their older-looking leader.

"Honestly, we're willing to resign and hand you the championship in that moment. This is a squad decision."

"My goodness. So you didn't sign up for SJ2 with the intent of trying to win?"

"That's right. We're just testing ourselves. As a matter of fact, we're a squadron of hunters who use guns in real life."

"Ooooh. That's interesting."

It was a safe bet that anyone who willingly talked about their real-life details in a VR game just wanted to brag. Pitohui's engagement with that statement prompted the squad leader to tell her lots of stuff.

Everyone in their squadron was a hunter living in Hokkaido. They had hunting licenses in real life, so they normally used the game to practice and then went into the great outdoors in the fall and winter.

"So we're pretty confident in our marksmanship. We've got good aim without having to rely on any dumb old bullet line. In fact, we sniped three guys earlier without them noticing us. I bet you folks can't even imagine being able to snipe long-distance without a bullet line to help you," he said, proud in ways both good and bad.

"Why, I'm amazed," Pitohui lied. Neither M nor the masked men said a word.

Then the leader bragged about how high-spec the rifles were that they had stashed away and how excellent the aim of his teammates was.

"So we can snipe and back you guys up. It'll give you an overwhelming advantage in battle. What do you say? Think of it like hiring mercenaries. Why don't we go and be champions and runners-up?" he suggested.

"I understand your proposal," Pitohui said. "At first glance, it's not a bad deal."

"Okay. And?"

"But I'm afraid I have to turn you down. When I put this squad together, I had an idea in mind. I thought, 'If I lose with this lineup, then I've really failed.'"

"I see… That's too bad. Well, I can't force you, if that's the case," murmured the leader of the team of hunters. "Tell you what. Let's make a clean break of it. We'll go vanish into that overgrowth over there," he said, pointing to a group of trees over two hundred feet to the northwest. "After that, we won't make contact until the next scan. We'll swear on our pride as gun-owning hunters."

"Okay. Then we'll stay here until we can't see you anymore,"

Pitohui replied. She turned to M and the masked men who'd been watching the horizon and said, "You all heard that. No shooting. A real man keeps his word."

They grunted brief acknowledgments.

"They're true warriors. Well, best of luck to us both," the leader said, then turned on his heel and started walking. The three men who looked worried at the turn of events followed after him, as did the green-haired girl.

Pitohui watched them go, and at about a hundred feet, she waved her left hand. "Is that far enough?"

She picked through her menu and selected an automatic pistol called a Springfield XDM. The XDM floated in the air until Pitohui grabbed it with her other hand. She extended her arm—and in the next instant, she yanked back the elbow of the arm holding the gun with tremendous speed.

It was so fast, it practically left an afterimage. The inertia of the motion pulled the slide of the XDM back. It sprang back forward, loading a .40-caliber pistol bullet into the chamber.

This was the kind of one-handed pistol reloading that only real tough guys could do in real life. To pull it off in *GGO* required a huge strength stat.

"Shall I start with the one on the left?" Pitohui wondered, lazily pointing the gun at the back of the tall man on the left end of the line. She fired with one hand.

"Huh?" wondered the audience watching the slack scene play out.

"Huh?" wondered the man who got shot at the same moment.

"Whoopsie, not quite."

Pitohui's first shot only hit the man in his left shoulder. She took closer aim this time and fired the XDM. The second shot sank directly into the back of the blond man's head. It was a good enough shot that even a weak pistol hit was lethal.

Naturally, the other four turned around in shock. "Wait, wha…?"

They saw Pitohui clutching a fist to her chest and aiming a black pistol with her other hand, and a bullet line extending in their direction.

Pow.

This time it was a black-haired man who was the target. He took a bullet to the collar.

Pow. Pow. Pow.

The first one didn't kill him, so next came the cheek and eye and forehead.

The team leader watched his second comrade's HP bar plummet as the man himself toppled to the ground.

"Hey! What in the world are you doing?! You promised!" he bellowed. A bullet entered his wide-open mouth. "Glrrk!"

The inside of his mouth glowed with the bullet-wound effect, and he fell backward.

With her gun aimed in one hand, Pitohui gloated at the dying opponent and said, "Well, I'm not a man!"

"This is like target practice."

"Looks more like an execution to me," muttered some men, watching the not-even-a-battle on the monitors. Three men were dead in seconds, leaving only one man and a woman. Once the second member had fallen, the survivors wised up and started sprinting for safety.

"No time to pull their guns out of the inventory, I guess…"

It wasn't clear what weapons they had, but it would take a good ten seconds for them to produce the guns, load them, then aim and fire back; flight was the only option in this situation.

There was another crisp *pow*, and the fleeing man's left leg lit up with a bullet effect. He stumbled forward and suffered a second shot, this one hitting him on the fingers of his left hand.

"…"

Shirley watched her fallen companion in silence.

"Run!" he urged, but she did not. Instead, she rushed to the fallen man, crouched, then got down on the ground. She went to lie down on top of the man—who was about her same size—so that her back was resting on his stomach. Then she grabbed his thighs and bolted to her feet, carrying him behind her as she ran.

"Ooooh!"

Pitohui was still firing away one-handed, until the target got a distance of forty yards away, at which point she added a steadying hand for better accuracy.

She spread her feet apart perpendicular to the target, holding her arms in front for balance...

Pow.

The bullet was perfectly accurate. It landed in the spine of the man Shirley was carrying. It took two seconds for his HP to drop, and then a tag reading DEAD appeared over him with a little chiming sound.

But Shirley kept running with him.

"Oh dear." Pitohui kept firing the XDM.

It produced a series of pops, emptying golden cartridges to the right. The shots flew with unerring accuracy, but they hit only the man's corpse.

Pitohui fired all sixteen shots in the magazine, then the XDM's slide did not retract, just as Shirley vanished into the overgrowth.

M ordered, "Machine gun."

"You got it. Someone lend me a shoulder," said a large masked man, producing his favorite gun from storage. An MG 3 with a silencer attached and an ammo belt of a hundred bullets appeared.

With practiced ease, the man loaded the gun and rested the barrel on the shoulder of a smaller man hunched down in front, then started blazing fire at the bushes where Shirley had just vanished. Even suppressed, the sound was loud and high-pitched, and the plants in the way jolted and swayed with the force of the bullets.

Once the man had fired all one hundred bullets in an unbroken run, M peered through the binoculars and reported, "She's still running."

In the middle of his rounded view, he could see her running in the area beyond the overgrowth, still carrying the body with DEAD floating above it.

"She's good! She knew that a dead body would be impervious to bullets and ran off with it. That chick never gave a single thought to actually helping her teammates!" Pitohui marveled, opening her window with the left-hand gesture.

She made a few quick operations as her spent XDM dangled in her other hand—and then she transformed.

On the screen, the patrons of the bar saw the woman who initially dispatched eighteen unlucky souls from an unarmed state now building up her arsenal.

First, a backup magazine for the XDM appeared in the air. She dropped the empty one from her gun and slammed the fresh one in, pressed the slide-stop button, and loaded a new bullet into the chamber.

From that point on, it was a transformation sequence.

In VR games, you could set a particular equipment layout to a preset, meaning that a single action from the inventory screen could equip all the gear at once—and that was what she employed now.

With a simple tap of the OK button, gear began materializing on her like magic, fitting into place on her cyborg-esque body. First was a thick belt around the waist of her deep-blue suit. Hanging off the belt on the outside of her right thigh was a plastic holster, followed by a support belt around the thigh itself.

The same thing appeared on her left thigh, and this one already had an XDM inside it. She put her other XDM in the right holster, giving her dual pistols. As she loaded the left XDM one-handed, thin combat knives appeared on the outer side of each of her boots.

With each new piece of equipment, the audience in the bar marveled and cheered.

"Dual pistols!"

"That's so cool!"

"Yeah, it looks sweet, but what's the benefit?"

"That it looks freakin' cool, dumbass!"

"Ooh, knives, too!"

"I wish she'd slice me up..."

The camera zoomed in on her upper half. A black combat vest with bulletproof armor in it appeared over her taut, muscular torso. There were plenty of thin magazine pouches along the belly of the vest, making it look like armor.

On her back was a bulletproof plate that would protect her heart and other vitals from behind. There was also one large, long pouch of unknown contents fixed near the lower part of her back.

"Think she's got plasma grenades in there? Could be a special-order type protected by ultra-thick fibers to prevent herself from getting blown up by a stray bullet."

"Ahhh. That would be clever."

"At the very least, I'm guessing it's not a makeup brush."

"But wait, my friends. Perhaps she's a huge glutton, and it's just a packed lunch she's got in there?"

"Nah. And don't try to pass that off like it's a serious suggestion."

At some point, her black hair broke free of its ponytail constraint. On the screen, it danced and splayed like a living creature. The audience wondered why, until the answer was made clear to them.

Headgear appeared and covered her forehead. It was the kind of armor that circled the outside of the head, like in a combat sport. But since *GGO* was a sci-fi setting, its design was sharp and cybernetic. It was a bit like the metal headbands that ninjas used.

Its materials were a mystery, but it had to be bulletproof, too. Naturally, it was black, like the rest of her equipment.

Once the headgear was on, her hair naturally swooped together. After it formed one solid lock, the ponytail tie appeared again, resting low.

"Holy crap! It really is just like a transformation sequence!"

"Is it just me, or was watching her change kind of, um…a turn-on? Anybody?"

"I've been wondering, is there anyone in this bar who isn't a pervert?"

There was yet more gear. On her left hip was a lengthy, narrow sheath, about twenty inches long and six inches wide, right at the point where you would attach a katana.

The sheath was empty now, but its intended contents soon appeared: a gun. It was a Remington M870 Breacher—an M870 shotgun with a short barrel and pistol grip, just twenty inches long.

It was called a Breacher because of its ability to blast holes in things. With its short barrel and large ammunition, this gun could easily blast the lock right off a door. Naturally, a shotgun with a shortened barrel was going to have considerable spray. It was the perfect weapon to use against a close-range, speedy target.

Someone just like Llenn, in fact.

She pumped the handle and loudly loaded the first round. Holders in red and blue colors appeared all over her vest. She pulled one out and added it to the shotgun.

Then she fit the M870 back into the sheath—and as though on cue, there was another flash of light that congealed into a solid shape in space. This new and final object was the woman's main weapon. It was a long, narrow black assault rifle.

"Ooh! A KTR-09!"

"I haven't seen one before. Didn't know you could get custom guns like that in *GGO*."

"That's a real rare piece…"

"She's finally shown off the real deal!"

The gun fanatics were in an uproar. The KTR-09 was a custom model of the ultra-famous Russian AK series. It was made by the American manufacturer Krebs, and KTR stood for Krebs Tactical Rifle.

AKs were known for their toughness and reliability, but the

engineering was old, and they weren't as easy to use as more modern guns. The KTR was designed to improve on those weak points.

On either side of the front half of the gun were rails with optical instruments on them; the grip was designed with better safety measures, and the stock was the same as the rival M4A1.

She grabbed the KTR-09 and brought out a fresh magazine. It wasn't the typical, thirty-round type that was curved like a banana, but a seventy-five-round drum magazine, cylindrical in shape. It could cover twice as many 7.62 × 39 mm rounds.

She fit the magazine into the gun, then pulled the lever and let go, sending the first bullet into the chamber.

In the span of mere seconds, her transformation sequence was over, and now she had weapons all over: two pistols and two knives, and a shotgun and an assault rifle. She was as heavily armed as the historical hero Benkei.

Despite the proliferation of heavy gear, it didn't change her mobility, as this had all come from her own inventory. A character's carrying limit was the same whether items were held in the hand or in storage.

"That equipment capacity is out of control! How high is that chick's strength stat anyway…?" someone in the bar grumbled.

"Oh, it's been so long since I was decked out like this. Hell yeah, let's do this for real." Pitohui grinned wickedly, dressed like she was preparing for the final battle.

"Gosh," said the chubby masked man nearby, "at this rate, you don't even need us, do you?"

"If only that were true. But our enemies ahead are no pushovers. We're going in like our lives depend on it, okay?" she replied. She sounded relaxed, but there was no mirth in her eyes.

While Pitohui was transforming, one character ran and ran and ran, swearing in a most unladylike fashion. "Shit! Shit! Shit!"

Shirley, the green-haired girl and the sole survivor, made her

way to freedom through a hail of ferocious machine-gun fire. And pulsing around her mind were thick black storm clouds.

"That bitch! That bitch! That bitch!"

*   *   *

Nobody in SJ2 had wanted to participate less than Shirley.

Her name in real life was Mai Kirishima. She was a twenty-four-year-old woman in Hokkaido making a living as a nature guide and hunter. However, unlike Karen, she was not born and raised there; she hailed from the heart of Tokyo.

Ever since she was a child, it had been Mai's dream to have a job involving nature. So she enjoyed outdoor activities like camping and mountain climbing, and she even practiced some horseback riding. She'd been an active teenager, preferring to spend time outdoors rather than dress up.

When she got into college, she joined an outdoors club that participated in all kinds of activities. On the recommendation of an older girl, she got a shotgun license and a hunting license and started hunting right at the minimum age of twenty.

After college, Mai's hopes came true, and she found a job as a nature guide in Hokkaido. She got to help show tourists and mountain climbers the great outdoors. That was her job in the spring, summer, and fall. When tourism dried up in the winter, she switched to hunting Yezo sika deer for fun and profit.

In 2018, eight years ago, the laws on guns and weapons were reformed, relaxing the requirements to own a rifle from "at least ten years of continual shotgun ownership" to just three years. Because the deer population had exploded recently, leading to increased damages, the government needed more hunters with powerful rifles to help curb their numbers.

With increased interest in wild game and an improved public image of hunters, this helped bring fresh blood into the aging hunting population, including more women. In fact, the term *hunting girl* had become commonplace.

Mai got more and more experienced with age. In the first three years with her shotgun, then the one and change with a rifle, she had bagged a number of deer.

When they had the time, Mai and her hunting companions traveled by car or foot or skis in search of targets to take down and prepare. Once they had some quality deer meat, they could sell that to high-end restaurants in the big cities that served more exotic game.

It was in the midst of this fulfilling time in her life that one of her hunting partners brought up the topic of VR games and *GGO* last summer, in 2025. VR was practically the same as the real thing, he'd said, and they had realistic models of real-life guns in there.

You could practice shooting in the game, and aside from the 3,000-yen monthly connection fee, it didn't cost extra, and there were no shooting accidents. In America, they actually used it as a method to practice hunting—though the targets were monsters instead of animals.

There were even clay shooting ranges in *GGO*, so you could shoot discs if you wanted or even do classic bird shooting with a shotgun.

So the younger hunters, who had less resistance to the idea of picking up an online VR game, began checking out *GGO*. Within just two weeks, they had even formed their own squadron abbreviated KKHC, for Kita no Kuni Hunter's Club, named after their "northern country" home.

As more of the younger folks started it up and recommended it, Mai eventually got roped into *GGO*, too. Naturally, it was her first VR game. She'd never even played a regular video game before, and she wasn't too keen on the idea.

Mai's avatar was Shirley, a well-endowed woman with green hair. That was a nickname that a friend in middle school had given her once. It started by changing the *mai* character she spelled her name with from "dance" to another *mai* that meant "rice," which by free association turned into *shari*, the word for vinegary sushi rice. From there, the vowels were extended into the Japanese pronunciation of the name Shirley. She was embarrassed to be called by the name in public back then, but she had no such problem in this alternate-dimension world.

As for *GGO* itself, Mai had to admit that it was useful when it came to practicing your shooting. In Japan, the only places you could shoot your gun were at shooting ranges or in hunting areas. Also, the distances at shooting ranges were fixed, so you couldn't go closer or farther away.

On top of that, you were only licensed individually to your specific gun. It was absolutely forbidden to shoot another person's gun. The law even stated that you couldn't "test-shoot" a gun, the way you could test-drive a car before you bought it.

But in *GGO*, you could shoot any gun anywhere you wanted. Real guns and bullets were re-created in exacting detail, so you could test all kinds of things, without any fear of accidents or injuries. Therefore, it worked well as a way to shoot a wide variety of guns and practice firing from different positions and different distances.

GGO's special "busybody" assistance tool, the bullet circle, was both good and bad, but as long as you didn't touch the trigger until you were going to shoot, it didn't matter. The hunters eventually picked up the knack of firing without the tool.

In the game, animals like deer, bears, and wild pigs showed up as zombie-like monsters. Their actions were very similar to the real-life animals, so even chasing and shooting them in the game was a beneficial way to practice hunting. You just couldn't eat these ones.

So Shirley and her friends got better at shooting and hunting in *GGO*. They—or she alone—would choose terrain that most resembled their local Hokkaido and go hunt monsters there. These would be hilly areas, forests, and snowy mountains. Sometimes they would walk long distances, and sometimes they would wear skis to track and hunt their prey.

In this year's winter season, she felt the benefit of all that practice.

In order to produce the tastiest sika deer meat, you need a one-hit kill shot on the head or neck, where there is little edible meat. This is called a clean kill.

Compared to pampered human beings, wild animals have a far greater resistance to pain, and they will desperately run for safety even after being shot. The increased circulation decreases the quality of the meat and, in a worst-case scenario, might leave nothing that can actually be used after death.

Also, bullet wounds in the guts will cause damage that splatters various bodily liquids around and contaminates the meat, leaving it inedible.

Of course, shooting through the head or neck is far more difficult than hitting the body. The hunter's rule is "Don't shoot unless you're sure you can hit it," and that often means not taking a shot that is lined up and ready.

In the latest hunting season, they found that their clean-kill rate was far higher than before. It was clear that practicing in a virtual reality setting had a considerable effect on the outcome. Mai was grateful that she had started *GGO* and realized she shouldn't be so picky and judgmental about things.

All until one of her companions texted NOW THAT THE HUNTING SEASON IS OVER, EVERYBODY WANNA TRY OUT THIS EVENT CALLED SQUAD JAM?

Until that point, they had studiously avoided any kind of man-on-man combat in *GGO*. Their reason for playing was to practice hunting and shooting, and given that they actually owned real guns that could easily kill people, the act of intentionally attacking another person was a huge taboo.

GGO was designed to get players to kill one another, but simply by never attacking anyone, they were able to avoid just about all PvP combat. If another player or squadron attacked them during a hunt, they just ran away, simple as that. If they couldn't get away, they stashed their weapons in inventory space to protect them against the random-drop penalty for dying, then logged out on the spot.

In *GGO*, if a player logged out anywhere outside the safety of town, their body stayed put for some time, and if it got killed, they'd lose some valuable experience—from the avatar only, though. But since they were doing this for player experience, that wasn't a problem for them at all.

They would just say "I bet that attacking team feels really disappointed right about now" and laugh it off.

But despite having successfully done it this way the entire time, now they were embarking on the insane choice of proactively entering a team battle royale event against other players.

Mai was utterly annoyed by the idea and assumed that her squadmates would never go along with it.

"Sounds fun! Let's do it!"

"I've been wondering if we've got what it takes for the real thing."

"I'm in! What about you, Shirley?"

To her surprise, out of the group that had the time for it, she was the only one who didn't show any enthusiasm for taking part. She suppressed her anger and typed a very calm and polite response that expressed her concerns about the SJ2 question.

Instead, she got an aggravatingly patronizing response: "Really? That's what you're worried about? This is just for fun—you don't have to take it seriously. A game's just a game. If anything, I think it would do you good to participate in this, just to make it clear where the boundaries are between real life and a game."

She thought she might burst a capillary in her brain. Mai actually considered cutting off all ties with them, but they were both valuable companions in real life and her seniors, with ample experience and knowledge. And in even more practical terms, it wouldn't be easy to cut them off and lose the valuable winter income she received by hunting as a group.

"C'mon, join up! We'll have five if you're in, Shirley! Four's just not enough!"

"We'll buy you a bowl of ramen with extra pork!"

"And throw in an extra piece of your favorite cake, too!"

She'd been planning to skip out by faking illness or making up some other errand to do, but the cheerful, happy-go-lucky way her partners begged her to go overrode her own concerns, and she had no choice in the end but to reluctantly agree.

But secretly, she swore to herself, *I'm going to make up a dumb reason for not firing a single shot, and I'll drag them down with me!*

If she simply said "I've never shot a person before, so I couldn't bring myself to pull the trigger," they wouldn't realize she was actually sabotaging the team.

The day of the prelims arrived, much to her chagrin. Shirley and her four friends did not have combat gear, so they went in their usual virtual hunting outfits.

Upon calm consideration, it seemed ludicrous that they, with no combat experience at all, would have a chance at beating any other team that signed up for a competition like this. So Shirley expected they would get easily defeated in the preliminary round. Once they got thrashed, her friends would see the light and never be interested in a PvP event again.

But instead, their opponent engaged in a most incredible and unfathomable course of action.

All six from the other squad charged at them, bellowing and holding up photon swords—those sci-fi blades made only of supercharged light. And Shirley's team was made up of people who were "only" good at firing their guns. And fire they did, using their practiced technique of avoiding a bullet circle and giving their foes no bullet lines to dodge.

The unfortunate squadron of swashbucklers lay dead on the ground after exactly six shots, all pierced through the chest. Shirley could not for the life of her understand why they chose to use lightswords and charged in full view of their opponents' guns.

In any case, their team made it through the preliminary round. Now Shirley *had* to participate in the big event—so she decided to be as useless as she could here, too.

She didn't fire a shot in the first battle and even exposed herself to harm by pretending to search for the enemy, hoping she'd get shot so she could leave early. But nobody shot at her.

For some reason, none of the enemy squads approached them after that, either. As they stayed in place, waiting to snipe from cover, they missed ample opportunities for battle, until there were just seven teams left.

Then their squad leader suggested teaming up with one of the contenders and made contact with them, only to be turned down.

"That bitch! That bitch! That bitch!"

The tattooed woman named Pitohui had shot at their backs. During her escape, Shirley had heard the sound of a bullet at supersonic speed whiz past her ear for the very first time. She ran like the wind through the weaving red bullet lines, grappling with the terror of possibly being shot at any moment.

Shirley didn't know how long she'd been running anymore. The next thing she knew, she was facing nothing but a snowy mountain ahead.

"..."

She'd picked up her squadmate, intending to save him, but now he was nowhere to be seen behind her. She couldn't even remember dropping him.

On her right, she could see an enormous dome; on the left was a rocky, wooded mountain; and stretching onward through the grassland between them were her footprints. She looked to the upper left and checked on their hit points. All four of her teammates were dead, including the one she'd thought she'd saved, and now the leader symbol was on her name. It seemed like a miracle that she hadn't suffered any damage at all.

"..."

Shirley sat down out of sheer mental fatigue. The ground around her was damp with snowmelt, and her butt squelched as it landed.

"That bitch!" she snarled, gnashing her teeth hard enough that anyone present would have heard it. Her rear and hands were all muddy now.

"…"

Then the tension drained from her face, and she looked at the sky. The wind had stopped. The clouds were still, weighing heavily just overhead.

"Ahhh, forget it… Now that I'm the leader, I can just resign and put this whole stupid event behind me for good. I'll just tell them, 'You all died, so I figured it was a lost cause…' And I'll be able to get through it without firing a single bullet, just like I wanted…"

She lifted her muddy left hand and swiped at the air. A game window appeared, popping up an item list for quickest access. Shirley started to push it aside so she could reach the button to resign—when a particular graphic and string of text caught her eye.

"…"

It was a picture of a creepy-looking rifle, with a large scope and a stock that looked like it was broken in the middle. Like some kind of mutated fish that lived in polluted waters.

Below the image, the text read BLASER R93 TACTICAL 2.

It was a high-precision German sniper rifle that used 7.62 × 51 mm rounds. It differed from the normal R93 hunting model that Mai used only in that its stock had been modified for better sniping. The normal model didn't exist in GGO, so she chose this one to be her weapon, since it essentially fired the same way.

It also had power.

The power to stop any animal, no matter how tough, if it struck the right spot.

The power to help even a weaker woman like herself defeat a much larger opponent.

"…"

All she had to do was summon the resign command and hit the YES button, but Shirley's fingers stopped, hovering in midair.

"Her," she muttered with utter loathing. "That woman… She's… not human. She's a pest—a beast that only causes harm…"

She touched not the RESIGN button but the R93 Tactical 2. Light gathered in the middle of the air and began to form the shape of the rifle.

"Ah!" Shirley gasped, smacking her own cheeks. The mud on her hands splattered against her pale skin, and she wiped it across the bridge of her nose with one swipe. Then she reached for the rifle hanging in the air and clutched it to her chest.

"That pest…"

She pulled the bolt handle back and forward again. The straight-pull action, a notable characteristic of the gun, made a sound that suggested smooth, high-quality precision.

"…will be exterminated."

The first round was loaded into the chamber from the magazine.

With a bestial look, the woman with mud streaked across her face smiled and exposed her teeth. "I'll finish off my prey with a single shot."

She got to her feet and returned the way she'd come, taking her own footprints back.

"…"

But then she stopped.

Shirley slung the R93 Tactical 2 over her shoulder and glanced at the watch on her left wrist.

1:59. One minute until the next scan.

She turned around on her heels and took off running at full speed in the opposite direction of Pitohui, toward the snowy mountain.

CHAPTER 13
SHINC Runs

SECT.13

CHAPTER 13
SHINC Runs

Almost one hour had passed since the start of SJ2.

As she sprinted along, silenced P90 in her hand, Llenn learned from her watch's vibration that there were just thirty seconds to go until two o'clock. She craned her neck as she ran, looking for the nearest place to hide.

"Found it!"

There was a small divot in the ground that any regular person would not fit inside, but Llenn hit the deck and did a feetfirst baseball slide. The friction of the soft dirt slowed her down until she fit perfectly into the space.

If she craned her neck up to look around, she could see the top of the dome, the upper part of the hilly area, and the snowy mountain, all at about the same distance from her. There were no humans around, including Fukaziroh.

"It's time, Llenn. Are you ready?" said her partner's voice in her ear.

"I'm good. I found a spot to hide. We're sticking to the plan!" Llenn replied. Then she repeated, "We're sticking to the plan."

The sixth scan arrived at two PM.

"Whoo-hoo! We survived a full hour!"

"Yeaaaaah!"

"Bravo!"

"Hell yeah! Oh, *hell* yeah!"

"Yes, we can!"

The five members of the All-Japan Machine-Gun Lovers cheered and roared. They had barely moved from their starting location in the hills. The first battle had taught them that they didn't need to abandon an advantageous position.

In the last hour, they'd stayed at the top of a hill with excellent vantage. When they saw an enemy team approaching, they backed up a bit.

"Not yet, not yet...," they urged, making use of what little patience they had. "Almost there... Almost there..."

They waited until the enemy crested the hill and came into view, then started down the other side.

"Now! Fiiire!"

"Whoooo!" "Yahoooo!" "Ryaaaa!"

They leaned into it and unleashed a long-distance machine-gun assault from their useful spot. Since these were machine guns rather than precision sniper rifles, it took a lot of bullets to finish off an enemy team.

But in addition to plenty of bullets, they were also equipped with spare barrels to counteract the issues of overheating and friction. They knew as well as anyone that a machine gun without ammo and spare barrels was useless.

They'd blast the enemy squad to smithereens, then wait again. Another enemy, blast, wait—for an entire hour. They had beaten three teams, which was an unfathomable leap after their last result.

Now the sixth scan was coming in. It was a very slow one from the north again.

They hunkered down in the cramped spot atop the hill like they'd done all the other times, watching their device screens closely to check out their surroundings.

The northern edge of the hilly area was their current location. The massive wall loomed behind them, blocking all passage in that direction. Since no enemies would come from there, they only had to watch in three directions.

They peered at their screens, looking for the closest squad.

"Huh? What is this...? Is this a mistake?"

There was one team listed north of them. If they touched the dot, it displayed the name T-S. But that was completely impossible.

"Man, I think this scan is busted."

"Yeah. There's no way that's true."

There were two reasons they could be certain of this.

For one, the giant fortress wall was north of them, and the five hundred feet of space in between was a gentle slope, of which they could see the entire length. If someone was approaching the spot on the scan, the guys would have to see them, unless they were dealing with the Invisible Man. Some turned to the north to check, just in case. No one was there.

The other reason was that the team named T-S had been in the far northwest during the last scan—in the middle of the town. It was at least three miles from there to this spot. So they ran through the neighborhood and over the hills at over eighteen miles an hour without being seen? It was impossible.

"What the hell is this? A system error in the middle of a competition? Talk about a motivation killer!" groaned the guy with the Minimi.

The one with the M60E3 said, "The server's a computer, too, so it's not perfect. You know how a machine gun will break down unless you give it enough TLC? That's why I sleep with a model M60E3 air gun at home. I put it on the chair next to me at breakfast, and it watches movies at my side on the couch" without any apparent hint of irony.

"Oh, cool!" "That makes sense." "I admire that." "Nice one."

It was the kind of team that would accept that as an answer.

"For the other survivors... MMTM's on the north side of the dome. That's about a mile and a quarter away. They're coming this way leaving the dome. That'll be our next contact. The others are too far," reported the one with the M240B.

"The third-place powerhouse from the last time... Can we even beat them?" wondered the man holding the Israeli Negev machine gun.

"We're fine!" replied the FN MAG user with supreme confidence. "We studied the footage of the last one, right? The HK21 machine gun is scary, but that's the only 7 mm gun. The others are just 5.56 mm assault rifles. In open terrain like this, we've got an overwhelming firepower advantage!"

As his teammates murmured in impressed agreement, he continued, "We're gonna protect this spot and be winners! Shoot us with your arrows and cannons if you must!"

Just at that moment, red glowing damage effects appeared on his back, legs, shoulders, and head.

"Hebwoebe?" he said—a word that did not appear in any dictionary in the world—and died.

The other four didn't have the time to process why it had happened, either.

They, too, took a cavalcade of bullets to the back, losing massive chunks of HP until they died, one by one.

"Huh? Wait—what—?" stammered the last one, with the Negev. At the time he was eliminated from SJ2, only twenty seconds had passed since the first shot.

The All-Japan Machine-Gun Lovers were out.

The scan was still ongoing, so the surviving teams were watching the screen as the white dot turned to gray.

"Huh? Wow, the machine-gun dorks just got wiped out," one of the MMTM members noted with annoyance.

The team was checking on the scan from the transition into the slopes of the hilly area, keeping an eye on the horizon in the meanwhile. The hills to the north featured team T-S closing in on ZEMAL, so they were clearly the culprits.

"How did those idiots not notice someone right behind them...? Just when they lasted long enough that we were going to grace them with our attention."

"At that close of a distance, wouldn't they have already been in combat when the scan started? And maybe it just wrapped up now."

"Or was it...a mutual alliance that broke down in betrayal?"

Each member had his own ideas and questions, but it was the leader with the STM-556 who figured out the trick.

"Nope. You're all wrong."

"Aw, geez."

The audience in the bar was well aware of what the trick was already.

The T-S versus ZEMAL battle scene—more of a massacre, really—played out in its entirety for them starting at two o'clock on the dot.

There were no system errors in Squad Jam. The six members of T-S were indeed just five hundred feet to the north of ZEMAL. But none of the five Machine-Gun Lovers realized something very crucial: that the scan did not account for height.

On the screens in the bar, the camera looked downward from an incredibly high angle, taller than even the walls. Atop said walls was a concrete walkway about five yards across, with walls around three feet tall to protect against falling off.

And there were six people pointing just their gun muzzles over that wall and firing down at a distance of five hundred feet and a height of two hundred feet.

They were sci-fi soldiers.

They wore dull-gray armor made of unknown material all over their bodies, without a single square inch of exposed skin. They were completely armored from head to torso to thigh to shin to toe, even on all their joints.

And on their off hands, they each equipped a shield, a rectangular armored plate fixed to their upper arm. That way, they naturally covered their hearts whenever they aimed their guns.

Of course, they also wore what looked like space helmets. They had tough face guards that covered their cheeks, and goggles as well, so there was no way to make out their faces. It was as close as you could get in *GGO* to being perfect future soldiers.

In order to tell themselves apart aside from size, each one had numbers in a special font on the back of the helmet and the shield, from 001 to 006. The matching logo on the rear of each helmet was an orca whale bursting out of the water, sharp teeth exposed.

Normally, they used optical guns, but in this case, they were making a rare exception for live-ammo guns. Even then, they had chosen ones with the most futuristic looks.

The machine gunner had a 5.56 mm HK GR9. It was known for having a very rounded design, even down to the scope.

Four had Steyr AUGs and SAR 21s. These were both bullpup assault rifles, meaning that the magazines were located behind the grip. That made the overall length of the gun shorter than usual, but the empty cartridges also flew right past the shooter's face, so in order to properly use it, you had to prop it on your left side to fire.

One had the HK XM8, an assault rifle that never left the prototype stage. It had a very curved silhouette, too, almost like a fish.

While they were all decked out in wild sci-fi gear, the actual abilities and overall power of the team itself were nothing to write home about.

In fact, they had lost to another no-name team in the preliminary round but won a spot in the loser's bracket. They had lost because the other team took advantage of their weakness: Their heavy gear kept their defensive levels high but made their movement very slow.

But one of the six had pointed to the walls right at the start of the game and had said, "Hey! Do you think…there's a place where you can climb up there?" and that had changed their fate.

"Y'know, if you look at the map, the walls are just barely inside the lines…"

"Since the first ten minutes are the easiest, why don't we spend the time looking for a place to go up?"

"Sounds good!"

So they stuck to the wall and continued investigating near it…

"Found it…"

…until they found a hidden door. One of the members pressing around on it saw part of the concrete-like wall open up. It was impossible to see from a distance, but once close enough, you could tell that there was a slight gap. It seemed there was a similar entrance about every hundred yards or so along the structure.

On the inside was a small, dimly lit room with a spiral staircase that led upward. Obviously, they wanted to keep going as far as they could, and they climbed until they reached the top of the wall. At two hundred feet up, they had an excellent vantage point.

"Whatta view, whatta view!" exclaimed one of the team members in the manner of the notorious thief Ishikawa Goemon as he looked out on the dome, fields, and town.

"Hang on a second! The game designers aren't doing their jobs!" yelled another one, staring at the other side of the wall.

They all agreed that it was an affront to their sensibilities. Outside of the specially designated map was nothing but clouds and space of the same color, both above and below. In other words, on the assumption that none of the SJ2 players would actually see it, they didn't bother to add any graphics outside of the walls.

But why could they reach the top of the wall, then? Was there some kind of communication lapse between the map designer who placed the stairs and the design chief?

No, they must have assumed that no one would be stupid enough to actually climb up there!

No, they decided that this surreal sight was a prize for the person who was bold enough to reach this place!

Their debate took them to all kinds of places that had nothing to do with the actual SJ2 happening around them.

"Hey! We're not just playin' around here, people!" They realized this as the first Satellite Scan approached. They'd climbed to the top of the wall, but what now?

From up above, they could shoot downward, but only if their targets were within their effective range of four hundred yards. Were they going to have foes coming into that very convenient circle at regular intervals?

They were split between wanting to go back down and fight in the normal terrain and wanting to stay up there to shoot whomever they could, then wait until the numbers were thinned out to go back down.

The "Let's Go Down" faction argued that moving atop the castle wall involved too much distance and effort. The "Let's Keep Going" faction had noticed something, however.

It was a distant game item. Through binoculars, they discovered six bicycles, arranged to facilitate speedier movement atop the walls. That convinced the "Let's Go Down" faction.

They chose to move around atop the walls, striking and escaping from danger. They made for a rather surreal sight: all sci-fi space battle armor and exotic guns, riding around on typical neighborhood bikes along an extremely tall fortress wall.

For a while, they had no enemies to shoot and simply enjoyed a breezy bicycle ride with breathtaking views, until finally, they had the All-Japan Machine-Gun Lovers in their sights. They won their first fight with a one-sided attack just an hour past the start of the event.

"They went on top of the wall. They were in the northwest corner ten minutes ago, so they must have some way of moving around real fast. The machine gunners didn't know that, and they got ambushed from behind," said MMTM's team leader. His members nodded along.

Jake, the one with the HK21, said, "They'd be a bad team to square off with then, yeah? Once they duck, there's no way to aim at them from below."

It was a good question. The leader patted his grenade launcher. "So we attack from above."

*   *   *

Back at exactly two o'clock.

"Checking the scanner!" Llenn called out, staring at the screen as she hid in the hollow.

Elsewhere, Fukaziroh, Boss's team, Pitohui's team, and every other living thing focused on the sixth Satellite Scan.

Even the patrons at the bar.

The scan scrolled down slowly from the north, first showing T-S and ZEMAL—and the destruction of the latter.

With the scene itself on display in the bar, some lamented the loss of the Machine-Gun Lovers, who had put up quite a good fight by their standards.

"Awww."

"Darn..."

"They really did their best."

The results of the scan continued to develop on a map screen on the monitors. SJ2 was heading toward its final act. The only teams left at this point were either very tough or very lucky, or even both.

After this scan, each team would actively and forcefully proceed toward its closest opponent to engage in battle. There was little reason left to wait. The fighting would get fiercer and, like the last Squad Jam, should probably wrap up within about thirty minutes.

Thus, in order to follow the remaining teams and their locations, the audience in the bar studied the scan just as hard as the players in the event did.

As the scan moved south, powerhouse MMTM showed up at the start of the hilly area, more than a mile south of T-S. Since there was no other battle happening, the screen showed them, zooming in on the smile of their leader, who was patting his STM-556 grenade launcher.

"Looks like MMTM's locked on to the sci-fi boys."

"We'll see who's on top: the guys with more skill or the ones who are literally on top…," murmured the spectators.

Llenn's team, LF, was next. They were about a mile-plus to the northeast (upper right) of the dome. On the screen, a tiny girl in pink huddled in a dip in the ground, watching her terminal.

"Hmm… They went way northeast after leaving the dome… They tryin' not to hit PM4?" someone wondered. Of course, no one had an answer. The camera pulled out slowly, making Llenn appear smaller and smaller. It was just damp ground without any grass around her and no other players.

"How come the grenade-launcher girl isn't nearby?" someone asked out loud. Again, no one could answer.

The scan crept south across the map, until another dot appeared another mile-plus to the east of Llenn. The screens in the bar automatically showed the team name, so they knew it was KKHC. The dot was still moving, running to the northeast in the direction of the snowy mountain.

The monitor promptly switched to show a green-haired girl wearing a camo jacket with a realistic tree pattern. The camera angle showed only her back and head, from a close angle.

The shape of a black, crude rifle was visible behind her.

"Oh! The girl who survived didn't resign yet!"

"The Blaser R93 Tactical 2? That's a pretty neat gun to use."

"Go on! Get your revenge!"

The audience could keenly remember how the rest of her team had been slaughtered, which invested them in her struggle.

"Yeah, but what can she do on her own…?"

"Plus…she's running in the opposite direction, isn't she?" someone else noted. They couldn't see her feet, but the changing scenery behind her made it clear that she was running straight up the mountain, pushing farther away from any other team.

"She's gonna run and hide until there's just one other team left. Then she can snipe from the mountaintop."

"I guess. There's not much else you can do with just one member."

Farther south, the scan showed the location of PM4—the team with M, the four masked men, and that dangerous woman. They were over a mile to the east of the dome, right around the entrance of the valley between the two mountains, north and south. It was a good two miles from Llenn's location.

Then the image switched to the team of six from overhead. Short grass covered the ground. It was the greenest place on the map, excluding the jungle inside the dome. Little brooks caused swampy marshes here and there, like a natural park. It would have been beautiful if they weren't reflecting a dull, reddish sky.

There was one building among all the green. It was a two-story log house about twenty-five feet tall and over one hundred and fifty feet across. Literal log houses couldn't get all that big in construction, but this was a big one. It was very well preserved for a *GGO* building, with glass windows that were actually still intact. The exterior was rather fashionable, like a fancy hotel.

The four masked men were about a thousand feet away from the log house. They were spaced thirty feet apart, down at the edge of the brush, watching the vicinity and ready to shoot at a moment's notice.

The short one with the bizarre UTS-15 shotgun looked through a large pair of binoculars.

The tall and thin one who acted as a mule stood to the left of the large fellow with the MG 3 machine gun, ready to feed the gun its linked-belt ammo.

In the middle of them all was M, watching his device in a crouch.

The M107A1 antimateriel rifle that had wreaked such havoc earlier was placed before him next to the M14 EBR. He could pick up either one if needed.

The five men were wearing camo, so they were extremely hard to see among all the green.

As for the woman, she was facing the other way behind M, still dressed in all her gear with her KTR-09, pressed flat against the grass. The huge backpack stuffed with M's bulletproof shield was placed in front of her.

Her right hand was on the grip, her index finger extended, but the gun's safety selector was disengaged for automatic fire. She was ready for battle. Her expression was fierce.

"Oh? I figured that chick would be kicking back in confidence... I didn't expect this," said someone in the bar.

But another person said, "She knows the remaining teams are all tough cookies. She can't be lazy. A single stray bullet can kill you in this game."

"Good point. The mighty can't afford to let their guard down."

Six squads were left, and the last one to appear was SHINC. They were in a field to the southeast of the dome. It was about a mile or so to the southwest from M on a straight line. The area around them was all fields with long sight lines, but even the M107A1 couldn't cover that kind of distance.

The screen switched to the women. The Amazons had flattened down in the middle of the field in an outward circle to prepare for the scan, so they could see around them.

From the prior scan, they knew it was unlikely there would be any foes to their south or west, but they were smart enough to stay ready.

"Those girls had the truck last time around for speedy travel. They must be ready for enemy teams to do the same this time."

"Don't act like that was some impressive nugget of knowledge. We all knew that."

"Well, it reminded me that we haven't seen any vehicles this time."

"Good point. Either they haven't shown up, or nobody's spotted them yet."

"What do you mean? You didn't see those eco-friendly bicycles?"

"Do those count?"

On the monitor, Boss was glaring at the map in a crouch. Her brow furrowed as she frowned, then furrowed even deeper. Her face shot up.

That glare was trained on PM4's location. A wide-open space of farmland.

The slow scan finally came to a finish, and the dots vanished, both on the devices and in the bar. For the next nine minutes, the only way to detect enemy location was by the naked eye. The tactical decisions of where to go and what to do were up to the squads now.

The patrons at the pub had their fun offering predictions, but as the battle royale approached the climax, everyone was in agreement.

They all thought that MMTM's excellent teamwork and their leader's grenade launcher would easily help them beat the team atop the wall, T-S.

Llenn was avoiding a battle with PM4, so she would keep moving until the next scan. Since their team was just a duo, they would wait for the bigger squads to become fatigued and lose members.

The lone member of KKHC would keep running and not engage in any more battle. She would wait for the very last team before she found an opportunity to snipe.

SHINC and PM4 were going to clash in an open space at this rate. But they were both smart, so they would avoid going into the open, and they'd try to flank the other instead.

And none of the audience members had the slightest inkling that all those expectations would fail to come true.

＊　　　＊　　　＊

After a full minute, the scan was over at last.

"Let's do this, everyone! Get your heads in the game!" shouted Boss, tucking her device into her left shirt pocket.

"Daaa!" said Tohma, the black-haired beanie wearer with the Dragunov sniper rifle.

"Ushh!" grunted the red-haired, freckled mama with the PKM machine gun.

"Let's go!" yelled Sophie the dwarf, prepping her ammo box nearby.

"Yes, Boss!" said the blond Anna, the other Dragunov sniper.

"Uh-huh!" murmured Tanya, the silver-haired fox with the Bizon.

Boss hoisted her silent Vintorez sniper rifle and said, "Okay! Target PM4! Commence Operation Snacks!"

In the bar, they saw SHINC start marching.

The six women put distance between one another and began to walk or trot at a decent clip. Rosa with her PKM was in the center with Sophie at her side, then the two snipers on either side of them, then Boss in the middle, then Tanya at the rear.

They knew their foe was far off, so they didn't split into two teams, so one could move while the other took point. All six were moving as one. Toward...

"Huh?"

"Oh!"

Based on the locations of the dome and the snowy mountain on the screen, it was most definitely in the direction of PM4, their biggest enemy. They were heading straight across flat, clear land, with no cover or obstacles.

"What?! What are they thinking?"

"Aren't they just asking to be shot?" the crowd wondered.

They were a mile apart at the moment, but it hardly seemed like a good idea to approach head-on this way. PM4 had an M107A1 with an effective range of nearly a mile, and once they were in range of the Savage 110 BA, they would be sniped to oblivion.

"What's up with them?"

"Are they just giving up?"

But then someone figured it out.

"No! The Amazons don't realize that PM4 has some ultra-long-range sniper rifles! They're probably more cautious of M's M14 EBR and his fancy shield, right?"

"Oh, good point! We only know about that stuff because we've been watching the stream."

"So they're probably thinking they're safe as long as they only approach to 7.62 mm range—about half a mile!"

While the rest of the audience seemed to find this understandable, only one person pointed out, "Hey, even that doesn't work for them! They'll get shot either way!"

2:03 PM.

"Here they come," M announced.

He stood up at his full, considerable height, staring through the binoculars, facing southwest. In the middle of the circle, he saw enemy soldiers marching toward them.

"That's Team SHINC, the Amazons. One PKM, two Dragunovs, one Vintorez, one Bizon. The last one is machine-gun support, perhaps? She's not carrying anything. Distance, one mile. Approaching directly on foot."

The heavyset sniper facing the other direction with the Savage 110 BA said, "So they're coming for us. Nothing on this side, I'll go join you."

He began crawling across the grass, black sniper rifle in one hand. The large man with the MG 3 machine gun stayed in position but swiveled his muzzle in the other direction.

Only the small man with the UTS-15 shotgun and the tall courier stayed looking the other way. They both used binoculars to keep an eye out for attacks from the rear.

"We don't know how they'll attack, but we should strike at as long a range as we can. I'll use the M107A1 from behind the shield. I'll get it ready now, but wait until they're within fourteen hundred yards, just in case," M said.

"What do I get to do, then?" asked Pitohui, who was watching their flank from beside the backpack.

He said, "Stay back and find a dip where you can watch our rear and sides."

"Awww! I don't get to shoot the Barrett? Please, please, pleeease?" she whined.

"These aren't easy pickings. Do you think you're a better sniper than me?" he asked without mercy.

"Tsk," she snapped, shrugging. "Oh well. Guess I'll reserve my stamina for Llenn, then."

Ultimately, she withdrew, like he'd ordered.

In the bar, the monitor switched to PM4 getting ready for action. Pitohui left the side of M's backpack and headed for a lower spot on the flatland so she could watch their rear.

Then M opened the top of the backpack.

"Here we go! It's shield time!"

He pulled out an object that looked like a connected stack of tiles. Each piece was about twenty inches tall and twelve inches wide. He spread them apart to form a horizontal line of eight slabs. With links connected on the top and bottom, they fanned out into a crescent-angled wall that was twenty inches tall and nearly eight feet across.

This was the iron wall M had employed behind the waterfall and the same one Pitohui had used at the foot of the mountain against the group of team leaders—and now M would be using it again.

"That thing's…just not fair."

"Did you mean to say 'That thing's gonna be mine someday'?"

"Yeah, I might have," admitted the onlooker with all honesty.

"Enemy sighted! M's shield! One mile ahead! One building's worth to the left of the log house!" said Anna, looking through her binoculars as she marched, Dragunov over her back.

"No one stop! Keep moving as though you're not aware of them!" Boss commanded immediately. "Anna, give me as much detail as you can."

"Roger that. M's got the shield set up on the plain facing us. There's a guy next to him, the fat one with the mask and goggles. He's got a black sniper rifle—never seen its shape before."

"He's spreading out the shield?" Boss asked again, surprised.

"Absolutely," Anna said.

"I can confirm," said Tohma, the other sniper.

Boss's expression grew dark as she walked. "Why...? They've still got a mile. Why would he...?" she asked herself.

Kana, the vice-captain of the gymnastics team who controlled Sophie, agreed with her. "It's too early, Boss."

"Exactly... The effective range of M's gun should be half a mile. It doesn't make sense that he'd get set up so early, just because he's ready for us..."

"Right. If they stayed down, we wouldn't have seen them. But setting up the shield is a dead giveaway."

"Which leaves...just one possibility," Boss concluded, arriving at the answer by the process of elimination. She told her squadmates, "M's team has a gun that can shoot farther than half a mile!"

"They've probably noticed us now," said the chubby sniper. On the right edge of M's shield, he had the Savage 110 BA set up on a bipod.

While he wasn't quite as well guarded as M, who had the M107A1 set up in the middle, over half his body was protected by the shield. He pressed his masked cheek to the stock and looked through the scope with a goggle-protected eye.

M opened the caps on either side of the M107A1's scope, set the magnification to full, and lay prone. "Not a problem. We'll just keep shooting at them to minimize their number. They might open the machine guns on us. If you see the line, get to cover."

"Roger. But let's wipe them out before it comes to that!"

"Exactly."

The two men saw the enlarged terrain through their scopes. Beyond the fields, six women approached on foot. The chubby sniper read off the distance from his scope's internal sensor.

"Sixteen hundred–plus yards to go."

"A little more than sixteen hundred yards," read Anna.

The six members of SHINC pressed onward.

"It's probably a 12.7 mm antimateriel rifle they'll use. This is close enough, so the fact they're not firing means they're waiting for us to get close enough to hit reliably. At the very least, they're going to shoot before we get to our range of half a mile. I just don't know if it's going to be eleven hundred yards or thirteen hundred," Boss said tensely to six sets of ears.

"M will fire on us without a line. Be cautious!" she ordered, but no amount of caution could protect against a sniper without a bullet line. The only thing you could do was use your sixth sense and feel for someone breathing down your neck.

"It's a bit farther than expected, but we're going to carry out the anti-shield plan anyway! Get prepared for the order! Tohma, Sophie, Tanya, it's on you!"

The three murmured acknowledgment in unison.

"They're gonna clash now. This should be good…"

"Who do you think will win?"

The audience at the pub was raring for another battle already. Since nothing else was apparently happening, all the in-game cameras were capturing PM4 and SHINC from different angles.

It was a mystery that the imminent MMTM versus T-S battle wasn't happening, but the audience didn't seem that bothered; they were more excited about a clash between two titans.

PM4 set up their perimeter and waited. Protected by the shield in the grass, they had two long-range sniper rifles: M's M107A1 and the other man's Savage 110 BA. There was also a 7.62 mm MG 3 machine gun for support.

And toward that buzz saw walked SHINC, the team of Amazons.

"Which side will win? M's side, obviously! Those women are going to get blasted from a distance, and that'll be it! Just like the team leaders from that alliance! And if they shoot back, everything will get deflected by that huge shield!"

"But even if they can't see the bullet lines, they can still avoid the sniping with that kind of distance, right? I mean, if it takes

two full seconds for the bullet to arrive, who cares if it's within range? They know where the opponent is, so there's no way they'll just let themselves get picked off."

The crowd was split on who they thought stood a better chance.

"Can they shoot M while he's behind his shield, staying mobile and out of harm's way the whole time? Even if they move to his side, there's still the rest of his team. So they might put up a good fight, but they're all going to get shot in the end, I bet."

Nobody was able to argue against that logic.

"Distance, fourteen hundred yards," reported the chubby man.

"We're going to start soon," M replied.

Through their max-zoom scopes, they had a clear view of six women walking across a dead farm field. All they needed to do was pull upward a little bit to account for distance, then pull the trigger.

"Behind them?" M asked.

"No hostiles as far as I can see," reported the small man, who was on his belly, peering through binoculars.

"This is all you guys. Wrap this thing up quick," added Pitohui, who sounded bored.

"Okay." M put every ounce of his concentration into the circular world of the scope. He put his whole mind into his dominant eye, keeping his left eye open all the while.

Six women in the distance. Some were so burly and imposing that they didn't look particularly feminine, but they were all women. The first step was deciding which person in the horizontal line to shoot first. Then they had to compare answers, to make sure they didn't both shoot the same target.

The chubby guy with the Savage 110 BA was an excellent sniper in *GGO*, but he had no practical experience with real guns. He couldn't hit a target at this range without the help of the bullet circle.

So it would be best for him to generate the circle, and thus the line, at the same moment as M's first shot. M calculated quickly.

It would take two seconds for an M107A1 bullet to reach a target at thirteen hundred yards.

There was a fraction of a second between contact with the trigger and the visual generation of the bullet circle. If it worked well, he might be able to fire before the opponent took the hit.

He didn't know how quickly the enemy side would react to one of their number getting shot, but if it wasn't lightning quick, he should be able to land a shot.

"Okay. I'll take the leader. The tough-looking one with the braids and the Vintorez. When I shoot, you take the blond sniper with the shades on the right end."

"The blond one. Got it."

Satisfied, M stared at the menacing face of the woman with pigtails. Her mouth was moving, saying something.

"They should be just about to try us…," Boss muttered.

"I'm ready whenever you want," said Tanya from the back. She had stopped watching behind them and was now up closer to Boss.

The members of SHINC walked onward, their faces resolute. Bullet lines could appear from behind that shield at any point in the next two or three minutes. In fact, the bullets themselves might simply come roaring at them without warning.

They had to withstand that fear and keep walking as though unaware of the enemy.

"Well done. Here we go! Don't forget, 'three seconds' and 'two seconds'! Now charge!" yelled Boss.

The order reached six sets of ears.

Six pairs of feet moved as one.

First was Tanya in the back, Bizon in her hands, silver hair swaying as she began to sprint. In no time at all, she had flown past the rest to take the lead.

"Yahooooo!"

A character with max agility running at full speed in *GGO* was beyond the limits of the human body. Tanya wasn't as swift as

Llenn, but she was the fastest on this team. Her feet kicked up little clouds of dust as they pounded the dry field. The brown clouds floated upward as she charged at the enemy.

Tanya wasn't the only one running, of course.

The other five began sprinting, too, to keep the gap from growing. But they, on the other hand, were zigzagging, changing directions every few seconds to keep from being easy targets.

This change was apparent through the rifle scopes.

"M!"

"Yeah, I see it… Shit!" M swore, a rarity for him.

They were just getting ready to fire on their walking targets, when they got the jump, two seconds early.

"Their leader has good battle instincts. Change targets. I'll get the little one in the lead. Take whichever one in the back you want. When they get in range, I want machine guns to hold them off. Only at minimal ammo cost. Continue checking the rear."

"Roger!" "Roger!" "Roger!" "Roger!" "Okeydoke."

M fired the M107A1 while his teammates checked in. It was still quite loud, even with the silencer on. The gas exhaust from either side of the muzzle swept the nearby grass aside.

The 12.7 mm bullet gently arced toward Tanya and roared past her right side by a foot, after she had abruptly changed directions.

"Yeow! I saw it! That was scary!" Tanya yelped, the shock wave fresh on her cheek. "If that one hit me, I'd be even smaller right now!"

"It's started!"

"She dodged it!"

The audience members in the bar clutched their mugs so hard, they could've broken the glass.

One screen displayed an image of M firing his gun from behind the shield.

The other featured small Tanya, just barely dodging out of the way.

"About eleven hundred yards away, I think? How close can they get while avoiding shots?"

"Why, you…"

The chubby guy with the Savage 110 BA kept it darting back and forth in his aiming position. Every three seconds, the women he could see through the scope switched direction. Since they were very far away, it didn't take much fine movement to cover the shift, but it was hard to keep his aim steady.

He could see the bullet circle, because his finger was resting on the trigger. All he had to do was put it on one of the women at the right time for the shot to land.

"Tch!"

But they could see his bullet line, bright and red, so they could dodge it. Still, he had to shoot them to keep them away. Even if it didn't land, as long as it forced them to keep their distance, that was a win.

The Savage 110 BA roared. A .338 Lapua Magnum rocketed forward, sending up concentric shock waves.

"Whoa!"

It passed right before Tohma's eyes—she had stopped when she saw the line. She spun around, Dragunov in both hands. "I'm not done yet!"

She resumed charging toward the enemy without firing.

They had practiced how to lead an assault on the position of an enemy sniper with good visibility. Using real bullets, firing at one another. The trick they had learned? "Move the same way for at least three seconds; get shot. Stop for at least two seconds; get shot."

"One Mississippi, two Mississippi, three Mississippi," Tohma counted to herself as she ran, then abruptly changed direction. It was a quick, sharp shift, one she'd practiced while doing gymnastics training in the simulation.

A bullet passed through empty space.

*   *   *

"Damn! This is pretty tough, M. They cut really sharp," complained the chubby man, loading his next shot with the bolt handle.

M fired at Tanya and missed for the third time. "So it seems," he agreed. Then he ordered, "Change of plans. Alter the independent shooting. Use your line to freeze them, and I'll pick them off when they pause."

It was the technique they'd used earlier to defeat the pack of squad leaders. Of course, the one shooting the M107A1 at that point had been Pitohui, who ranted, "Let me shoot the Barrett, lemme lemme lemme lemme lemme—or I'll shoot *you*!"

The chubby guy said, "Roger that! Start with the blondie!"

He trained his aim on the beautiful blond woman running along the right edge.

"Under a thousand yards! Almost there!" shouted Boss as she ran.

Running without a moment's rest, while constantly changing direction, was a mentally exhausting task, but if she stopped, she'd get shot. One hit from an antimateriel rifle meant instant death.

If they didn't get just a bit farther, to half a mile, their shots would never reach.

Just seventy-five more yards… Now sixty…

At that moment, a bullet line intersected with Anna, who was running on their left flank. From behind her, Boss could see the line and watched Anna dodge out of the way.

The bullet rushed forward, erasing the line as it went, and hit nothing but the ground, right as Anna smiled at her successful evasion. "Ha-ha!"

The next moment, although she was still smiling, her body flew backward and out of sight.

"Shit!" Boss swore.

"Nice one!" cheered the chubby sniper.

"She's down!" yelled the crowd in the bar, all at the exact same moment.

                    *   *   *

As Boss ran, she let her eyes drift up to the corner, so she could see the HP bars of her teammates. Anna's plunged to the left until it hit zero.

"Damn! Anna's dead!"

Boss and the other four kept running, unable to even look back to confirm her death. They ran and wove and bobbed.

Then Tohma called out, "We can still make it! Let's go! Anna bought us time!"

That was all that Boss needed to make up her mind. "Okay! Let's do it!"

With 930 yards to go, the five initiated their plan.

"Which one next?"

The bullet-line feint had worked, and M picked off the blond sniper. The chubby man put a new magazine in his gun and looked back, full of anticipation.

"Next is… No. Wait," M cautioned.

Then the other man saw it. The women who had been running desperately toward them just moments ago abruptly came to a stop, then dropped flat on the ground. Given how level the ground was, they were practically invisible at that angle.

He squinted through the scope, but the best he could see was the tip of a helmet above the curve of the earth. It was hard enough to know if he could actually hit that kind of target from this distance, and they could see his line, so it was just a matter of rolling out of the way.

"Distance of nine hundred and thirty-five yards," said the large man with the MG 3 machine gun, reading it off the distance measurement of his binoculars.

"How come…?" the chubby man wondered. That distance had to be farther than the effective range of the other team's guns. Why would they stop like that, when they could have charged even closer? Because one of them was dead?

No, if they were going to stop because a single member had

died, they wouldn't have charged like that to begin with. They should be pushing forward, even with greater casualties at risk.

"I can't figure out what they're thinking, M," he admitted. It was beyond his mind's capability. A good player knew not to lie and pretend he understood just because it would make himself look better.

"I don't get it, either. Just don't get careless," M said, equally honest.

At the bar, the audience was similarly dumbstruck.

"Why'd they just come to a stop? You oughtta keep going, even if you lose more members, right?"

"Okay! Let's do it!" ordered Boss to the rest of SHINC—the only people who actually knew the answer to these questions.

Sophie, the squat, heavyset dwarf, waved her left hand in the air with her head pressed to the dirt. "I'm ready!"

An item window that only she could see appeared, from which she quickly selected what she wanted to materialize, and she hit the OK button.

Meanwhile, Tohma, the black-haired sniper, crawled up behind Sophie. She did her best army crawl over the dirt. The Dragunov caught on the ground along the way, and she left it at her side.

"Here I am!" she told Sophie. Light began to bead together into a form between them, the sign that something was materializing out of thin air.

"Take it away, gang!" shouted Sophie with a huge smile, standing up.

"Wha—?" "Huh?"

Why would she stand up right in full view of the enemy snipers? everyone in the bar wondered.

"Huh?"

The chubby man, one of those very snipers, was equally taken aback. When the dwarf woman stood, she was nothing but a target. He took aim, expecting her to start running again.

"Whaaaa—?"

But instead, she plopped straight down on her backside. The wide-set woman sat cross-legged, looking their way with a confident grin. Then she extended the fingers of her bulky arms and jabbed them at the ground. It looked like she was going to dig into the dirt, but she stopped them in a thrusting position.

"…M, what is she doing? What is she trying to do?" the chubby man asked, still confused—no, more confused than before—and looking to his leader for help.

"I have no idea…but I'm going to shoot," M said, placing the sights of the M107A1's scope over the dwarf woman.

Then something even more unbelievable happened.

A bullet effect appeared on the head of the grinning woman. The left half of it glowed red, spitting off little polygonal chunks, and the large head on its thick neck base tilted to the right a bit.

After the three or four seconds it took for her HP to deplete, a DEAD tag popped over her body. She had died instantly—the sitting dwarf was now a sitting corpse.

"Wha—?"

M's finger stopped, just before it was about to touch the trigger of the M107A1.

He could easily tell it was an insta-kill, because she'd been shot in the head.

But who had shot her?

She'd been shot on the right side from his perspective, and the left from hers, but there couldn't have been a different team in that direction just now.

Still, M had to move the gun a bit to the right in order to learn the answer.

She dropped to the ground right away, before he could fire, but through the scope, he briefly but clearly saw…the boss of the enemy team, pointing her Vintorez at her own teammate.

CHAPTER 14
Bombardment Battle

SECT.14

CHAPTER 14
Bombardment Battle

Thanks to the camera with a close-up view of SHINC's situation, the crowd in the bar saw the entire sequence very clearly.

They saw the pigtailed leader of the Amazons use her gun to shoot her own teammate. She propped herself up, steadied the silenced Vintorez sniper rifle, and fired one bullet at the squat dwarf woman a hundred feet away.

The extremely heavy 9×39 mm round struck the woman's left temple, killing her instantly.

"Wha—?!"

"Whoa!"

"Hang on!"

"Did she go crazy?!"

"Huhhhh?"

"How come?"

The bar was filled with screams and bellows.

And before they could subside, the audience saw, right behind Sophie's body, the nature of the item she had just pulled out of her inventory moments before.

The particles of light coalesced into a long stick.

"What's up?" M and the other members of PM4 heard Pito-hui ask.

"The enemy leader shot one of their members in the head and killed her," M explained as concisely as possible.

Even Pitohui found this to be a surprise. "Whaaat? Why?" she yelped.

"No idea…"

"Infighting? I guess that would be like you in the last Squad Jam!" Pitohui added, needling him. But the number of reactions she got from the team, whether laughter or anger, was zero.

So Pitohui followed it up by saying, "Well, I didn't get to see it, so how did she kill her partner? Can you explain in detail?"

M said, "Huh? Okay. They were charging to close the distance between us, and we sniped one of them. Then, at a distance of 930 yards, they all dropped to the ground. But one got up and sat cross-legged, then her own teammate shot her from behind for an instant—"

He was unable to say *kill*.

Pitohui cut him off at the end of his explanation by screaming, "Get down as flat as you can!"

The audience at the bar had a better grasp on the full situation than the ones actually fighting in it.

At the point that the dwarf woman's final item materialized, they understood at least half of SHINC's strategy. The motes of light gave shape to an enormous gun.

It was nearly seven feet long, as a matter of fact. The barrel was just a raw metal pipe with a bipod halfway down its length for support. There was a muzzle brake at the end to minimize recoil and vent exhaust.

The barrel alone was over four feet long. That was longer than the entire length of nearly any assault rifle. In order for it to be usable for a human being, the trigger, grip, and stock were placed back behind the center of gravity. A sight sticking out to the left of the barrel was nonstandard, an aftermarket scope.

And this obnoxiously long gun that looked more like a fishing rod than anything else was named—

"The PTRD-41!"

"Degtyaryov's anti-tank rifle!" two people shouted at the same time. It was in the nature of a gun fanatic to want to be the first person to identify and call out the model of a gun.

Both answers were correct. It was a Soviet Army anti-tank rifle used in 1941, during World War II. Degtyaryov was the name of its designer and represented the *D* in PTRD. Thus, the weapon was often known as a Degtyaryov anti-tank rifle in Japan.

Because tank armor at the time was fairly thin, this extremely large-caliber rifle was designed to pierce it. The reason that such weapons did not exist anymore was because they were effective only into the second half of World War II. Since then, the anti-tank rifle category had been replaced by the much-improved antimateriel rifle instead.

The bolt-action single-shot rifle used a 14.5 × 115 mm Soviet Russian round. In other words, the bullet was 14.5 mm around, and the cartridge was 115 mm long.

The .50-caliber rounds for M's M107A1 were 12.7 × 99 mm, which meant these ones were a full size bigger and used more gunpowder. Naturally, the bullets were far more destructive as well.

The entrance of this monster gun enthralled the rest of the crowd, stricken with gun mania.

"What the hell is that?!"

"What a relic we've got here!"

"How do you get your hands on something like that?!"

"Are they gonna fight back with that thing?"

"And they kept it stashed away in storage to hide their secret!"

"Very methodical… That's the kind of power that can take down M's shield."

"They didn't have it last time, right? They must've done some superhard quest to loot it since then."

But then someone wondered, quite understandably, "But how will it work? They can't aim against a flat target on their stomachs like this."

Both sides were fortified on flat land. M's team couldn't snipe well at SHINC when they were flat on the ground, so it only made sense that the women couldn't get a decent shot at M's group without lifting their guns higher.

But if they stood up to shoot, or even sat up, they would make themselves into targets. And most importantly of all, standing up was no way to fire such a heavy gun. Even sitting wouldn't give them precise aim.

These superheavy weapons were meant to be propped up on something to shoot. How were they going to use it?

The audience's question was answered with action.

It was the black-haired sniper who would fire the monster rifle. And anyone who saw the last Squad Jam knew that the one with the black hair and knit cap used a Dragunov with an adjustable scope. She was the one who sniped Llenn and nearly took her out of the first Squad Jam—the best shot on the team. She was also the last character to die in that event.

She sat behind the dead body and carefully lifted the gun there, nearly seven feet and thirty-five pounds of metal. Then she rested the front end of the long barrel atop the left shoulder of her deceased teammate.

"Ohhh…"

The audience understood, with a shiver of horror down their backs.

That was why the dwarf woman sat down facing the enemy.

That was why the leader had shot her dead.

That was why she shot the left side of her head.

"They used their own teammate as a shield and stand!"

In Squad Jam, all dead bodies remained in place as indestructible objects for ten minutes.

In other words, they were invincible shields.

Tohma lifted the silver bolt handle of the PTRD-41 and pulled it toward her. In a waterproof pouch nearby, she had ten bullets that looked big enough to be used as fatal bludgeons on their own.

She plucked one out of the pouch, leaving oil on her glove. The bullets were coated with plenty of oil to ensure the gun operated smoothly. Then Tohma loaded it into the gun through a slot on the underside and pushed the bolt forward to load it.

Kneeling about three feet behind the corpse with its arms jammed into the ground, she took aim. Through the scope, which was quite a distance from her eye, she took aim at the shield twenty-eight hundred feet away.

The moment her finger touched the trigger, a pale-green bullet circle appeared, and upon its first contraction, the Russian named Milana who controlled Tohma chanted, "Your life will be mine!"

The gun fired.

It was less of a gunshot and more of an explosion.

"Get down as flat as you can!" yelled Pitohui.

"Ngh!" M let go of the M107A1 and threw himself against the ground. Grass and dirt entered his mouth.

"Huh?" The chubby man was just a bit slower.

And unfortunately for him, the shield was blocking his view of Tohma's bullet line, so he did not notice it.

The 14.5 mm round struck the rightmost plate of the fanned-out shield—and ricocheted.

There was that spaceship-exterior metal coming into play. Thanks to the diagonal angle, even a 14.5 mm bullet from 2,800 feet did not puncture the material. It sent up a shower of sparks and made a tremendous noise, but it did hold.

However, impenetrability was not the same as shock absorption.

The kinetic energy the bullet delivered was tremendous. It slammed into the plate of the shield, inflicting tremendous pressure on it.

The shield was hardy, meant to stand up to any amount of heat and pressure. But the metal joints that folded to connect the shield, top and bottom, were not as strong as the plate itself.

The two joints that supported the piece that received the brunt of the pressure instantly twisted like soft candy and snapped apart. The

shield part then bounced right off its bearing backward—and struck the face of the man holding the Savage 110 BA right behind it.

He couldn't do a thing. No scream, no complaint, no surprise.

After the hardy metal sheet struck him, his head was twisted at an angle the human body was not meant to support, generating the red glow that indicated damage had been inflicted on the flesh.

A DEAD marker sprang up, identifying PM4's first casualty of the battle.

A blast of air buffeted the area around the PTRD-41 with its shot, whipping up a dust devil from the dry ground. The tremendous kickback did shove Tohma's body, but on her knees, leaning forward, she had enough momentum to withstand the recoil.

It was a bolt-action gun, but with a unique system that utilized the recoil to open the bolt and eject the empty cartridge—a feature that was faithfully re-created in *GGO*. Upon firing, the body and grip of the gun—essentially everything other than the shoulder stock and cheek pad—shifted backward about two and a half inches. That momentum caused the bolt handle to strike the metal bit in the rear and deflect upward. It happened automatically, rather than forcing the user to manually release the bolt.

The inertia caused the released bolt to retract, and the greased-up empty ejected itself from the chamber to fall beneath the gun.

Tohma picked up another oiled bullet and slid it into the gun from below. She pushed the retracted bolt forward to lock it on the right. The gun was ready to fire again.

"Next!"

*　　　　*　　　　*

For their counterplan against M's powerful shield, SHINC's philosophy and choice of action were simple: "We just need to get a weapon that's way more powerful than what we have now!"

If they couldn't beat him with their current firepower, they just needed a more powerful weapon to break through his shield.

So what would that be?

First, they considered the same kind of grenade launchers that Fukaziroh was now using. They could use the projectile arc to go over M's shield and reach behind it.

But with a range of not much more than four hundred yards, it just wouldn't have enough reach. They needed to be able to surpass the range of the M14 EBR (which was twice as long), or at the very least match it.

That left only one option.

They needed a high-caliber, high-powered antimateriel rifle.

That way, even if it failed to puncture the shield, the force would likely destroy the joints. Or perhaps knock the shield out of place.

So in between their busy studies, team practice, and hellish battle training, they gathered what information they could. They'd thought there were only about ten antimateriel rifles on *GGO*'s Japanese server, but the rumors said otherwise.

"That was last year. They started adding more recently, so not only are there more opportunities, it's easier to get them than before." There was hope.

Next, they tried collecting information from people who already had antimateriel rifles about how they got theirs. First, they needed rumors about who might have what, then they could search for that person. In the end, they tracked down four, and only two took their questions seriously.

Both said, "I miraculously beat a superhard quest, and it dropped from a boss encounter." As they'd expected, there would be no way to buy one from a normal store.

Of course, the chance that a person who owned one would part ways with it was much lower than for another kind of weapon. The last time one was auctioned off, it commanded a shocking price: about 200,000 yen when converted into real money.

One of the two people who answered their questions was a

woman. She was a cute girl with light-blue hair named Sinon. That was her avatar's appearance only, of course, and the player behind it might have been an old woman. Sinon was an expert in the game, a finalist who reached the end of the BoB tournament. Nobody in SHINC could beat her in a one-on-one fight.

It was Boss and Anna who got to talk with Sinon, because they finished up their homework earliest. Sinon was very helpful and accurate in answering the questions, perhaps as a favor to fellow women in the game.

According to her, the dungeons deep beneath SBC Glocken were harder than the ones in the wilderness outside and had better loot drops. The odds were much higher in the places where traps dumped you deeper in. At least, that was how she got hers.

That day was the start of a very reckless campaign for the gymnastics team in their attempt to earn an antimateriel rifle. They headed into areas they couldn't possibly handle at their current level and got chased around by super-huge boss monsters and giant machines—and occasionally stepped on. They repeatedly wiped as a squadron, respawning back in the safe part of town for no experience gain.

After they had stopped counting the number of times they wiped out and tried again, Lady Luck finally smiled upon them.

They were fighting in a long and narrow dungeon that was most likely originally a subway station. The enemy was a monstrous machine like a giant tank with multiple power-shovel arms, and the squad was blasted to bits by its laser beams. Rosa the machine gunner was unable to dodge its ramming attack, and she got crushed under its treads and splattered to pieces.

But out of some kind of vengeful spirit, her severed right hand continued to pull the trigger. The PKM kept firing, exercising its owner's last act of rage.

For the brief span of time until her body evaporated into polygonal shards, the gun shot about twenty rounds toward the walls of the tunnel. Some hit the pipes that ran along the sides, punching holes in them.

They burst forth with hot water meant to keep the subterranean tunnels warm. The spray of hot, pressurized water hit the machine monster. Suddenly its movements weakened, perhaps because of electronics shorting out. The thick steam that filled the area halved the effectiveness of the laser beams it shot from the ends of its arms.

"This is our shot! Attack at once!"

"Yeaaah!"

"Get it!"

"Destroy it!"

"Raaaah!"

The remaining five set upon it all at once, paying no heed to the boiling water.

They were wiped out in moments.

This was because of how much damage they had accumulated over the course of the fight. If it were that easy to win a battle with spirit alone, no country would ever lose a war.

But they had found the key to victory.

The next day, they went into the same dungeon and set explosives on the heating pipes. Then they lured an enemy closer and drenched it right off the bat with even more water than the day before.

At that point, it was just a matter of overpowering it.

They shot and shot and shot at the incapacitated enemy. Just shooting the arms equipped with laser beams caused the monster's accuracy to go haywire. Even still, the ferocious battle continued for some thirty minutes. Once the enemy began to run low on HP, Boss took all the plasma grenades she could carry and charged in for a suicide attack.

They won at last.

In the end, it was Tohma's Dragunov that shot through what looked like a power reactor that had been exposed by loose armor plating. But because it exploded into pieces so spectacularly, only she and Anna, the snipers shooting from a distance, actually survived.

A flashy sign congratulated them on their victory in the moldy corridor, and for landing the killing shot on the enemy, Tohma saw a small game window open for her. When she touched it, an anti-tank rifle like a giant fishing rod, the PTRD-41, appeared before her.

The girls pretty much exclusively used Soviet-era weapons, and this fit the bill, almost as though they'd been aiming for it specifically.

Anna remembered how Sinon said she'd used a French sniper rifle and got a French antimateriel rifle back. "Ah, that makes sense. I guess the gun you receive as your prize depends on what you used to beat the boss."

But of course, nobody could say if that assumption was actually correct.

When Tohma and Anna brought the massive PTRD-41 fishing rod back to the teammates who had died and spawned in town, everyone was delighted. With the way they hugged and laughed and cried and jumped, you would never imagine they'd gotten along poorly at first. The girls' school gymnastics team had been through many battles to the death with their guns, and they had become inseparable friends.

And now they had the weapon they needed.

They just had to be able to use it.

At twenty-five pounds for just the gun alone, the PTRD-41 was heavy and required a character with a very high strength stat to wield it. Only Sophie and Rosa could make immediate use of it and actually run around carrying it. They had the strength because they typically used heavy machine guns and carried huge boxes of backup ammo and barrels.

But this was a sniper rifle. Tohma and Anna were best prepared to use it, with their sniping ability and various passive skills that assisted sniping, so they trained hard in an attempt to raise their strength fast. With the arrival of spring vacation, they focused on their own efforts at all times outside of club practice.

Eventually, Tohma reached a point where she suffered a weight penalty walking around with the gun, but she could at least shoot it. At that point, the gun was effectively hers.

The first time she shot it, following the in-window instruction manual, she thought that the incredible kickback it had was going to separate her shoulder. It didn't seem like something that a human (avatar) should be able to fire.

But if she couldn't tame this beast, their team wasn't going to win. They procured a bunch of 14.5 mm bullets, and Tohma practiced with it. She got mentally tougher, teaching herself to deal with the recoil.

The gun had no scope. Anti-tank rifles at the time did not have them. But this wasn't going to help them fight long-range against M.

"If the cuckoo does not have a scope, give it one. That's how the saying goes, right?"

She used the gun-customization function to attach one. She crushed the metal aiming reticle on the left side of the barrel and welded a scope mount on instead. It was a crude method, but all that mattered was that it worked.

If she used a normal rifle scope, there was a danger that she'd damage the area around her eye when the gun kicked back on her. So instead, she used a pistol scope with a longer eye relief, meaning the distance between the lens and the eye. That worked better.

It was the creation of the "PTRD-41 Anti-Tank Rifle, Girls' School Gymnastics Team Special."

Also known as the Anti-M Ultimate Weapon, or simply, the M-Gun.

As a test run, the girls went back to challenge the same monster that had dropped the gun. They used the hot water to lock it down, then let Tohma shoot it repeatedly from a distance. The armor just peeled right off the enemy that had been so hard to defeat.

"Now we can wiiin!" Boss roared down the tunnel.

They defeated the machine like their previous hassle had never happened. Of course, they did not receive another antimateriel rifle for their trouble, but they did get good experience and money.

As the rest of the team celebrated, Tohma wondered, "But what happens if I can't get set up with a bipod in an advantageous spot? I can't exactly carry this gun around with me…"

The bulky weapon wasn't going to move once they set it up on the ground. Tohma's concerns were well-founded.

Both Rosa and Sophie, the two machine gunners, grinned at once.

Rosa said, "You guys know how sometimes you act as a base for us to prop up our machine guns when we don't have a level surface?"

Sophie said, "Exactly. We just need to do the same thing. One of the two of us will plop down on the ground, and you can fire the gun off our shoulder!"

Tohma's eyes bulged. "But…that means one of you might get shot and killed!"

Sophie said, "Yeah, that's not great. In that case, I guess we'd better commit to being a base."

"That's not what I meant by…"

"Well, this should be easy to solve!" said the dwarf woman with a grin. She was as dutiful as a team vice-captain should be. "Just kill me first. Then I'll be an invincible stand that will absorb all enemy attacks for ten whole minutes!"

*   *   *

"Next!"

Tohma had loaded the second shot before the dust of the first had even settled.

Her aim drifted a bit right this time. Right into the center of the fanned-out shield.

If she scored a hit with this one, it wouldn't just knock the shield away; it should deliver big damage to M and the gun he was using right behind it.

SHINC had not counted on M bringing in an antimateriel rifle. They'd practiced and planned to shoot from just outside the M14 EBR's effective range of nine hundred yards, but there was no complaining now. They knew they were bringing in a big gun; it was their fault they didn't expect the enemy to do the same.

"Eat this!"

She fired.

With an earthshaking blast, a hunk of carbide weighing two ounces hurtled forward at an unbelievable twenty-three hundred miles per hour, or Mach 3.

The next instant, it hit the shield.

Tohma's aim was a bit off. It struck the left edge of the shield and knocked one of the panels loose.

If M hadn't dropped to the ground like Pitohui directed, the shield panel would have smashed into his head and killed him. He looked up and clung to the M107A1.

M knew what the enemy was after. They used their own teammate's corpse as an indestructible object and set it up to be the base for a large-caliber gun in the open. A gruesome but very effective strategy.

Through the scope, he saw the dwarf woman sitting with her eyes closed and, behind her, another woman loading a bullet into a gigantic metal pipe.

"Enemy! Degtyaryov anti-tank rifle! Even a graze will kill you! Absolutely do not look up!" he ordered his squadmates, then fired the gun. While it wasn't as powerful as theirs, his gun was still devastatingly powerful. The bullet roared away and simply deflected off the sitting body's head.

"Shit!"

The monitors inside the bar faithfully showed this exchange of cannon fire. One of the Amazons fired the PTRD-41, using her own comrade as a base. The blast of sound boomed through the speakers, rumbling the air in the room and the guts of the avatars present.

When the chubby member of PM4 got bludgeoned to death with the loose piece of shield, the crowd cheered.

"Whoaaaa!"

"They did it! It worked!"

"They broke through the invincible shield!"

The shooter quickly reloaded and fired a second round. It knocked another piece of the shield off, but M did not back down. He shouted a command and fired back, but the indestructible body bounced his powerful bullet away.

Meanwhile, the woman had loaded her third bullet and was quickly sharpening her aim. The camera zoomed in on her face, displaying a fierce but delighted smile on her lips.

"It's a bombardment battle," someone muttered, but the thunderbolt of the gun firing drowned it out.

Tohma's third shot roared over the dry earth. The shock of the bullet's route traced a straight line of dust on the ground as it flew. It hit the shield, twisting off a third panel.

The panel hurtled directly over the head of M, who ducked after his own shot, then it stuck into the ground over fifteen feet away.

The eight-panel shield had lost material from either side and was down to five now. But M did not falter. The opponent's gun had auto-discharge, manual reload. His gun was a semi-auto, with five rounds left in the magazine.

"Come on!" he barked, lifting his head and aiming with the M107A1. He stared through the haze of dust at the distant enemy as though trying to kill with a glance, and he pulled the trigger.

"Taaa!"

Tohma fired her fourth bullet at the exact same time as M's shot.

It was a repeat scenario of the end of the last Squad Jam.

Tohma's and M's weapons belched fire simultaneously. The empty cartridges discharged and pinged off the ground.

The bullets passed in midflight at a distance of no more than eight inches. One struck the left shoulder of a dead body, stopping its momentum completely in an unnatural way. It fell harmlessly to the ground.

The other bullet hit the center part of the shield and pried it loose. The shield bounced backward, hitting the M107A1 and slamming into the side of M's body.

"Oof!"

He toppled to his left, grabbing the gun closer and examining its side.

"…" Then he understood.

The gun was unusable until he took it to a weapon shop. It would not do anything more for him in SJ2. The edge of the shield, which was made of that sturdy material, had carved a deep groove in the side of the gun barrel.

If he'd tried to fire it again without noticing that, the bullet would have caught on that groove, and without a place to go, the pent-up pressure would have burst the barrel. This was the kind of attention to detail in terms of how guns could get damaged that drew so many gun fanatics to *GGO*.

"The .50-caliber is down. I can't shoot it until it gets repaired," he announced. He tossed the M107A1 to the side, then carefully slid backward. When he was about ten feet away from the shield, the fifth shot hit the now unoccupied shield.

If not in *GGO*, the resulting sound would have ruptured eardrums. The panel in the center of the shield blew off. The frame was no longer able to support its curve, and the remaining pieces fell in a heap.

They'd lost one team member, their fancy invincible shield was destroyed, and their long-range rifle was unusable.

"…" "…" "…"

The three other masked men, lying facedown, all took a silent breath. No one needed to see their faces to know what expression they were making.

"Not baaad!"

Only Pitohui seemed happy about it, cackling away.

"Damn, not bad at aaall!" the bar roared with delight.

The Amazons had sacrificed one of their own, but they'd destroyed the shield of M, returning champion, and inflicted PM4's first loss. Naturally, the crowd was in an uproar.

"Yeah, yeah, yeah! SHINC could win this thing now!" cheered those who were on the side of the Amazons.

"You never know! It's five on four! And M still has the M14 EBR, plus that vicious woman is still in prime condition!" said others, who were rooting for PM4.

The crowd was split evenly between the two teams, leading to a whole lot of excited cheering. Meanwhile, one lonely man sipping whiskey from a shot glass mumbled, "What happened to my dear Llenn…? What is she doing…?"

"Huff…huff…"

Tohma panted, holding the PTRD-41, its long, long barrel issuing a trail of smoke.

"I…beat…it… I beat it, Sophie! Thank youuuu!" she cried tearfully to her friend, the steadfast corpse sitting in front of her.

"Yessss!" exulted Boss, still facedown in the wide-open field. They had lost Anna and Sophie, but they'd succeeded at the goal of getting rid of M's shield. Her watch read thirty seconds past 2:08 PM. The time had passed so slowly.

"That was perfect timing! Prepare to charge again! Tanya, you're back in the front. Tohma, give your thanks to the Degtyaryov! Rosa, provide covering fire when you're in range!" she ordered her surviving teammates. They all replied in the affirmative.

The PTRD-41 couldn't be used anymore. With Sophie dead, nobody could actually carry it around. Not only would it be too heavy for Tohma to go at more than a crawl, she'd also be unable to carry and use the semi-auto Dragunov, which she'd need in the fighting ahead. If she had to pick between the two, it was going to be the Dragunov, obviously. The same was true for Rosa and her PKM.

"Thank you for everything. Until we meet again," Tohma said to the gun that had done its job so admirably. She set it down next to Sophie's body. Then she put the remaining bullets back in her inventory, just in case someone else tried to pick up the gun and shoot it.

Boss stood and told four sets of ears, "We broke M's shield! The opportunity is ripe! Charge!"

"They're coming!" said the macho man in the mask and goggles. He fired his MG 3 machine gun at the approaching Amazons. The sound it made with the silencer was very odd.

They were very far off, still just dots by the naked eye, but he was placing the sights over them and firing in bursts of five anyway. The cartridges fell to the ground and vanished as bare polygonal models.

He kept firing. Even if he didn't hit them, the point was to force them to watch the line, dodge, and duck. It kept them from lining up any shots in return. One of the targets he'd come close to hitting stopped zigzagging and hit the deck. He assumed that he'd successfully kept them in check for now, but he hadn't actually landed a hit.

"Pull back!" M suddenly shouted, and the man obeyed, immediately hauling his gun away. A number of bullet lines appeared around the position he'd been in, and after a beat, a hail of bullets burst through, leaving brief orange lines in the sky. The grass swayed and hurtled, while dirt flew into the air.

"Eep!"

He'd been focused so much on beating the enemy that he'd been slow to react to the lines approaching on a diagonal angle. Without M's instruction, he could well have been shot just now.

The enemy was still firing. Bullets whizzed and cracked directly over his head.

"Crap!" He couldn't see it, but it was certain that while the enemy machine gunner was keeping them down, the others were moving quickly. Once the other guys—no, girls—had gone far enough, they would hunker down again, and another teammate would provide their cover fire.

"It's all right. No need to panic," M said. "It's still far enough that you have time to dodge the line. Even from the side, they don't have any cover to hide behind. If they get a bit closer, I'll ask you to hold them off again. Until that point, I'll keep sniping."

"Yes, sir."

M then took out his M14 EBR and rushed through the grass in an army crawl. The land was essentially flat here, but there would be enough slight undulation that he could find a slightly higher spot, set up the bipod just behind it, and shoot from there. It would give him more ground to hide behind and a better angle for shooting.

As he crawled, M couldn't help but wonder, *Why are they pushing at us so hard?*

His team had chosen a flat piece of land because they had the shield and the super-long-range sniper rifle. The other team had an anti-tank rifle, so they chose to fight back in that location. And they emerged triumphant. That much made sense.

But now that they had destroyed the shield and achieved their goal, SHINC had no reason to rush them head-on anymore. Shouldn't they normally pull back and regroup for a different maneuver? Why would they choose to press onward in the worst possible location, a wide-open field that was ideal for getting picked off?

Had they lost their minds with anger after the loss of their teammate? The possibility was greater than zero, but it seemed very unlikely for a squad as good as theirs. In which case...

"They must have some strategy...," he mumbled, finding a suitable spot and setting up the M14 EBR where there were no bullet lines to worry about. He aimed at the silver-haired woman through his scope.

She was quick. In her hands was a Bizon submachine gun. This was the person who'd encountered Llenn among the rocks for that ferocious dogfight last Squad Jam.

She ran for three seconds, changed directions, and approached. She was about 760 yards away.

Would she turn right or left at the next juncture? What would the angle be?

Without having the answers, M could rely only on his instincts. He aimed at an empty space.

"Let them fall where they may."

He pulled the trigger.

Tanya was in the process of changing directions in the middle of her sprint when she screamed. "Kyahrg!"

The shot went directly through her left shoulder. Even she could see the glowing damage effect. She crashed spectacularly, sending up a cloud of dust. Her hit points dropped about halfway down at once, from the green zone into yellow.

"Dammit! I got sniped! He did it without a line again! He read my mind!" Tanya swore in frustration. She pulled out an emergency med kit and stuck it into her neck. Very slowly, her hit points began to recover.

"Boss! I don't think we can get much closer than this!" Tanya complained with her typical good cheer.

"I know that! But we've got to do it regardless! Just like we planned!" Boss replied, her face still in the dirt.

Five seconds later, right as she was about to get up, her wrist-watch buzzed, and she looked at the readout.

2:09:30.

"Here we go! It's time!" she called out.

"Roger that!" replied Llenn.

CHAPTER 15

It's Just a Game

SECT.15

CHAPTER 15
It's Just a Game

Although it wasn't shown on camera at all, from about 2:05 to about twenty seconds past 2:09, over four minutes in which SHINC and PM4 carried out their intense long-range battle, there were two characters who were crawling along the entire time.

One was Llenn.

She had a brown camouflage poncho on to hide her pink battle fatigues, and she was army crawling at absolute top speed over earth of the same color.

With her incredible agility stat, what would happen if she tried to crawl as swiftly as possible? It turned into an ultra-high-speed crawl, like watching a video on fast forward. She was scrabbling over the dirt at about the speed of an ordinary person trotting along, only it looked like some giant crawling insect.

The other person was Fukaziroh.

Her camo was already well suited for this terrain, so she didn't need a poncho. She dragged her two MGL-140s along at the slow crawling speed of a normal person. "Heave-ho. Heave-ho. And there we go." She was more like a caterpillar.

The rigors of an endless crawl were impossible to understand unless you did it yourself. The act of sliding across the earth with nothing but elbows and legs sapped stamina and wore down the mind.

There was no physical stamina in *GGO*, but mental stamina

was a different matter. The fatigue of the mind was something that did take a toll on a player.

But Llenn pressed on.

Defeat Pito. Defeat Pito. Defeat Pito. The mantra echoed in her mind. She pushed her right elbow and knee forward on the beat of *Defeat*, and the left elbow and knee on *Pito*.

Occasionally, she would look up, using the distant scenery as her guide, to make sure her direction was correct. Over the low brown horizon, she saw a small patch of green earth.

And she was heading right for where Pitohui had been on the two o'clock scan.

The place where SHINC was fighting now.

✳   ✳   ✳

Slightly earlier, at 1:50, inside the dome…

After the scan had passed, Boss wished Llenn a good clean fight, but Llenn was unable to respond in kind. She'd hemmed and hawed, unable to explain why, until Fukaziroh spilled all the beans in one go.

They had explained the situation as thus: Llenn was only fighting in SJ2 so she could save the life of Pitohui's player. It was the biggest spoiler she'd ever dropped in her life.

"Hmm…," Boss had mumbled. Her expression looked bitter at first, but after several seconds of contemplation, she asked, "In that case… Is there anything we can do for you, Karen?"

Llenn and Boss came up with their plan in a very short span of time.

It would be a two-team pincer attack. Boss's group would leave the dome from the south; Llenn's team would leave from the east and wait for the two o'clock scan. They would identify the location of PM4, most likely southeast of the dome, and converge on the spot from different directions.

SHINC would attack first, from the south. While PM4 was preoccupied with the battle, Llenn and Fukaziroh would attack from behind.

Defeating Pitohui would be Llenn's job, but SHINC would help with that by whittling down as much of PM4 as they could.

"It'll work! We have our own plan to get rid of M's shield, as a matter of fact! We can keep PM4 occupied for at least that long! And hey, if we get wiped out, that's that!"

Llenn knew best of all that the girls just wanted to win.

"..."

She started to say something, then thought better of it. Instead, she bowed her little head low.

"Next time, I'm buying you more snacks than you can possibly eat! That's a promise!"

Moments before the two o'clock scan, Llenn burst out of the dome and began sprinting almost directly north, not even toward the likely location of PM4.

All in order to create an impression: *She's running away. No likely contact in the next ten minutes.*

At two, after running pell-mell, Llenn reached the foot of the snowy mountain. She watched the scan come in there and confirmed that PM4 was where she expected them to be.

"Taaaaa!"

When the scan was over, she began racing like a demon for that spot, over a mile and a half away.

Meanwhile, Fukaziroh stayed behind, hiding inside the dome, and began to slowly make her way toward the same location. They proceeded toward PM4, Llenn covering massive ground at superhuman speed, and Fukaziroh making her way slowly from a much closer location.

But because it was a highly visible area, they would be spotted if they simply ran up. PM4 was a very capable team, and they would not fail to notice what was happening around them.

So Llenn and Fukaziroh got within a certain distance before getting down and crawling the rest of the way.

In under three minutes, Llenn ran over a mile, then put on the camo poncho and began to crawl over the dirt for the rest of the distance. Fukaziroh did the same.

Llenn could hear that SHINC and PM4 had begun battle, just as they'd planned. The gunshots were distant but audible.

Then she heard Boss say, "Okay! Target PM4! Commence Operation Snacks!"

This was possible thanks to the comm that Boss had taken from the team they'd beaten very early in SJ2. Any weapon or gear taken from another character was usable until the end of the event. So this whole time, Boss had been giving orders to her entire team, *plus one*.

That was why, while she was crawling, Llenn knew that M had sniped Anna with an ultra-long-range sniper rifle, and that Sophie had died to become a shield, just as they'd planned.

"We broke M's shield! The opportunity is ripe! Charge!"

And she knew that Boss and her three teammates broke through the shield and were engaging in a diversionary charge.

She could hear the sound of SHINC's machine guns and M's M14 EBR. It sounded like a merciless shoot-out.

It was impossible to see, because she'd been crawling the whole way, but there had to be less than a third of a mile to go until she reached PM4.

Their perilous and painful plan had paid off.

*   *   *

Llenn's wristwatch buzzed, signaling that it was thirty seconds past 2:09.

"It's time!" Boss said in her ear.

"Roger that!" Llenn replied.

The final stage of the plan: get as close as possible before the 2:10 scan and attack before PM4 saw them on the map.

"Do it, Fuka!" yelled Llenn at 9:40.

"You got it!" Fukaziroh shot back. She readied the MGL-140 while lying on the ground. "Hi-yah-yah-yah!"

Between 9:45 and 9:50, she shot off six consecutive grenades.

They were aimed at a location between where she believed PM4 to be and where Llenn was. Her job was to paint the space pink and allow Llenn to make a high-speed charge.

The six smoke grenades she kept back for this purpose landed right where they wanted and began issuing smoke. Llenn could see the space before her turning the proper color.

"Okay! I'm going for it!"

"Best of luck!" "You got this!" Fukaziroh and Boss replied together.

Llenn tore the poncho off and stood up. Once her feet pushed off the ground that supported her body, they would not stop until she clung to Pitohui's throat.

Here goes!

On her feet, her eyes looking upward for the first moment in minutes, Llenn noticed a dark blob to her left.

At first, she thought it was just a mound of dark, damp earth, like a large anthill.

But the next moment, she saw the short black line extending to the side.

Then she recognized that it was a gun barrel.

And once she knew it was a gun, her mind could then process the human figure behind it. It was a seated person with legs in front, looking like a black mass. A person cradling a long rifle and aiming it. About 650 feet away.

And the gun was pointed right in the direction that she was about to charge: toward PM4.

The possibility was still only one in five, but a terrible premonition ran down Llenn's spine.

"Noooo!"

She gave up on running and pointed the P90 instead.
She opened fire.

*   *   *

Shirley's plan was almost the same as Llenn's: snipe and kill Pitohui.

Once her mind was made up, she suppressed her burning desire for revenge and calmly considered what she could do to achieve it.

The most important thing in hunting was not to shoot a gun well. It was getting yourself to a situation where you were guaranteed a clean hit. In other words, how close you could get to your target. The better the hunter, the closer they were to the animal when they fired.

At 1:59, Shirley began climbing the snowy mountain. It was to try to fool them about her location on the upcoming scan, whether it was going to work or not.

And in order for this to work, she opened up her inventory and brought out an item. It was an item that she actually used in real hunting off-line and one to help her deal with snowy slopes in *GGO*, too—a pair of skis.

These were no ordinary skis for enjoying the feeling of sliding down snow. They were a special pair made for hunting and other mountain activities. They were probably called mountain skis popularly, but all the Japanese hunters knew them as sommerskis, or summer skis.

They were about five feet long, with no binding at the ankle, so you could walk with them like cross-country skis.

The biggest feature of them all was a special layer called a seal on the underside of the skis to keep them from sliding. They were named for the sealskin they were traditionally made of, which always grew fur in one direction. This meant they would slide forward but grab the surface of the snow and hold tight in reverse. Just by shifting their legs forward and backward, skiers could climb right up a slope.

Mai had plenty of experience with sommerskis. It was the

best possible tool for making your way quickly around the back-country in the snow. As Shirley, that still held true. She kept the R93 Tactical 2 on her back and hurtled up the slope like an alpine soldier with her poles in hand.

At two o'clock, a very slow Satellite Scan started up. Shirley checked her device with one hand as she climbed. She glanced at PM4's location, driving it into her memory.

She continued climbing the snowy mountain for as long as the scan was going. She wanted all the other players to think she was running for safety.

After a full minute, the scan was finished.

"..."

The woman with mud across her face stopped and turned around. She'd climbed quite a ways. Down the smooth slope, the massive dome was visible on the right. On the left was the valley with the long bridge, with the rocky mountain on the other side.

Straight ahead was a grand, wide-open space filled with green—and a small log house.

"Haah!" she barked, a smile on her lips.

She rearranged her feet and began to slide downhill, toward the target she meant to shoot and kill.

She was more than twice as fast going down the hill than she was climbing it.

Shirley shot down the slope in moments, as straight as a shot put. She didn't have the Skiing skill in the game, but because she was an expert skier, it was no issue for her.

She had about a mile to go until she reached her target.

Then Shirley used a strategy identical to Llenn's. She started crawling. It was the only way for her to approach without being spotted by her target or any other hostiles in the area. The difference between her approach and Llenn's was that she crawled for a much longer period of time, and her terrain was sludgy with snowmelt.

She put two gloves over the end of the R93 Tactical 2 to keep the mud from getting inside the muzzle. Then she laid it sideways across the crook of her elbows and began to wade across the muddy ground.

Instantly, she was covered in filth. Her torso, her legs, and even her brilliant green hair turned black with mud.

While she crawled, she learned from the sound of gunshots that some other team had started fighting PM4. It was probably someone coming from the south. There were huge gunshots like thunderclaps. It sounded like they were firing cannons.

This battle was exactly what she needed. Shirley smirked to herself, white teeth shining in the middle of her muddy cheeks.

She kept moving, onward and onward...until her wristwatch told her that it was past 2:09, and she stopped.

In fifty seconds, her position would be made obvious on the scan. She didn't know how much closer she was to that woman now, but at this point, her only option was to set up her gun.

Shirley moved slowly to avoid detection. First, she rolled over onto her back. Then she circled around 180 degrees, pointing her feet toward the enemy.

She took the gloves off the muzzle of the R93 Tactical 2 and pulled herself up to a sitting position with ab muscles alone. By raising and spreading her knees a bit, then bracing the outside of her elbows against her inner thighs, she could stabilize herself in a firing position.

Shirley opened both ends of the scope and peered through the lens, pulling the gun up slightly.

"There..."

She found PM4's location right away. It was about a third of a mile away, atop a patch of grass. The enemies a few hundred yards on the opposite side were shooting off machine guns, and the tracer rounds made it easy to spot them.

To Shirley's good fortune, she found the woman who had killed her partners right away. She was down on a dip in the grassy slope. But she was being cautious and staying down, leaving only a bit of her ponytail visible. The only thing Shirley could do was give her a haircut.

She considered aiming a bit lower with the hopes of hitting her in the face, but she abandoned that idea. Knowing that woman, she probably did stuff like dropping her gun down to guard her face or something like that.

"Dammit!"

She'd successfully snuck up to firing range and had her target in her sights, unaware—but she was unable to take her shot and score a vital hit. She looked at her watch: 2:09:45.

The scan would start in fifteen seconds.

If she stayed there, she'd get busted immediately, and PM4 would take appropriate action. Whether that would be a hail of machine-gun fire, a deadly sniper shot, or more of that horrible woman's shooting, she didn't know—but with nothing but a single bolt-action sniper rifle, Shirley knew she didn't stand a chance.

Perhaps she should accept that her approach was a failure and run away while she could. Or should she attack, expecting to die in the attempt?

As she pondered these extreme options, Shirley heard a distant sound of gunshots.

It was something else, not the machine-gun rhythm she'd been hearing already.

This was almost cute, like *pom-pom-pom-pom-pom*.

It sounded louder in her right ear, so it was probably coming from her right. But before she could determine the source of the sound, she caught sight of something truly unbelievable out of the right side of her vision through the scope.

"Huh?"

There were little bursts of pink smoke appearing one after the other, one, two, three—six in all. With no real wind passing by, the smoke rose upward and outward.

Why...smoke?

No... Why pink?

It didn't make sense to Shirley.

She hadn't seen any footage from the prior Squad Jam, so she wouldn't have known that a little shrimp wearing pink was the winner. So the pink shade of the smoke meant nothing to her. It just looked festive.

And then, grappling with confusion, more visual information entered her right eye. Within the enlarged world of the scope lens, the woman—the horrible one who had cheap-shot all her friends—raised her head.

There was new armor covering her head that hadn't been there before, but the snotty tattooed face was clearly the same.

And she wore a happy smile. Shirley could see her pearly whites.

Why? How come? For what reason?

The woman who had been so cautious—and hadn't let down her guard for even an instant—raised her head and smiled when she saw the pink smoke. Shirley couldn't fathom what this meant.

But she wasn't going to let this opportunity pass. Even without a bullet circle, at this distance, she was confident she could hit any still target.

Shirley instantly put the crosshairs of the scope just a tad higher than the woman's right eye. The scope was set for about a hundred yards shorter, so this accounted for extra distance. The woman was facing slightly to her left, so if it hit her right eye, the bullet would bury itself deep into her brain.

Once she was sure she could kill the woman, Shirley felt her heart leap like never before.

"Ha-ha-ha-ha." She laughed to herself.

What a comical thing. After all her stubbornness about never pointing her gun at someone else, even in a game, she had let her fury carry her up and down a snowy slope, crawled in the mud for minutes straight, then readied her gun and was about to seize her shot.

What would her old self say if she saw this?

But it didn't matter.

It was just a game. It was just for fun, she told herself, mind clear in a single instant.

Just because she shot guns in real life, it didn't make any sense to get angry about pointing them at people inside a game. Just

2ND SQUAD JAM: FINISH   153

like her friends had once laughed, there was no need to treat real life and games the same way.

That woman had two-timed Shirley's teammates and shot them as part of the game.

In a battle royale where everything was permitted, it was their fault for turning their backs and letting themselves be tricked.

She was attempting to snipe her target now as part of the game.

It was the woman's fault for showing her face.

This was a game.

Your avatar dying didn't mean that you died.

Their avatars dying didn't mean that they died.

At last, Shirley felt like she understood what it meant to enjoy Squad Jam.

She was going to shoot and kill that woman—but only in SJ2. When the event was over, they could share a drink together as fellow female players and have a fun conversation about how they got back at each other.

And so, without anger or resentment, out of nothing but enjoyment, Shirley pulled the trigger of the R93 Tactical 2.

Her gun roared, high-pitched, letting off all the steam that had built up over an hour of disuse.

It was only an instant of relaxation.

"Ha-ha! That's gotta be Llenn!"

Pitohui figured it all out when she saw the pink smoke. Llenn was going to come charging through that smoke to attack.

Then she lifted her head. She was smiling.

And a bullet without anger or resentment burrowed into Pitohui's right eye.

"Got her!" shouted Shirley, almost as loud as the gunshot, when she saw the damage effect light up on Pitohui's eye through the scope. Just the way the effects had appeared on Shirley's teammates in the preliminary round—and after the battle in the fields.

Her white teeth sparkled in the middle of her muddy face.

A swarm of 5.7 mm bullets assaulted her location, sending up plumes of mud all around her.

Crack. One struck her right temple.

"Huh?"

That vital hit knocked Shirley's hit points all the way down. She watched them go on her bar in the upper left.

"Awww. I got shot. Darn. I guess someone else was close by. I got sloppy," she groaned happily, falling back to the ground.

The shot had been a one-hit kill, knocking her HP to zero.

A sign reading DEAD appeared over the muddy woman's body.

Shirley died in the midst of SJ2, gazing up at the sky with a satisfied smile on her face.

"Huff...huff..."

Llenn had emptied her fifty-round magazine at the target 650 feet away.

"Yes!"

Three seconds later, a small red sign appeared. She didn't know who it was, but she knew she had beaten them.

It was right at the edge of the P90's effective range, and she wasn't good enough to aim from that long of a distance. It was pure "spray and pray"; she dumped her ammo and was lucky that one hit the target in the head.

"Wh-what's up?" Fukaziroh asked her, startled.

No wonder she was. She'd just used the last of her smoke grenades to set up a screen, and rather than charging through, Llenn had started shooting off to the left. That had probably revealed Llenn's location to the enemy, too.

Llenn crouched and changed out her magazine, telling Fukaziroh and Boss, "There was a sniper from a different team right nearby! They were aiming at Pito's group! So I shot at them first and managed to beat them!"

Fukaziroh's response was "My word! Brilliant! But...did they actually shoot anyone?"

"I—I don't know! The sound was all mixed together!" Llenn admitted. She'd been so busy shooting her P90 that she was totally unable to tell if the sniper had fired any shots.

If they had…and they were after Pitohui…and they had landed the shot…

Llenn went pale, right as the ticker on her wrist crossed 2:10.

The scan was starting, but neither Boss nor Llenn had the time or wherewithal to pull out their terminals to view the results.

Neither did PM4.

M hit Tanya with a shot and was looking for his next target when the small man with the shotgun reported, "Behind us! Smoke grenades! Newcomers!"

There was no mention of color, so M let the gun drop and pulled back before turning around. Then he saw the impossible pink color of the smoke.

He figured out everything—all of it—in an instant.

He knew that SHINC's wild push was in coordination with Llenn's team and was meant to grind them down and occupy their attention. He just didn't know when and where they had come to this agreement.

And of course, the pink smoke was meant to hide Llenn's charge. It was hard enough to shoot Llenn with her size and speed even when you *could* see her, so having her blend in among smoke of the same color made it nearly impossible.

It was a good plan. Llenn was going to charge them from the smoke while the scan was happening.

"Llenn's coming! Watch the rear!" M warned his squadmates, glancing at Pitohui, who was ten yards ahead and to the right.

"Ha-ha! That's gotta be Llenn!" Pitohui marveled, reaching the same conclusion as M. She lifted her head.

Three seconds later, she collapsed to the grass, spraying red damage effects.

*   *   *

"That chick got shot!"

One of the cameras had a close-up on the woman, red light streaming from her right eye.

"Whoa!"

"Yikes! Damn!"

"Hyaaa!"

The bar was positively buzzing. Half the crowd was certain that the woman on that team was the strongest and craziest in the battle and was a shoo-in to triumph. And she'd just been sniped—in the face.

"From where? Who did it?" someone asked. As if to answer, one of the screens switched to a muddy woman clutching an R93 Tactical 2 from a seated position.

"It's her! Way to go!"

And the next moment, she was hit by a swarm of bullets and died.

"Aaah!"

"And she's down!"

The angle switched yet again to display Llenn furiously firing her P90.

"It's Llenn! She's gettin' it done!"

The time was 2:10. The scan had just started, so one of the screens in the bar automatically displayed the map, but no one was paying attention to it.

"Pito!" screamed M, racing over to Pitohui. He grabbed her facedown body and flipped her over to cradle her, using his massive size as a shield.

Pitohui's right eye was bright red with gunshot damage, the color flickering with polygonal effects rather than blood.

"Ha-ha, ah-ha-ha-ha-ha! Ah-ha-ha-ha-ha-haaa-ha-ha-ha-ha!" Her left eye was open wide enough that it threatened to split down the sides. Tears streamed out of it like a waterfall, and her mouth was turned up and emitting raucous laughter. "Ah-ha-ha-ha-ha-ha-ha-ha-ha-haaaa!"

M pulled an emergency med kit from his own pouch and stuck it in Pitohui's neck without hesitation. Then he glanced to the left to examine his team's HP bars.

"…"

Pitohui's was dropping rapidly, down into yellow—

"Ah-ha-ha-ha-ha! So this is it! This is my deaaaaath!"

And then into red—

"I'm gonna die now! It's finally happening! Ah-ha-ha-ha-ha-ha-haaa-ha-ha-ha-ha-ha-ha!"

And with that final burst of laughter, it stopped.

Her remaining hit points were so few that he couldn't even see the bar anymore.

"Haaah…"

M exhaled at last, cradling Pitohui. On his craggy face was the same flood of tears he'd shown in the last Squad Jam.

"Hya-haaaa! What's with the crying, Goushi?!" said the one-eyed woman, slipping out of his grasp like a snake. "I haven't died yet! Ee-hee-hee-hee-hee-hee! I haven't died yet!"

She rolled over onto her face in the grass and continued screaming.

"This is so much fuuuun! Isn't it? It's so fuuuuun!" Her slender body writhed and flopped like a dying cicada. "Ah-ha-ha-ha-ha-ha-ha-ha! Aaaah-ha-ha-ha-ha-ha-ha!"

She seemed to be having too much fun.

"Please, Boss! Let's not do this!" M cried tearfully. "I know you've figured it out! You're just as scared of dying as everyone else! So let's not do this!"

"What are you saying, Goushi? You really think I can *stop* doing something so scary and fun?" Pitohui said, answering him with a punch.

"Gahk!" M's head turned on his thick neck.

"I can still do this! I can, I can, I can, I can—"

Her shriek abruptly froze, and she flopped backward against the ground.

The DEAD tag did not appear over her.

*   *   *

"..."

The small man with the UTS-15 shotgun, who was closest to Pitohui, had no idea how to react to this. He simply watched the whole scene play out after she got shot.

Pitohui's right eye had been shot from a long distance, so it had certainly been done with be a rifle. Somehow, she'd managed to escape death by the slimmest possible margin.

GGO was just a game, so it worked on very simple mathematical formulas: subtract the attack number from the character's number. If you were as tough as Pitohui was and got shot somewhere between the right eye and right brain, the same thing might happen to you.

He could only admire Pitohui's incredible luck in battle.

The man listened to the conversation that transpired after that, too. He actually got a little bit jealous about how seriously Pitohui and M were taking life and death in the game. No matter how realistic it got, a virtual game was still virtual. "Dying" never meant actually dying.

And yet, they were so agitated that they were literally crying.

Yeah, they were probably getting a little too deep in their own role-playing, but it really looked like fun. In fact, he felt like he heard some real-life names among all the passionate emoting, but he was a conscientious gamer and decided that he did not hear it after all. Sometimes the Ignoring skill was very important.

Lastly, the man was left with one question.

Pitohui was so agitated that she passed out. So why didn't her AmuSphere shut down?

In the past, he had witnessed multiple occasions of VR newbies who were so overwhelmed by the experience of virtual battle that their minds were tricked into thinking that they were actually about to die.

The virtual experience of getting cut or shot or burned or blown up was plenty scary on its own, even if it wasn't as bad as the real thing. But there was no need for them to be more frightened of it—the VR world would expel them before their terror could reach its peak.

Most extreme mental states led to bodily repercussions: a rise in pulse or breathing, a sudden outbreak of sweat, extreme blood pressure, and so on.

The thoughtful safety measures of the AmuSphere, once detected, would forcefully pull a panicking player out of the world of dreams and back to reality. It was just like waking up from a nightmare and realizing with relief, "Oh... It was just a dream... Thank goodness..."

So based on how agitated Pitohui and M had been acting earlier, the AmuSphere could easily have butted in and addressed things.

Unless...

An unsettling possibility occurred to the man.

No, no. It couldn't be that. Anything but that...

It was such an unlikely thing that it was pointless to even consider it.

It couldn't be true that Pitohui was using a first-generation home VR machine that was capable of opting out of the Health Monitor safety detection systems: the infamous NerveGear.

He glanced to his upper left and confirmed that the unconscious Pitohui's hit points really were increasing, as slow as a snail crawling. His problem to consider now was that Pitohui, who made up the core of the team's power with M, had suffered great damage and would need time to recover.

The tall man, who hadn't let down his guard in the least, peered through his binoculars from a kneeling position. "Sniper was to the north-northwest, about sixteen hundred feet. She's the surviving member of that team of hunters. Now deceased. High possibility that another nearby team shot her, probably located behind the pink smoke," he reported.

M was instantly their leader again, no longer crying. "That's Llenn. She was planning to charge us through the smoke, but she spotted the sniper first and shot her. The other member of LF has a powerful six-shot grenade launcher. Don't get sloppy," he cautioned.

There was a burst of suppressed fire from the MG 3 machine gun, about twenty rounds of automatic fire. "We're still fine over here! All the Amazons are standing their ground!" the shooter reported confidently, before admitting, "But if they go on a suicide charge all at once, spread out the way they are, I don't know if I can hold them all off!"

M immediately replied. "We're pulling back. I'll take Pito. Leave the Barrett. You guys grab the M14 and Savage," he ordered the three other men.

The tall man who'd transported the M107A1 in his inventory replied in the affirmative.

"We retreat to the log house. We need to hunker down in a high-altitude location until Pito recovers. Everybody needs to sprint. Let's do this!"

"Is the chick…dead…?"

"But I don't see the DEAD tag…"

In the bar, the topic of discussion was Pitohui, after she fell backward and stopped moving. Before she collapsed, she'd been yelling with excitement about something or other, but for better or for worse, the cameras didn't pick up any voices unless they were very close.

The special rules of Squad Jam said that if a player had an automatic shutdown due to an overabundance of emotion, their avatar should vanish, but that didn't happen here.

So what happened?

M and the rest of the team burst into motion without any consensus among the crowd.

The tallest man on the team crawled around in the grass, picking up M's M14 EBR and the chubby sniper's Savage 110 BA, and made the movements with his left hand to open his window and drop them in.

The Savage's owner was dead, but the team was still going to make use of the gun. He also pulled spare magazines from the body's pouches. As for M, he crawled quickly over to the pieces of his shield and picked up the two still-intact pieces.

"Oh! What's he gonna do with that?" the crowd wondered. He promptly demonstrated—M lifted Pitohui, battle gear and all, in a so-called princess carry, and placed the two shield plates over her stomach to protect her.

"Oh, I see… He really cares for her…"

"Well, she's the team's best attacker, clearly."

"Nah, I think it's love. There's love between them!"

"Love…? Say, where can I buy some of that?"

"Don't ask me, dude."

The large machine gunner hoisted the MG 3, equipped with a new ammo box, onto his shoulder and stood up. He started firing in short bursts in the direction of the Amazons to keep them at bay.

On that cue, the others started to run. It was clear to any and all what they were trying to do: get away from that spot as quickly as possible.

"Yeah, I guess they need to run…"

"Can't blame 'em."

Everyone in the pub understood that it was the best course of action.

Lastly, one of them noted, "That's one dead and one maimed for PM4… Now there's no saying who should be the favorite at this point…"

Through a high-powered lens, Tohma watched PM4 flee. With the MG 3 sending bullet lines all over the area, she stood up, essentially saying, "I can dodge *after* the line hits me," and looked through a large pair of binoculars at a higher elevation.

"They're moving toward the log house. Current distance: one thousand yards. Distance to log house: twelve hundred," she reported to Boss. Boss repeated that information to Llenn. Llenn passed it on to Fukaziroh.

"M's carrying the woman. Damage effect on her face. Looks like she got sniped. I don't see the tag, so she's not dead, but she's not moving, either."

The message made its way through the game of telephone to Llenn.

"Gyaaaa! So that person *was* aiming at Pito! She got shot!"

"Calm down—she's not dead. She probably lost almost all her HP from getting shot. I just don't know why he's carrying her," Boss said calmly. She asked Llenn, "What should we do? Follow at once? I don't think we can catch them before they escape into the log house, of course, but we could do a pincer attack before they can get set up and fortify themselves. If you can manage to get inside, I bet you could attack Pitohui before her hit points are all recovered."

"…"

Crouched with P90 in hand, Llenn wasn't able to answer right away. The smoke over the plain was almost entirely clear now. She'd wasted the six shots they'd saved to be their final secret weapon.

Boss's idea made sense. PM4 was on the run. If they all rushed to circle the log house, and she snuck into the house while SHINC was keeping them busy, the plan in general would work the same way as the last one.

But Pitohui had just suffered a ton of damage. It was going to take six minutes at minimum for her HP to recover to full, perhaps longer. If she attacked her before recovery…

"If I finish her off while she's damaged, does that really mean that *I* beat Pito…?" Llenn wondered aloud.

"I have no idea." "No way to know," replied Fukaziroh and Boss at the same time, one in each ear.

"The one who decides that," "The one who decides that," they said in perfect unison, "is you, Llenn."

Llenn closed her eyes.

She spent four seconds in contemplation, feeling the weight of P-chan in her right hand—then lifted her head.

"Let's hit them from two sides! We'll slaughter all of PM4! But Pito will be mine! She's damaged? That's her fault for being careless! That's *GGO*! No matter what, I'm going to beat Pito! That's why I'm here right now!"

Her eyes glimmered with murder.

CHAPTER 16
Memento Mori

CHAPTER 16
Memento Mori

2:13 PM.

In the bar, the screens showed an aerial view of the log house.

It was a two-story building about 150 feet across the facade, thirty to fifty feet from front to back, and twenty-five feet tall. The walls and roof were built with astonishingly large logs. Each looked to be over two feet in diameter.

Thinner logs were cut to make the gabled roof, which sported four brick chimneys. There were four balconies in a line on the south face of the second floor.

Around the log house was a pleasant lawn, and there were even a number of gravel walkways leading out from the eastern side. Little streams trailed alongside the paths, widening into ponds here and there.

But as the camera approached, something rather mysterious came into view. There was actually a copious amount of steam rising from the streams and ponds.

Someone in the audience noticed and wondered, "What is that? Hot springs?"

"Bwa-ha-ha. Well, it ain't gonna be that!" Someone else laughed.

At that precise moment, one of the ponds erupted with water. A fountain nearly two feet wide and seventy feet tall burst upward, spraying water and steam all around for ten seconds before it abruptly ended.

The crowd was stunned. Eventually, someone commented, "Uh… If only it were a hot spring. That's a geyser. Those things that shoot heated underground reservoir water out at regular intervals."

"Ohhh! So the reason there's actual plants around that area is because of the thermal energy and the presence of water."

"I'm guessing that the log house is actually meant to be a hotel for geyser tourists. And the number of chimneys makes sense, too. There are as many rooms as chimneys on the second floor."

The crowd was rather observant, it had to be said.

"Bellhop, see the M party to their room!"

On the screen, PM4 was just arriving at the building. The small man with the boxy UTS-15 shotgun on his shoulder went to the front door, in the center of the building. He did a quick check for traps, then pulled on the large door. It wasn't locked.

M was next, still carrying the woman in his arms, followed by the tall man who put the weapons into his inventory, and lastly, the large man with the MG 3 with a silencer. There were no enemy attacks as they filed in.

"They're all in the log house," Tohma reported. Boss passed on the message to Llenn again.

"Got it!" Llenn said. Boss passed that back to the surviving members of SHINC: Tanya, Tohma, and Rosa. They didn't attack, but both LF and SHINC had a handle on what PM4 was doing.

Llenn and Fukaziroh were about a third of a mile north of the log house. They were lying flat on the grass, spaced about ten yards apart. Llenn was wearing her green camo poncho again, to keep from being spotted and sniped at.

Boss and her team were on the opposite side, a third of a mile south of the log house, where they could see the entrance. Aside from Tohma, who was on her knees, the rest were on the ground to protect against M's deadly lineless sniping.

Llenn used her monocular to observe the north exterior of the structure in great detail. From here to the building, the land was basically flat, covered with grass about knee-high. There were no obstacles, impediments, or cover.

The log house was built on a concrete foundation about four inches thick. There was no large entryway on the north side, just side doors on each end. This side of the building seemed to be a straight hallway on both floors, with small windows set at regular intervals. By the standards of GGO, it was a remarkably well-kept building. Not a single window was broken.

The lights didn't seem to be on inside, but the windows didn't have curtains, so it was probably bright enough already.

In her ear, Llenn heard Boss say, "Like we planned, we're going to put on full-bore covering fire. Just wait for us to get to a better distance and position. I'll send a signal."

Llenn gave her an affirmative and relayed the message to Fukaziroh.

Oh, geez... Thank you so much, she thought. The members of SHINC were surely crawling forward at great risk for her sake at this very moment.

While the location may have changed, the plan was the same. While SHINC fought fiercely from the south, Llenn would approach from the north and somehow find a way to defeat Pitohui.

But this time, Llenn had to charge into that building.

The issue was where to enter.

The log house's windows were very small and set into tough, thick wood frames. They looked like the type that pulled upward, rather than sliding to the side.

The idea to get a running start and break through the window, like she did in the very first battle, was probably a valid one, but it was too likely to end in failure. She could envision herself bouncing off the window frame or colliding with the logs because she got the angle wrong.

That left only the side doors at the corners of the building.

"I'm going in the door on the west edge of the building. Don't shoot that way," Llenn told Boss and Fukaziroh, waiting for their acknowledgment.

There was no more smoke screen to be had; she would need to sprint straight for the building. If anyone in PM4 foresaw their plan and set up in wait, she'd be running right into a hail of gunfire.

"Whew…," she exhaled, squeezing the P90 under her poncho and looking resolute.

Through her comm unit, she heard Fukaziroh reassure her from ten yards to her right. "Relax, relax. You got this," she said. "You're still the lucky girl, Llenn. That sniper took Pito all the way down, so she's easier to beat, and now that you'll be fighting indoors, there's no imbalance in range between their rifles and P-chan. Being tiny and fast is a huge advantage indoors. Now you just have to charge in safely! Go on, then! Get in there!"

Llenn stared ahead. "All right… Thank you for everything, Fuka. I mean it. Thanks for coming this far with me," she said to her trusty partner.

"You bet. It's the final battle. Go give it everything you've got. Finish Pito off."

Llenn took her eyes off the log house and glanced over to Fukaziroh on her right.

Pitohui had told her so many times that when you were on a lookout, you should never make unnecessary eye contact. It was absolutely forbidden—but this one time, before her big charge, she wanted to see her partner's smile.

Yes! I can do this! she was about to say, as soon as she could see Fuka.

"Huh?"

But then she saw, past the grass and Fukaziroh, a long stretch of brown land.

And off in the distance, a dust cloud rising.

At first she thought it was just a whirlwind. It simply looked too big to be real. You couldn't kick up that kind of dust from one or two—or six—people running together.

It took three seconds for her to realize her mistake.

"Ah!"

As it grew larger and larger, she could see that the source of the rising dust was cresting the horizon and approaching.

Three vehicles were racing side by side across the dry earth.

When she saw the boxy silhouettes of four-wheel-drive vehicles, Llenn shouted, "From the west! A caravan, a car, a van!" She was so agitated that the message slipped away from her.

"Bwa-ha!" Fukaziroh snorted.

"Whaaaat?" Boss reacted belatedly, taken aback by the corny wordplay. But when she tilted her head to look in the indicated direction, she too saw the rising dust.

At about the same time, Tohma lifted her upper half just a bit and turned the scope of her Dragunov, which had been trained on the windows of the log house, toward the western horizon.

"Cars! Three off-road vehicles! They're coming this way—I mean, toward the log house!" she reported. Just then, a bullet from a second-story window of the building struck her in the right shoulder.

"Kyah!" she shrieked adorably, lying down flat.

There hadn't been any line at all, which meant it must've been M. The elite sniper's legend still lived. He could fire instantly at any visible body part and hit it, too.

"Dammit!" Boss swore to both parties.

"Now we're cookin'!"

In the bar, the screens showed a trio of 4WD vehicles kicking up a dust storm as they drove.

They were vehicles well-known for their transport use in the American military: Humvees. Sand yellow in color, fifteen feet long, seven feet wide, boxy and flat in shape.

The Humvee's large tires and high suspension gave them a distinctively high minimum ground clearance. They could drive over terrible conditions without worrying about contact with the underside of the body.

There were many different types of Humvees; the ones on the screen were M1114s used by the US Army, covered with thick armor. There was a round opening in the roof with a rack for an M2 .50-caliber heavy machine gun and armor sheeting to protect the gunner. It was also surrounded by bulletproof glass, so you could survey the surroundings without exposing yourself to danger.

Of course, it wouldn't be fair to give players extra weapons, so there were no M2s on these vehicles.

The three Humvees formed a diagonal line, spaced apart by twenty yards, roaring over the dusty earth and sending up plumes of dirt. The aerial camera view made it look like either an off-road rally or a commercial for a new car.

You couldn't personally own a vehicle, so like the hovercraft and trucks the last time around, someone had to have found these on the map.

The glass reflected enough light to hide the occupants, but it was pretty easy to imagine which team was driving them. There were only two other surviving teams at this point.

"It has to be them!"

"Let's go, boys! We're going to neutralize that log house!" shouted the leader of MMTM, the team that raised hell on the hovercrafts last time, as he sat in the passenger seat of one of the Humvees.

He was a long-term *GGO* player who had been active in the community since its early days. As was mentioned in the pub, he'd been in a squadron with Pitohui back in those days.

He never cheated on *GGO*. He stayed faithful to his game and avatar, until he had the skill to reach the final match of the Bullet of Bullets tournament, which decided the game's strongest player.

Now he was excited about fighting alongside his teammates in Squad Jam. With a boyish smile, he exulted, "This fight is the real final battle for this competition! So don't hold back! Ammo, courage, life—don't waste an ounce of any of it!"

* * *

"Ah-haaaaa! It's you guys agaaain! Get the hell outta heeeeere!" bellowed Llenn at the three Humvees, a true scream from the soul. It did not stop their advance.

When she spotted them, they were still over half a mile from the log house, but that gap was closing rapidly.

Then the shooting started.

Deep, heavy consecutive fire from a distance—that was Rosa's PKM. It was on the far side of the log house.

She saw the glass break on a west-facing window upstairs as bullets flew out from it. She hardly heard any sound from that one, for some reason, but the series of glowing tracers made it clear that this was a machine gun, too.

PM4's machine gunner was set up toward the back of the room to hide the sight of the muzzle and flashes. He started blazing at the Humvees at full strength.

"Oof…"

If Llenn had charged to the western door as she'd planned, the shooter would have spotted her, and she'd need to weave her way through that gunfire. So in that sense, perhaps the cars had actually saved her? That was a complicated feeling to have.

Llenn took out her monocular and turned it to the approaching Humvees.

Please! Take 'em out! she wished, hoping the two machine guns would mercilessly punch those vehicles full of holes. If they did, she could start her mad sprint immediately afterward.

Through the little magnified circle, she could make out the cars' details much better.

"Huh?"

The bullets that landed on the vehicles' bodies merely created sparks and did nothing to slow down the Humvees as they continued their approach. Llenn recalled how Pitohui had told her that car exteriors and glass windows were very flimsy and couldn't actually stop a bullet.

"No fair!" she yelled, completely forgetting that MMTM had lamented the same thing about her own team the last time.

"Dammit...," groaned Boss, staring through her binoculars from the other side of the log house.

She didn't know a lot about military vehicles, but she knew enough to tell that those four-wheel-drive armored vehicles weren't going to blink at some measly 7.62 mm machine-gun fire. If only they still had the anti-tank rifle, they'd give those damn things a show.

But there was no point lamenting it now.

Tohma gave herself a med kit after M's shot took her health down a third, then she aimed her Dragunov sideways at the Humvees. "Why, you—!"

"No. Don't shoot," Boss warned. "You too, Rosa. You're just wasting your bullets, sadly. Get yourself ready to shoot them when they leave their cars, and watch out for M's sniping."

The booming PKM immediately went quiet.

Tanya's weapon couldn't even reach that far. "So what are we going to do? At this rate, they're going to raid that log house. Based on what we saw in the video of the last Squad Jam, MMTM is really good at indoor combat! If they manage to beat PM4..."

She didn't finish that sentence, but everyone understood what she meant.

All of Llenn's hard work would be for nothing. Boss didn't say it out loud, because the other girl would hear, but she did wonder, *Does this mean Llenn was the unlucky girl this time around?*

"Go, go, go! Bust into the place!" cheered the crowd in the bar, which tended to side with whichever team was doing the most attacking at any one time.

"Crush all three teams in one go!"

"Show us the kind of men you are!"

They were all pulling for MMTM now.

*   *   *

As if the excitement from the bar was somehow reaching them, MMTM's mad burst continued.

"That's LF on the left and SHINC on the right, but you can ignore them now! There's less pushback from them, so we're busting into the log house! We know PM4 is licking its wounds!" the leader explained.

Based on the locations from the last scan, they were definitely taking refuge in the log house, which would give them a big advantage.

The fact that they were fighting back with only a single machine gun said that their combat ability had taken a major hit. There were no guarantees on the battlefield, but whenever you made a decision, it was always wiser to assume the higher probability outcome as your base assumption.

"I'll shoot a grenade through the upstairs window before we go! No need for fire support. Keep your heads inside! After that, it's our bread and butter: indoor combat! We'll clean the place out!" the leader ordered. His comrades chirped back.

A pair rode in each vehicle. Driving in the left Humvee was a man with an Italian ARX160 assault rifle. His name was Bold. He had the darkest skin and the most fit physique of the team. Add in his short dreads, and you had the most exotic member of the team.

He was the only member whom Llenn had killed in the previous Squad Jam. Naturally, he was fuming for a chance to get his revenge.

In the passenger seat next to him was a guy with a German G36K. His name was Lux, and he was the biggest gun freak on the team, as well as the one who got knocked off the hovercraft and drowned at the bottom of the lake last time.

He was of average height and build, not particularly notable in any way, but just for fun, he wore sunglasses with a single connected lens this time around. It couldn't be "too sunny" in *GGO*, so sunglasses weren't necessary at all. He was just trying to be cool.

The middle Humvee was the one the team leader was sitting in. Driving that vehicle was a man named Summon, who used a Belgian-made SCAR-L assault rifle. His avatar was the buffest of them all, and it made his gun look tiny. But he was also the newest member of the squadron—and the weakest character. For that reason, he was sometimes charged with being Jake's ammo carrier.

The driver of the last vehicle was the other G36K guy, Kenta. He wasn't very tall, with short-cut black hair, and along with his name, his avatar looked Japanese. But his avatar name didn't come from his real name or anything like that. It was actually derived from his favorite fast-food fried chicken.

They liked to call him Chicken as a nickname, but in fact, he was a bold fellow who regularly charged into dangerous locations.

And seated in the back, rather than in the passenger seat, was Jake, the team's only machine gunner and de facto second-in-command. He was very thin and didn't seem strong on first glance, but that was the magic of the avatar system. In fact, he had the highest strength stat of the team.

MMTM's main trade was 5.56 mm assault rifles, so Jake's HK21 7.62 mm machine gun was valuable firepower. His HK21 also had a variable scope. It was the rare kind of machine gun with semi-auto fire, so that meant he also filled the role of the team's only long-range shooter.

He stayed in the back seat, preparing to use the roof mount to fire. On the other hand, it was difficult to do so when the high speed over a rough surface meant it was all he could do to keep his balance without a seat belt, so that he didn't smash into anything.

"Eep!"

Based on the experience last time, they had learned that if you survived for a certain length of time, vehicles would start appearing to make traveling to other targets easier. So MMTM had kept their eyes open at all times for vehicles, even while on the move.

At last, they found what they were looking for.

Around 2:03, after they had raced through the hilly region to attack T-S, they spotted an object covered by a camo-pattern sheet at the bottom of one of the little valleys. They descended the slope and pulled off the cover to reveal three sparkling treasures.

The leader made an immediate decision: They would leave the retreating enemy atop the fortress walls behind and use this new mobility tool to lead a surprise attack on the three big teams. Beating the teams already in combat was how they would win.

They circled counterclockwise around the dome; at the 2:10 scan, identified the place where the three teams were engaged in a major battle; and took off at top speed to catch them.

Under her camo poncho, Llenn watched the vehicles racing along from her right to her left, dust flying behind them, and gnashed her teeth. "Dammit…"

Head down at her side, Fukaziroh added with frustration, "If only we were a bit closer…I'd blow up the ground right under their feet."

The three cars were about to pass just a third of a mile in front of them. Neither of their weapons was going to reach that far.

If only it were just a thousand feet, Fukaziroh could have blasted them with twelve straight grenades. It might not have hit the vehicle body, but it might've succeeded in knocking a tire off.

Llenn was seized by an urge to run full tilt and attack the three Humvees, but she knew it would only get her killed. "Ugh…"

If one of them hit her, she was light enough that it might just knock her clean over those towering walls.

"M, Pito, run away!" she shouted, practically praying for the people she was swearing to destroy just moments ago.

The Humvees approached the log house for about six hundred feet. The machine gun firing from the second-floor window scored a number of hits on its armored body, creating quite a show of sparks, but eventually fell silent. Either it was out of ammo or overheated, or the shooter just gave it up because it was pointless.

Only in the last five hundred feet did the three vehicles finally slow down. The center one slowed down the quickest. From the armor-protected roof enclosure, a grenade shot forth.

"Ah!" "Whoa!"

As Llenn and Fukaziroh watched, the little black dot disappeared into the open window with admirable aim. A beat later, it exploded. Window glass and the frame itself blew outward and fell to the ground.

There was no way to tell how big the room behind it was, but if the PM4 machine gunner was still in there, he would've taken major damage.

The Humvees approached the entrance on the west side of the log house and stopped right next to one another. Frustratingly, they were even excellent drivers.

Promptly, the men exited the cars. They wore blocky patterns of green camo. That was indeed MMTM's look, as Boss had explained.

There was another sound of PKM gunfire, and a Humvee burst with sparks.

Quickly and carefully, one of the men approached the door and opened it, one man watched the upstairs window, and the remaining four slid right into the log house as though pulled by suction.

One of the two remaining men patted the other on the shoulder and passed by him, and then the last one went inside, too.

It took just seconds from when they stopped the cars next to the building. Not a single one of Rosa's shots hit them.

"What are those guys, a SWAT team?!"

"They just slipped right in there."

"That was too easy…"

The audience in the bar was stunned.

"Didn't you see the video of the last one? Their battle inside the spaceship was like a model demonstration of interior combat. They eliminated blind spots, never stopped moving, and cleared out sectors one after the other," explained one person, just as the camera switched to inside the log house.

It was placed above the entranceway, looking down the hallway of the first floor. It was much dimmer than outside, but not enough that it was hard to see anything.

The men of MMTM made their way down the hallway with its wooden floor and thick log walls. They held their rifles in compact positions and filed into a room directly on their right, one after the other.

The time was two fifteen.

"They got inside…"

M's craggy face was etched with panic and frustration. He was in one of the guest rooms on the second floor of the building.

It was quite spacious, over thirty feet to a side. Along the walls were four sturdy-looking beds with wooden frames. There was also a heater in the corner near the window, as well as a closet and a sofa. Part of the room was a kitchen. Like all aspects of the building, it was beautifully preserved. It was practically ready to host guests even now.

This room was the one just to the east of the staircase in the center of the building. On the wall consisting of bare logs, there hung a large frame, containing a map of Geyser Park. It was an introduction of the area with all the grass and water to the east of the building, including how deep each pond was, how often each geyser erupted, and how high the plume would go—all in English, of course.

Pitohui was lying on one of the beds. The damage effect over her right eye was gone, but the eye itself was still closed. In the left corner of M's and his teammates' vision, they could see that Pitohui's hit points had risen above the halfway point. The bar was colored yellow. It would still be a few minutes before she reached full health.

But there was a problem.

"Hey, wake up. We don't have time for you to be unconscious," M said, slapping her cheek a bit, but Pitohui did not wake.

PM4 was in unprecedented trouble.

Pitohui had gotten sniped and been so agitated that she had

passed out. They successfully evacuated to this log house to recover, and none of this was that big of a problem so far. The log house had good visibility from the second floor, with much more visibility than lying flat in the field.

It would've been easy for them to keep SHINC and Llenn's group away to the north and south with machine guns and sniper rifles. M had already hit that woman sniper in the shoulder when she'd been sloppy enough to lift up off the ground.

They'd take refuge here, wait for Pitohui to make a full recovery, then continue fighting with her help. It was a good plan for M and the masked men, one with a good chance of working.

Until MMTM's shocking arrival.

There was no point in regretting it now, but he really should have taken the possibility of cars into account.

"Nope! Gotta head back to you!" said the voice of the machine gunner in M's ear. He was fine. But a large machine gun was not going to be much help when fighting indoors.

It was a bad situation atop a bad situation, but they weren't just going to sit around and let themselves get killed.

"Okay."

M promptly thought of their best move to play next and told his three companions. The one with the UTS-15 shotgun was at the top of the center stairs, and the tall man was in the hallway outside the room. The machine gunner would be running down the hall toward them now.

"The central staircase has to be the absolute line of defense. They're the only stairs in this building," M explained as he opened his inventory, materializing a ton of grenades. They were normal shrapnel grenades, not the dangerous plasma grenades that were so powerful they posed a threat to their owner.

"We're not going to let them get up here."

While he waited for the grenades to finish popping into existence, one at a time, M pulled the HK45 pistol out of his thigh holster. He checked that it was loaded, then put it back. He was going to fight with his pistol, not the M14 EBR.

Just then, there was a voice.

"M… We agreed to shut up and follow orders, but can I just ask one thing?"

It was the tall man, who rarely spoke up. He was walking into the room in the process of producing the Savage 110 BA from his own storage.

"Sure, go ahead."

"All right. What exactly is Pitohui to you, M?"

"Huh?"

It was such an unexpected question that M's mind completely blanked.

The tall man wearing a mask and goggles faced M directly and said, "Well, I mean, I just wanted to know if she was really worth this much desperate protection."

"……Yes!" he said, once he regained his footing. The other two men heard it, too.

"Heh," chuckled the tall man. The Savage 110 BA and its ammo magazine appeared and fell to the floor. "Did you hear that, boys? This is our time to shine."

The shotgunner said, "That's more like it!"

And the machine gunner on his way back added, "You know it!"

The tall man pulled a Glock 21 from his holster and switched out the magazine for a long one that jutted way out of the grip with twenty-five .45-caliber pistol rounds.

"We can keep the stairs protected on our own up to a point, so make sure you wake up Sleeping Beauty before then. Then we can leave the rest up to the princess. You'd better ask her to kill them all for us," the tall man said, then spun on his heel.

He left the room.

MMTM's brutal room-clearing efficiency was on display in the bar.

It was more like "cleaning," really, a close-combat technique of clearing out every space where an enemy might be hiding.

One person pointed his gun down the hall for protection, and the other five rushed into the next room, instantly covering one another's blind spots by thrusting in with their assault rifles. Needless to say, if they found anyone, they would immediately open fire.

Once a room was clear, they exited to the hallway again and headed into the next room, mindful of the hallway windows. They never stopped moving.

MMTM searched two small guest rooms on the first floor and a larger room that appeared to be an office. They passed the stairs in the center of the building, leaving one member as a lookout, and headed into a different room. Within moments, they had cleared the entire first floor.

No one spoke a single word in that time.

The audience in the bar held their collective breath, expecting a ferocious interior battle to break out at any moment.

MMTM headed to the center stairs.

Whoever stood point when going in depended on their particular formation. Anyone aside from Jake the machine gunner could take the lead.

Summon, the macho guy with the SCAR-L who had been lead earlier, took on support in the hallway, so the ones who headed first down the hall were the two G36K shooters, black-haired Kenta and Lux in his shades.

The staircase in the center of the building was about ten feet wide. You started climbing from the first floor, north side, until you reached a wide landing, then turned around 180 degrees to reach the second floor.

The two climbed the steps, pointing their muzzles upward.

Ba-gong!

A hail of buckshot rained down on them.

"Oh… They're definitely fighting…"

Less than a minute had passed since MMTM busted into the log house. Llenn was looking through her monocular, still in the same location. Through the windows, she saw flickers of MMTM's camo and could tell that they were going in and out of rooms.

When they finally headed into the center of the building, she heard a muffled gunshot and saw something flash inside.

"You know it's pointless to go in there, Llenn," Fukaziroh warned her calmly.

"Y-yeah, I know! I know…," Llenn repeated, admonishing herself.

It was obvious that Llenn was not going to be able to slip inside and take out Pitohui in all the confusion. In fact, it was quite possible that she would get picked off by MMTM in the process of approaching the log house. They still had six members, making them the strongest in terms of battle potential right now.

I'm sorry, God; I just need you to protect Pito until I can kill her!

All Llenn could do was pray that Pitohui's side won the battle, even if she was the only survivor left.

"They're above," Kenta told his teammates, the first words they'd uttered inside.

Lux maintained his aim at the upper part of the stairs to hold the enemy at bay, and they both returned to the foot of the stairs, preparing themselves for a hand grenade attack from above.

They had essentially expected that the enemy would shoot from the top of the stairs already.

Pouring into an area wasn't the only way these guys fought. They could expect that with a staircase of this style, they could reach out a little bit and draw an attack from the enemy. Therefore, they could pretend to rush up the stairs to lure their opponent into firing first, just like they did now.

The short man who was tricked into firing his UTS-15 marveled "Ha! Very clever!" and pulled the boxy shotgun's foregrip back, expelling the empty cartridge.

"But this will help us buy time," he muttered. Adjacent to him, the large man crouched, busying himself with something.

He was wrapping up M's pile of grenades in tough, sticky gray duct tape. It was a more powerful adhesive than what was typically sold in Japan, often used for all kinds of repairs and other things in the United States.

It was one of those items that everyone carried around in *GGO*. Some players found it so useful and versatile that they started ordering it online in real life.

The man was quite dexterous with his hands for a person that size; he taped twelve grenades together into a long band, like a seven-foot-long grenade belt. Lastly, he put a long piece of tape around all the grenade pins so they would be easier to pull out. Then he draped the band around his tall frame like a sash, wrapping the pin-detaching piece of tape around his right hand.

"All right. You guys take it from here," he said as casually as if he were asking them to turn out the lights when they left, and he started stomping down the stairs.

Kenta and Lux, waiting at the bottom of the stairs, were startled by the man's sudden descent, and they fired their G36Ks the instant he appeared on the middle landing.

It was a quick burst of fire, about five shots that sank into his body, but he had his arms folded over his face and was wearing a bulletproof vest, so it did not kill him.

"Raaaah!"

As he descended, the masked man yanked with his right arm, pulling out the safety pins of all the grenades attached to his body. In that moment, Kenta and Lux understood what was happening: He was a suicide bomber.

If he simply dropped the grenades from above, they could clear out and avoid the blast. So instead, he strapped them to his body so he could chase after them. He was going to use the few seconds that it would take to shoot him dead to be close to them when the grenades exploded.

It would mean dire consequences for them—and possibly their teammates as well. But even if one attempted to sacrifice him- or herself to stop the bomber, they wouldn't be able to push back all the kinetic energy of that large body hurtling down the stairs. Any collision would surely send them flying instead.

So what could they do?

Both men reached the same answer at the same time and took the same action.

They aimed their G36Ks ten feet away, at about the fifth step up the staircase—right at the spot where the man's left ankle landed.

Two guns barked in unison, sending 5.56 mm bullets into his black boot. The narrow strip of flesh and bone tattered with the impact of multiple shots. Unable to bear his full weight, his foot and shin separated.

"Guh?"

He'd lifted his right foot, using the left as a support, and now his body lurched to the left. He toppled sideways along the stairs and slid down the other three steps.

Kenta and Lux leaped in opposite directions out of his way, and the man groaned, "Shit, they got me," then exploded with the impact of a dozen grenades all going off at once. His torso went fully red and shattered into pieces.

Duh-duh-duh-duh-duh-duh-duh-dummm. The entire building shook with the explosion.

"..."

M stood, looking down on the face of the sleeping princess on the bed. Her tattooed face was the picture of tranquility.

He'd already administered a third med kit, and her hit points were up over 70 percent by then. They would be green very soon.

M no longer attempted to wake Pitohui up. He did not smack her cheeks or call her name. He just waited in silence.

In his ear, the small man said, "M, the self-detonation attempt failed. But I'm up next, so I'll buy you some more time. Don't worry!"

Several seconds later came the massive sound of the UTS-15 firing consecutively. It was obvious, even through the thick log walls. It was matched by the sound of multiple assault rifles tearing a man to shreds.

M didn't even bother to check his teammate's HP. He didn't need to.

Right when the members of MMTM returned to formation and were preparing to charge up the stairs, another masked man descended, rapidly firing a UTS-15.

Summon promptly shot back with his SCAR-L, as he was now the point. He sent several bullets at the man's chest, but the shotgun hit his leg and sent him sprawling. That was a loss of 20 percent of his hit points.

In a one-on-one fight, that might have meant Summon would be blasted with more shotgun shells until he died.

"Raaah!" "Haah!" "Hi-yaa!"

But Kenta, Lux, and the team leader behind them all returned fire, preventing the small man from shooting again. They hit his left hand, which he needed to pump the handle, and that was all it took.

He died standing, his body covered in glowing marks. Then he toppled over, sliding on his face down the stairs and coming to a stop where the large man had blown up seconds earlier.

The DEAD tag appeared right at the moment the larger body began to recompose itself, limbs reappearing and forming a human body. When the first man's corpse was whole again, it settled and pressed down atop the smaller man.

"That looks heavy...," Bold grunted.

The team leader gave his final order by hand.

Go on up!

Kenta and Lux, followed by Bold and the leader and, lastly, Summon, who had gotten up from his damage, rushed in a row up the stairs.

The staircase was the most dangerous location in an indoor battle. Especially when you were attacking from below, as in this case. One dropped plasma grenade could spell the end of their entire team.

So if one was to go up, time was of the essence. The team simply had to burst upward all at once and instantly pacify the top of the stairs.

The men of MMTM cleared the landing, and the second floor came into view—followed by a bed, sliding down toward them.

"Whoa!" "What the—?" "Oof!" "Huh?"

Even the practiced members of MMTM had not expected this.

At the top of the stairs, a sideways single bed was descending in their direction, its feet rocking, *gtonk, gtonk*, as it shuffled down the steps.

It collided with their legs, one after the other, and pushed them all back to the landing. Their backs hit the log wall. They were sandwiched by the bed.

Their feet, legs, and rifles were trapped beneath them. There was even a very slight damage indication from the impact.

"Ha!" The team leader couldn't help but smile. It was all so unexpected.

They looked up to see a tall, masked man standing at the top of the stairs—holding another bed high over his head with both hands.

"Huh?"

Then he threw it at them.

"…" "…"

The crowd watching the footage in the bar was stunned into silence by the last masked member of PM4's exhibition of tremendous arm strength.

While his teammates were being taken out in battle, he dragged two beds out of the guest room closest to the stairs. Everyone watching felt like they had just learned something. *Oh, so if you get your strength stat high enough, you can actually do that.*

"You know... There used to be this game ages ago where there was a big gorilla at the top who threw barrels...," someone muttered.

The second bed hurtled down atop the four men who were already trapped by the first one on the landing of the log house's stairs. There was a dull sound of wood hitting wood.

"Gwah!" "Arrrh!" "Bmf!" "Gahk!"

The squashed men shrieked helplessly. They took damage again, although it wasn't nearly enough to kill any of them.

Trapped under the beds, the leader could see the man pulling a Glock from his waist holster.

The black pistol, sporting a very long magazine, was slowly pointed toward them. He was going to empty the entire thing, of course.

The tall man took a step closer to get a better, steadier shot. He stood right at the lip of the staircase.

But before he pulled the trigger, the leader shouted, "Jake! Now!"

Naturally, the tall man heard him, too. "Ah!"

His aim with the Glock wavered. The bullet line from the pistol moved from the four trapped men to the corner of the landing.

But no new enemy appeared there. Instead—

Bwak-bwak-bwak-bwak-bwak-bwak-bwak! Holes appeared in the floorboards under his feet. The bullets from below pierced his legs and body. His lower half glowed here and there with signs of damage.

"Hnng," the tall man groaned, but he focused through the pain and aimed the Glock at MMTM's leader. He fired once.

The .45-caliber bullet hit the bed in front of the leader. A piece of its wood frame splintered off and split his cheek.

"Raaaaahh!"

On the first floor, Jake was blazing his HK21 machine gun. He had it pointed straight up and held the trigger down to let it fly.

The belt of ammunition rolled up from the ammo box to his

gun, where it was very loudly expelled. The bullets pierced the ceiling boards of the first floor, then the insulation material, then the floorboards of the second.

Click.

Right when the last bullet of the fifty-shot belt was gone, the man up above became a corpse. The tall man wavered and toppled, DEAD marker hanging over his head.

"Jake, watch out!" the leader yelled.

"Ah!" Jake took a step backward.

The body tumbled through the tattered floorboards and downward, right onto where he had been standing.

"Yikes!"

The sound of machine-gun fire was clear through the heavy log walls—and so was the sight of his teammate's HP dropping like a rock to zero.

M knelt at the side of the bed. Sleeping Beauty's slumber continued on the second bed out of four from the west-facing window.

"…"

M picked a plasma grenade up off the floor. The timer was set on the longer side, five seconds.

His mouth opened to emit quiet words.

"You…saved…me…"

Tears streaked from his eyes and dripped onto the plasma grenade.

"Thank you."

He stood, leaned his large frame over, and planted a short kiss on the lips of the sleeping princess.

Then he straightened up, plasma grenade resting in his left palm, and pressed the activation switch with his right.

This scene did not play out on the cameras.

Grab this!
Thanks!

Without saying anything, the MMTM members worked at freeing

the four trapped members on the landing. The leader slipped out first, and Summon never got stuck. While they pushed the beds, the other three eventually worked their way free. All the while, Jake kept his reloaded HK21 trained on the top of the stairs.

Seconds later, they all had full freedom of movement again and quickly checked their guns.

Okay, let's go up! the leader motioned. They were about to leap over the bed to charge up to the second floor.

A tremendous blast shook the foundations of the building, nearly deafening them.

And every last one of them had the same thought:

A plasma grenade explosion? But where?

CHAPTER 17
The Demon Returns

SECT.17

CHAPTER 17
The Demon Returns

The sound of the exploding plasma grenade that would put M at eternal rest came from outside the window.

"Huh?"

Even with his eyes closed, he could see the hit point gauge in the corner of his view. His was green. Pitohui's was also green.

Then M opened his eyelids.

"Hang on—what exactly are you doing? Is this a double suicide? Where are we? Is this the play *Love Suicides at Sonezaki*? Is this the song 'Roppongi Suicide'? No, we're in *GGO*!"

It was the avatar of the woman he loved, glaring at him.

Pitohui was sitting up in the bed, her arm stretching out of the window.

M figured it out. She had regained consciousness and hurled the plasma grenade out the open window, and it had exploded down on the ground outside.

"Ohhh!" M exclaimed, eyes wide and tears of joy streaking down his cheeks.

"You moron!" Pitohui swung a fist at him.

"Augh!" She hit his left cheek.

"You clown!"

"Gmff!" A backhand caught his other cheek.

"You dipshit!"

"Gahk!" She drove a palm blow right into his chest. His large body hurtled backward, and he fell, rattling the floor.

"I was having a really nice dream, you know!" Pitohui protested, hopping out of the bed and standing before M. "You little—!"

She pressed her foot to M's crotch and jammed it down hard.

"Gauuugagagagagaggg!" he shrieked, flopping his heavy limbs like he was being electrocuted. "Gugugugagagagaaah!"

"I never said you could kill me!"

"Gagagagagagah!"

Fortunately—very fortunately—this scene was not broadcast on camera, either.

A few seconds later, Pitohui had taken her foot off M and picked up her KTR-09 from where it was left next to the bed.

"Just the two of us, huh? Enemies?" she asked.

"MMTM. Downstairs. They're coming right up here soon," M said, totally straight-faced. He stood up and drew the HK45 from his thigh holster. Nothing about his manly demeanor now suggested the kind of pained writhing he was doing seconds ago.

"So let's kill 'em all!" Pitohui grinned. She reached behind her back, opening the top of a pouch back there and sticking her hand inside.

M asked, "What made it a 'really nice dream'?"

Pitohui withdrew her hand from the pouch. "A dream where I was in *Sword Art Online* when it was deadly, going wild with my sword alongside my hearty fellows from the beta test!"

Pale light glinted off her vicious smile.

MMTM flowed up to the second floor and charged directly into the room just to the left, on the western side of the building. That was where the tall man had brought the beds from, so they suspected they would find the remaining PM4 members there.

But the spacious guest room was empty.

Jake stayed in the hallway, training his machine gun on the eastern end, while the rest went into the adjacent room.

Clear!

This one was also empty. The room was trashed because of the grenade their leader threw inside, but there were no bodies. There was no place to hide, either. The masterless MG 3 machine gun sat silent.

In that case...

The leader made a simple hand signal.

"We're going into the rooms on the east side of the building."

The bar, in fact, did see this part playing out.

Six men, their center of gravity low, proceeding down a hallway no more than seven feet wide, doing their best not to make noise.

GGO players did their best not to walk along the wall. This was because of deflections. When a bullet hit a wall at an angle, it generally flattened out and continued along the wall.

So MMTM continued down the center of the hallway in a single-file line. They understood and expected that if an enemy came out shooting, the man in the lead was likely to get shot. If anything, his body would be a shield to protect his team. The people behind him would eliminate the enemy.

Just two rooms remaining.

M and the woman would be in one of the two.

On the six went, without sound or words.

They wove their way around the hole in the floor where the enemy soldier had died and fallen earlier, adjusting their guns so they were all pointing at slightly different angles.

Taking point was the quickest member of the team, the *non*-chicken Kenta with his G36K.

Next was Lux, the man with sunglasses and the same gun.

The black man with the ARX160, Bold.

Beefy Summon with the SCAR-L.

Then the handsome team leader with a short-barrel model STM-556.

Lastly, skinny Jake brought up the rear a bit later, to watch their six.

It was close to twenty-five feet from the stairs to the first room's door on the right side. The walls were round logs on either side.

Like deflections, the other big thing to be careful of in an indoor gun battle was wall penetration. As the name suggested, this was when bullets pierced right through walls and doors to hit you. In other words, a sudden attack from an invisible enemy.

It was possible to detect enemies on the other side of a wall in *GGO* with an item like a sonar sensor—or certain character skills that acted in a similar way. And there was always a good old trusty hunch.

But this effect was impossible if the player couldn't reach their target, whether they knew their location or not. This depended on factors like the size of the bullet, the type of obstacle in the way, the width of the wall, and so on.

Rifle bullets had fearsome penetrative power and would easily tear through the walls of typical wooden homes, the same way that Jake had killed the guy upstairs through the floorboards.

But now there were huge logs over two feet thick on either side of MMTM.

It wasn't *completely* impossible for any weapon short of an antimateriel rifle to break through that thick layer of wood, but it was very unlikely. Even if an attacker somehow succeeded at it, the bullet's power would be greatly reduced and totally incapable of killing them.

In that sense, they only had to worry about either end of the hallway and attacks from the windows, making it a relatively safe trip.

Or at least, it should have been.

When Kenta had just three steps to go to reach the door, there was a ferocious burst of gunfire in the hallway.

Just ahead of him, the team leader saw Summon's right flank light up with gunshot visual effects.

"Grnnf!"

His large body twisted to the right. There was a bigger flash of light, and the reinforced plastic stock of his SCAR-L split loudly. The bullet destroyed the stock and continued on to the person holding it.

His health promptly began to plummet. Once you'd seen this happen often enough, it was clear that this was the sign of an instant kill.

"Right! From the wall!" the leader shouted, breaking the silence. But even he didn't know what had happened. It was an attack from the room, yes. But how had so many bullets split the thick logs and maintained their power?

Were the logs like movie props, fake and flimsy? Is that how they could be penetrated like this?

"Take this!"

Bold was ahead of Summon in their line. He turned to the wall and blasted at it with his ARX160, sending chips and shards flying. It clearly wasn't punching through.

"Knock it off!" the leader commanded, right as the enemy's fire ceased.

Summon, who had taken a ludicrous number of bullets to the gut, groaned "Sheeeit" and collapsed to the ground, landing right on his left shoulder insignia patch of a skull with a knife in its teeth. The DEAD sign appeared over his body.

At this point, the leader knew they needed to get into the room as quickly as possible to take out the two hiding in there.

As if to prove his point, the door in front of Kenta burst with holes. There were several shots all at once, which meant it was a shotgun from inside the room. There were three such blasts in quick succession.

"Tch!"

If Kenta had been one step, or even a half step closer, he would have been punched full of lead, too. He pulled back, yanking his G36K away. It was too dangerous to stand any closer.

At that moment, MMTM's signature flowing movement came to a stop.

Bold ceased shooting and backed against the wall, leaning over to peer at the spot where his teammate had been shot. He quietly reported what he saw to his squad.

"It's a hole!"

Damn, they got us good! the leader of MMTM swore silently, realizing what a simple but effective trap they'd fallen into.

PM4 predicted that they would pass down the hallway, so while the masked men were dealing with the enemy, the others had bored a small hole through the thin part where log met log. It wasn't clear what method they had used. They couldn't have had the time to do it with bullets, so perhaps there was a powerful electric drill inside the room. That plasma grenade explosion outside may have even been meant to hide the sound of it.

Bold kept his back pressed to the wall next to the hole and stuck the muzzle of his ARX160 into the hole. If they shot now, it would only hit the gun. He pulled the trigger and started firing.

It stopped after just two shots.

"Gah...?"

He froze, his face trapped in a mixture of anguish and confusion.

Then the leader—and everyone else aside from Kenta, who was staring at the door—saw something bizarre.

Bold, his back against the wall, his right eye wide open and glowing blue.

The light grew stronger, slowly jutting outward in a cylindrical shape. It stuck an inch out from his eye socket and came to a stop.

"Gaaaaaaaaaah!"

Bold's face began to twitch and spasm. He released his gun, and the ARX160 hung there, muzzle stuck in the hole, part of the wall now.

The leader's readout made it clear that Bold's HP was dropping rapidly.

Oh... Shit... That's what it is!

He was too slow to realize. This time he could only curse his own failure—there was no time left for admiring the enemy's handiwork.

He had forgotten about a weapon that was easily capable of penetrating both a two-foot-wide log and a person's head next to it. He just didn't recall it because there was no reason that he would ever use one.

Even though in the recent third BoB tournament, some totally unfamiliar new player had caused such a stir with one.

It was an ultra-powerful, ultra-close-range weapon that did not exist in the real world.

A weapon that created a three-foot blade of light that severed anything it contacted.

A blade in a world of guns: the photon sword.

Bold passed away, and his legs lost their rigidity.

The photon sword slid out, and the ghostly pale light vanished from the hallway. The body crumpled to the floor.

The next moment, a bright circle was drawn into the wall. A circle about five feet across, in one single movement. Right in front of Kenta, at the front of the line...

"Watch out!" the leader shouted, just as the circle of wall attacked Kenta. The large, circular block of wood shot outward into the hall with tremendous force.

"Hwooah!"

It flattened Kenta against the far wall. Then an utterly ordinary hand grenade came flying out of the new hole. It landed on top of Kenta, who was trapped between the wall and the circle, and exploded.

Kenta's upper half from chest upward burst out, pieces of him flying and sending glowing red polygons all over the hallway. The circular chunk of wooden wall split apart from the blast and crumbled.

A number of shrapnel pieces from the grenade struck Lux, who was closest. The force of the blast knocked his sunglasses clean off.

"Dammit!"

He didn't cower away from the damage—he started firing the

G36K he had propped against his shoulder, shooting directly into the room through the newly created hole. The team leader followed, aiming his gun at the hole, which was ten feet away at an angle, and firing while sidestepping to get a more direct shot.

At this point, their only option was to approach the hole, shooting periodically, and plunge through it to finish off the enemy. Better to at least charge in first and fight where they could see the other team, rather than continue to be ambushed like this.

From low in the hole, something rolled into the hallway.

It was black and round, like a small watermelon.

A huge plasma grenade, colloquially called a grand grenade.

A part of it was flickering, the signal that the activation button had already been pressed.

"Aaah!" "Wha—?!"

Lux and the leader yelped simultaneously. They stopped firing.

Are they idiots?! Do they intend to die along with us?!

He wondered whether PM4 had lost their wits. Plasma grenades were already overpowered enough in a cramped setting. And now they were hurling a grand grenade, with three times that power?

However many seconds the timer was set to, when it went off, it would destroy not only them, but whoever threw it on the other side of the hole.

Then it all clicked.

Oh…no, of course… They would *do this. The madwoman Pitohui certainly would…*

She wouldn't think twice about dying in order to kill the enemy before her. He'd seen her do it multiple times back when he first started playing *GGO*.

She's going to destroy herself and take us down with her! Dammit!

MMTM's leader turned away, knowing that it was already too late. In doing so, he saw Lux cast aside his gun and throw himself on top of the grand grenade at his feet.

Throwing oneself onto a grenade to absorb the blast and save one's comrades was a noble act of self-sacrifice that had been practiced all around the world for generations. The tradition lived on in *GGO*, too.

But that counted only when talking about normal shrapnel grenades. What benefit would it have against high-powered plasma grenades and their bigger cousin, the grand grenade? Very little, if anything.

The team leader readied himself for death in a few seconds. But he also had hope—that at least their opponent would die, too.

The blast surge would pound the guest room and blow up anyone inside. He didn't know how sturdy the log house itself was, but it might blow off some walls and the roof, too. In that case, he might as well face the explosion directly.

The team leader settled in, refusing to run. He did not twist or writhe away from it.

And then he saw, emerging from the hole in the wall, the figure of a woman.

A woman slender and strong, dressed in a navy jumpsuit, outfitted with an almost comical amount of armor and weaponry.

A woman with her long black hair tied into a ponytail.

A woman with brown skin and a brick-red geometric pattern tattooed on her cheek.

A woman named for a poisonous bird deadly to the touch.

Pitohui.

Pitohui emerged into the hallway with her hands behind her back. First, she pulled the right one forward.

A bright, pale line emanated from the dull-gray cylinder in her hand and left an afterimage when she swung it. It went low, then high, grazing the floor and scooping upward.

That was all it took to separate Lux's head from his torso as he lay atop the grenade. His head rolled onto the floor.

Obviously, there was no need to check his team's HP readout. Even in the world of *GGO*, there was no surviving the loss of your head.

The sight of the grinning woman standing next to the corpse cradling that deadly bomb caused it all to click into place.

Of course! The grand grenade wasn't going to explode for a while yet. She must have set it to several minutes or more, the way you could when luring out a boss in a dungeon to finish it off. It was just a trap designed to get them to stop firing for a moment.

He should have considered the possibility, of course, but his traumatic past experiences had made him leap to the conclusion that *of course* the crazed Pitohui he knew would blow herself up if she felt like it.

Then this would be it.

He swung his gun at Pitohui right as she brought her left hand out in front this time.

A gunshot.

The STM-556 shot a 5.56 mm bullet faster than sound at Pitohui's chest, barely a dozen feet away—only to bounce to the side in a hail of sparks and burrow into the log wall.

In her left hand was a sheet of metal about twenty by twelve inches long, which had deflected the bullet. It was a single panel of M's shield. There was even a small handle welded to the back of it, just for this purpose.

"Taaaaaa!" Pitohui leaped with a high-pitched roar. The second bullet from the team leader's gun traced the bullet line and deflected off the shield.

"Goddammit!"

She nimbly sidestepped the third bullet, aimed at her feet.

And before the fourth could leave the gun, the three-foot glowing sword of light swung sharply forward. The blade made the short barrel of the STM-556 even shorter. It melted the metal right through, both gun barrel and attached grenade launcher, chopping off the front half of the weapon.

If he hadn't pulled his left hand away at the last moment, it would have been severed at the wrist.

"Raaah!"

He threw his now useless gun at her.

But she did not avoid the hunk of metal. Instead, she caught it right on the forehead of her headgear and tossed it aside with a little twist of her neck.

In that brief moment, the leader stepped back and reached for the holster on his right side. He pulled out the Steyr M9-A1 automatic pistol and started shooting right from the waist, without bothering to aim it. He just needed it to keep shooting.

One of the cavalcade of 9 mm bullets buried itself in Pitohui's thigh, and one passed through her flank.

"Hya-hee!"

But she swung her arm, hitting the M9-A1 with the end of her shield and smacking it right out of his hands.

Jake the machine gunner had been looking for his chance to shoot Pitohui for several moments. He'd been at the rear of the hallway, HK21 machine gun pressed to his shoulder, with enough time to switch it to semi-auto mode.

But Pitohui repeatedly managed to move so that she was on the opposite side of the team leader. It seemed like she wasn't even looking at him, but she saw him quite well. Her mobility and vision were pristine.

"Dammit!"

It was Jake's dangerous firepower that ensured he couldn't actually use it.

After knocking the leader's pistol away, Pitohui pulled her photon sword back, pushed the shield forward, and hissed "Shaaaa!" as she charged him.

"Gahk!" He took a direct blow from the sheet of metal from chest to face. She pushed and pushed, overpowering him, until his legs budged and slid backward against his will.

"Oof!" He slammed into Jake, who had his gun at the ready behind him. Her incredible strength and momentum knocked the other member and his machine gun backward.

"Not...so...fast!" The shift in momentum gave the leader enough grip on his boots to push down and hold fast. He clutched the shield in both hands and, with all his strength, wrenched it away from her and hurled it.

The next thing he saw was Pitohui, smiling at him with the photon sword drawn back over her head.

An overhead swing with a sword inside was the height of lunacy. The sword would hit the ceiling and stop there. Many samurai in the old days of Japan had accidentally done this in battle, caught the blade on a beam, and surely died.

But the photon sword had no concern about such impediments.

"Well, time to die," Pitohui murmured, bringing it down with both hands. The tip of the glowing blade carved through the ceiling board and picked up speed, heading directly for the team leader's forehead.

"Urrraaaah!"

It came to a stop.

His hands were raised, grabbing Pitohui's wrists where they held the hilt of the photon sword and stopping its progress.

For a moment, they were frozen, two figures about the same size, connected by their hands.

As she applied more and more pressure, Pitohui taunted, "Well, well, you don't give up, do you?"

The team leader pushed upward from below. "What, is this the best you can do?"

They heaved with all their might, locked in a battle of physical power.

Slowly, Pitohui's arms pulled back. The sword pushed up and up, until the tip brushed the ceiling again. It went past a vertical position and tilted backward, getting closer to Pitohui's forehead. He put even more effort into it, pushing her bit by bit.

"Ha! These lightswords are just toys in the end!" he barked, staring her in the eyes, but she just smiled.

"Oh dear. Says the man with zero interest in photon swords. You gun freak."

"So what?!"

"So you don't know, do you? Do you? That the Muramasa F9 has this handy feature!"

Her right thumb rolled a dial near the top of the grip to the left. The extended blade of light vanished, meaning they were grappling over a simple metal tube less than a foot long.

"Huh?"

He had no idea what she was intending to do. Then that bright bluish-white light reflected off his eyes again, brighter and richer than before.

Pitohui's thumb turned the dial farther left, much slower this time.

"Wha…?"

Then he saw it.

From out of the cheap little tube held trapped between her hands, the same light was appearing from the hole on the opposite end.

Stretching and stretching, bit by bit, toward his own face.

"Wha—?! N-no… You can't mean—?!"

This photon sword could extend its blade from the top or bottom of the handle. When that feature finally sank into his mind, all the hairs on his body stood on end.

"You'd better look out… It's going to stretch more… Long… longer…longest…"

With each little twist of the dial, the blade inched out a tiny bit farther. If he tried to loosen his grip slightly, she would do the same in response, maintaining the precise angle of the photon sword.

"You… You madwoman!"

"Oh, stop it. I understand myself better than anyone else."

"Do you find this fun? You monster!"

"I seem to recall someone asking me that earlier. Of course it's fun! It's the best! Are you enjoying this life-and-death battle? Well, are ya?"

All the while, the blade grew and grew…

"Pitohuiiiii!"

"That's my name! Don't—wear—it—out!"

The tip of the glowing blade touched his forehead.

"Gaaah!"

It made a nasty slurping sound as it burrowed into his head.

"Gwagagagaaaagagagagagagah!"

He was under such mental anguish that his face distorted to the point that his two eyes formed totally separate shapes.

"Sorry, what was that? I can only speak Japanese and English. You understand me?"

"Beeedophuuuuiiiiigh!" he screamed with the last of his life, the light corroding his brain. Suddenly, the strength left his arms, and they dangled at his sides.

"Oh no you don't! No dying yet!" yelled Pitohui. She left the photon sword stuck a few inches into his head and grabbed his shirt with her left hand. "Yaaaaah!"

She charged forward with him. His back slammed into Jake, who had finally just gotten back to his feet.

"Now—it's—over!"

She turned the dial to its maximum level.

With a fierce growl, the Muramasa F9 blazed out to its full length of over three feet long.

"Gahk!"

It went completely through the team leader's skull and plunged through the left eye of Jake behind him.

From before MMTM's charge at the final room to the moment the last two died, there was no other battle happening, so the entire confrontation was streamed on the screens in the bar.

Starting from the shooting of MMTM through the wall as they approached, the gruesome conclusion of the fight was less than two minutes later.

At first, the crowd was delighted with the outburst of combat and cheered lustily. It quieted down considerably about the time that Pitohui chopped off the fallen man's head, and by the end, it was absolutely silent.

"Ugh." The moment that MMTM was done for good, with the two men stuck together on the end of the same photon sword, someone commented, "You know those sardines they package by skewering them all through the eyes? Yeah, not gonna eat any of those for a while."

"…"

There was one other person who witnessed Pitohui's demonic rampage in silence, feeling more conflicted about it than anyone else.

It was the very girl who had entered SJ2 for the purpose of saving Pitohui—Llenn.

From a third of a mile away from the log house, she kept herself pressed down in a slight dip in the flat plain, hiding herself under a camo poncho, peering through her monocular.

"Oh… Yeah, they're fighting in there…"

From the moment MMTM charged in, she had been relaying the status of the battle, as much as she could tell through the windows, to Fukaziroh nearby and to Boss on the other side of the log house.

"Okay, they're at the stairs. There are two masked men upstairs— Oh, I think one just got shot!" she said.

"An explosion on the stairs! Was that a suicide attack? Self-detonation? But there are still six in MMTM…," she said.

"Wow, the masked guy attacked them with a bed! And another bed! Whoa! The machine gunner's running around below! He's getting shot! He's dead…," she narrated, and so on in that manner.

At the point that the beds got mentioned, even Boss had to ask, "Is that supposed to be the name of a gun?"

Eventually, the six MMTM men, essentially unharmed, reached the room where Pitohui was likely to be hiding.

"Run away, run away, Pito, run away, just run away!" she muttered, more prayer than description, which wasn't much help to the two girls listening to her.

But in a way, what she saw next was even more horrifying.

The members of MMTM were slaughtered one after the other, with hardly a chance to strike back. She could only watch through the monocular at the sight of Pitohui carving them up with her blade of light.

"Ummm, Llenn? What's up? Did you fall asleep?"

"What's going on, Llenn? What's happening?"

But she couldn't even respond to them. All she could do was stare.

The last two men were skewered through the head, and when the will-o'-the-wisp blue light vanished, they toppled to the floor.

"Eep!" She returned to her senses.

"What is it?" "Uh, Llenn?"

"Th-they got wiped out... Pito did all of them in...by herself...," Llenn reported. Then she let her innermost feelings slip out. "Great. And I have to beat that..."

All of a sudden, her left wrist shook.

"Hyaaaaa!"

She mistakenly thought that someone had grabbed it—and briefly had a vision of Pitohui, a hallucination that the woman popped out of the ground and seized her wrist, grinning wickedly. Her heart leaped into her throat, and it was such a shock that the safety features of the AmuSphere nearly pulled her back to reality.

But when she looked again, heart pounding, it was just the watch on the inside of her wrist, telling her it was time for the scan.

2:20.

The eighth Satellite Scan of SJ2 was about to begin.

CHAPTER 18

Llenn Goes Crazy

SECT.18

CHAPTER 18
Llenn Goes Crazy

When the 2:20 PM Satellite Scan began, everyone in the bar thought, *This has got to be the last scan in this game.* The last event had reached its conclusion at a running time of an hour and twenty-eight minutes, and there were only four teams left at this point.

This scan started from the west, and it ran over the left half of the map quickly, then the right half much more slowly. It didn't seem likely that any satellite would be that nimble, but nobody was complaining.

The map showed the surviving dots in a rough line from north to south: Llenn, PM4, and the Amazons. They were bunched close enough together—within a thousand yards—that you had to zoom in to make out the different dots.

The final team was the group of armored sci-fi warriors riding their bikes around on the walls, Team T-S. They were atop the eastern wall, in just about the center.

They'd been in the northeastern corner at the 2:10 scan, so their bicycles had taken them south along the wall from there.

"They're probably hoping to take the valley through to whichever of the three teams survives the fighting and attack them there."

"Keh! That's cheap bullshit! A man oughtta stand up and fight headlong! Aside from M, all the other survivors are women!" the men in the crowd opined.

"Hang in there, you guyyyys!" shouted Anna, the beautiful blond in sunglasses, who had returned to the bar from the waiting area for deceased players. She was wearing her camo gear, and the combat vest still had a huge hole from the .50-caliber bullet that tore through it. Damaged equipment stayed that way when you came back.

In fact, her camo wear was also ripped in the same spot. Fortunately, her T-shirt *was* fixed up, lest she expose a little too much cleavage.

The dirt from SJ did not carry over, so her long blond hair was clean but rather bedraggled. The sniper with the Dragunov certainly had the air of a defeated soldier about her.

The bar quieted down when they heard Anna's soulful shout.

"Yeah, y'know, I understand how you feel. Say, you wanna watch with me over here? I could teach you a few tips about sniping."

"Feel like going on a quest sometime? There's this one spot that has a really romantic view," offered some sleazy men, who took advantage of the absence of the other Amazons to hit on Anna.

"Step the hell off! Would you say the same thing to my face in real life? Huh? Shut up and watch the monitors!" she snapped at them, and they promptly backed down.

"Whoa, yikes... Offer retracted!"

"Crazy bitch. She must be a total freak in real life..."

The disgruntled losers slunk off with their final comments, but if they ever met Moe Annaka in real life and saw that she was a shy little teenager, they would probably die of shock.

The surviving players watched the results of the scan come in. They, too, had to wonder, *This might be the final time I make use of this device.*

Llenn, Fukaziroh, and the remaining members of SHINC—Boss, Tanya, Tohma, and Rosa—were still in the same locations they'd been when MMTM raided the log building.

It was a third of a mile away, close enough that if they emerged into the open, they could get sniped by M at any moment.

Thanks to the scan, they knew that PM4 was still inside, and that the team called T-S was right at the eastern edge of the map.

Boss suggested, "This team must be moving on top of the fortress walls. Probably on wheels, probably unharmed." Everyone agreed with her, because there wasn't any other obvious possibility.

After the overwhelming display she'd just witnessed, Llenn murmured, "Just one team left… It's possible that Pito might beat them anyway, without me needing to do anything…"

It was far from the first time she'd expressed a mixture of doubt and hopefulness today.

"…"

Boss said nothing.

"…"

Neither did Fukaziroh.

Llenn clutched her hands into fists with her face pressed to the ground. "No, I can't say that! I have to do this! But what'll I do, what'll I do, what'll I do?" she chanted, like a mantra. She set her brain to racing, trying to think of a plan.

If she just charged in there now, could she win? She was confident in her speed, so she might be able to reach the building unharmed. But could she fight and win at that point? When the six-man team MMTM had totally failed?

"What do I do, what do I do, what do I do?"

How could she get Fukaziroh to help in an indoor battle? Could she team up with SHINC? Would they take each other out? If someone else carelessly took out Pito, it was all lost. How could she prevent that from happening?

"What do I do, what do I do, what do I do?"

Can't just send everyone in at once gotta think of a plan or it's just like MMTM gonna lose gonna die gonna lose gonna lose gonna lose…

"What do I do gotta think gotta think gotta think gotta think of a plan a plan a plan a man a canal Panama plan a plan—"

Her brain was so overheated, her mantra was starting to lose meaning and meld into other things.

"Everyone prepare to charge the building!" Boss interrupted.

"Huh?"

"We can't wait for Llenn's orders. We'll do it ourselves! Commence covering fire!"

"Huh?"

Then she heard a PKM machine gun firing. They had to be shooting at the windows on the far side of the log house, attempting to keep Pitohui at bay while they moved.

"H-hey! Wait, I wasn't—," Llenn clamored, raising her head.

"Whassup?" asked Fukaziroh, who had crawled over next to her. Llenn was startled by how close she was, without any kind of warning.

"B-Boss says they're gonna rush the building!"

"Uh-huh…" Fukaziroh grinned. It was devilish.

"Wait, everyone! We still need to prepare!" Llenn protested to Boss.

But the other woman's response was "Not good enough! We're doing this our way!" Then she addressed her own team, saying, "All units move out!"

"No—wait—hang on! Wait, everybody!" Llenn begged, but Boss did not respond.

"Aha. So they're just going to charge without any coordination with us or tricks up their sleeve?" Fukaziroh asked.

"That's what it sounds like… But it's suicide! Why would they do that? We can't beat Pito without working together! We need a plan! A plan! A plan! A plan!" Llenn repeated, bashing her fists against the grass.

"Hmm-hmm," Fukaziroh hummed. She was doing something behind Llenn's back, and the other girl did not notice. Five seconds later, she stood up and said, "Then I'm going, too!"

"A plan, a plan, a… What?" Llenn lifted her face, which was nearly about to burst into tears.

Fukaziroh was wearing her same old smile, one MGL-140 in

her right hand. "Thinking without ideas is just a poor man's version of resting! Ranting about a plan isn't going to do anything for us! Look at you, you're just crying to yourself! You're a li'l crybaby who can't do anything on her own! Nah-nah, nah-nah!"

And with that schoolyard taunt, she turned and started running for the log house.

"Huh...?"

"Just you watch! We're going to take Pito alive, wrap her up, and serve her to you on a platter!" Fukaziroh boasted improbably, running off.

Llenn watched her run off with one MGL-140 in hand, growing smaller and smaller, and could not formulate a single thought about it.

Ummm?

Meaning?

What?

Two seconds later, she finally recognized the most basic fact of what had happened.

Her friends had all left her behind.

"Waaaait! Nooo, you can't!" she screamed. She scrambled to get up—"Whoa! Hrfp!"—and failed. She flopped onto her belly in the grass.

She'd tried to bound to her feet with her characteristic agility, but her left leg wasn't cooperating. She couldn't get fully upright.

"Wh... Why...?"

She twisted around to look down her side and saw the cause of her clumsiness.

"What? Whaaaaat?!"

It was so startling that she failed to register what she was seeing at first, but there was no getting around what her own two eyes were looking at.

There was a wide strip of nylon wrapped around the ankle of her left boot—connected to an MGL-140 grenade launcher on the other end. Whether it was Rightony or Leftania was unclear, but it was obviously one of Fukaziroh's weapons. The heavy weapon was a shackle that kept her tied to the ground, like some chained-up prisoner of old, but with a gun instead of an iron ball.

There was no question who had done this. It was Fukaziroh, while Llenn was lost in her own hesitant thoughts.

Why, that...jerkwad!! she screamed internally. "C'mon! Dammit! Get off!"

She tried to work the material off, but her fingers kept slipping, so she finally just took off both her pink gloves to try again, but even then, the sling was vexingly tight around her ankle.

"Arrrrgh!"

She couldn't get it off at all. The material was very tough, and with her brute strength, Fukaziroh had pulled the wide strip of nylon into a tiny little ball. Llenn had to keep her head down so they didn't spot her and shoot her as she desperately struggled and pulled on the knot. Her hand slipped again.

"Nyaaaaaargh!" she shrieked.

"Calm down. Just take your time, and you'll get it loose," said Fukaziroh's voice in her ear, almost mockingly. She could clearly tell what Llenn was having trouble with.

"Fukaaaaaa! What are you thinking?! Don't rush ahead without me!" she yelled, giving up momentarily and glaring at the small shape running across the field ahead.

Fukaziroh replied, "Whosoever succeeds in undoing the knot shall become the rightful king of the entire world! Ah-ha-ha-ha-ha!"

"You...dummyyyyyy!"

Boss smiled to herself as she listened to Llenn scream through the comm unit.

As she sprinted across the grass, Vintorez in hand, she reached up to turn off the switch to the device that allowed her to communicate with Llenn and gave an order to her teammates. "This is all to get Llenn to fight like she did before! Everyone keep going!"

Tanya was the first to understand the intent of the plan. "It's the only way to get Llenn to be at her most exce-Llennt!"

Tohma followed with "Let's sweeten the pot so she has no choice but to ante up more sweets!"

"Nothing like a sneak attack to set up a snack attack!" Rosa quipped.

"..."

Boss was silent for several moments, then offered, "And then we'll......... Dammit! I can't think of another good pun!"

"Four Amazons making a charge. Distance: a bit over four hundred yards and closing."

M had his M14 EBR at the ready. He was on the balcony of one of the guest rooms on the south side of the building. It was a very small balcony, so most of his considerable size was still inside the room.

The M14 EBR was propped up on a bipod, sticking a little bit out between the railing posts. Stuck to the round wooden railing was the shield that Pitohui had used earlier. There were two plates of the shield duct-taped to horizontal bars with enough space apart to allow the gun barrel through—but oddly enough, those horizontal "bars" were actually the G36K and ARX160 assault rifles that MMTM had used. The shield was fixed in place by wrapping the tape around two rifles.

The deceased characters had to spend ten minutes in the waiting area, but they were allowed to watch the stream to give them something to do in the meantime. The owners of those two guns had to be gnashing their teeth at this moment.

The bullet line of Rosa's PKM sparkled around the vicinity of the room. The spray of bullets she sent their way punched holes in the glass and thudded into the log walls.

The Dragunov sniper's bullets came flying at him, too, but coming from a lower location, they could only hit the logs of the balcony or the roof.

M ignored the many incoming shots, unconcerned with anything that wasn't going to hit him. "Seeking instructions," he reported to Pitohui, to whom he had conceded command.

"Well, let's see…"

Pitohui was on the north side of the building, where the hallway was. She had the Savage 110 BA bolt-action rifle that belonged to her deceased teammate. She wasn't using its attached bipod. Instead, the object propping the gun up was the body of one of the MMTM members. It was Kenta, his body whole again after his death by explosion. The body was facedown, the gun resting on the small of his back.

It was about the same plan as what SHINC had done minutes earlier—a body that wouldn't budge, blocked all shots, and was just the right height—except that they had used their own teammate, and she was using an enemy's body.

This still raised some moral questions, which did not trouble Pitohui in the least. One wondered how Kenta would feel about this, watching his body being used in this manner from the waiting room for the deceased.

There were no low windows in the hallway to allow her to shoot from a prone position, but that wasn't an issue. There was a hole about fifteen inches across she'd carved through the logs with the photon sword, through which she stuck the barrel and scope of the gun.

Through the circle of the lens, she saw a tiny enemy rushing closer through the field. She was alone and carrying a six-shot grenade launcher. She was still far off, at least five hundred yards.

"For some reason, Llenn's not coming from this side… It's just the six-shot grenade girl, making her way here on her own. What do you think, former leader?" she asked M, keeping the gun ready to fire at any moment.

"What do I think…? I cannot imagine why the enemy would want to charge straight for us. They're practically asking us to shoot them."

"Exactly… It's a bit creepy, really. I wonder if there's something more behind this…?" Pitohui said skeptically. If she hadn't had her cheek pressed to the rifle stock, she would have tilted her head out of curiosity.

"Still, we ought to thin out the enemy numbers while we have the chance."

"I guess that's the only real option. Okay, here's your order: You are free to shoot and wipe them out. We'll speak again if they get within two hundred yards."

"Roger."

One second later, M's M14 EBR and Pitohui's Savage 110 BA fired in absolute unison.

On the stream in the bar, they saw the head of the woman firing the PKM machine gun light up with a gunshot effect.

"Awww!"

"They got her!" the men wailed.

"…"

But Anna stood there with her arms crossed, watching her comrades fight in silence.

"I got shot, but I'm not dead yet! I've still got your backs!" reported stout mama Rosa, the right edge of her head glowing as she got to her feet with the PKM. Her hit points dropped until they stopped at 20 percent, in the red zone.

She didn't use a med kit—she didn't have time to bother. She put the heavy machine gun on her shoulder, aimed it at the light of the muzzle that shot her from the second floor of the log house a thousand feet away, and fired with all her strength.

"Ryaaaaaah!"

She used her sheer brute strength to keep the gun from jumping, the tracer bullets lashing the distant room. The PKM barked and roared, the personification of its owner's fighting spirit. Flame and exhaust shot from the muzzle, rippling the nearby grass. Empty cartridges hurtled to the left, then disintegrated into computer graphics, evaporating into the air.

Five seconds later, all one hundred bullets were gone from the ammunition box below the gun, and the world was suddenly quiet.

"Phew..."

Rosa lowered the PKM. A single bullet flew at her forehead—and continued through it out the back.

While this furious gun battle was taking place on the south side of the building, Fukaziroh heard something metallic over her head that she had never heard before.

Jragnk!

Her head tilted a bit to the right, like some unseen person had pushed her.

"Yeesh, the bullet grazed my helmet! Yikes! But lucky me!"

She kept running.

Pitohui grumbled, "It's not fair being so tiny..."

She moved the bolt of the Savage 110 BA, expelling the empty and loading the next bullet into the chamber. "How's it going over there?" she asked M on the other side of the building.

"I just finished the second one. I can get them all," he answered.

"This is a no-go."

"They don't stand a chance..."

The bar was in a mournful mood. On the screen, in the midst of Team SHINC's reckless charge, Tohma the Dragunov sniper got shot and went down.

She had been in a pattern of running, stopping to fire a few shots, then running again. But once Rosa's machine-gunning stopped, it was only natural that she became the next target.

Tohma emptied the ten-shot magazine, her bolt sliding back after its furious repetition while she reached to a pouch for her next magazine...

One shot to the head.

One high on her chest.

Tohma fell to her knees and toppled onto her face. Soon there was a DEAD sign floating over her.

"Well, I guess he got revenge for the shield…"

"Two members of SHINC left. The Bizon and the Vintorez."

"They're both pretty sharp, but they can't actually get to M."

"For having fought so well this whole time, it's turning into a pretty underwhelming ending…"

One of the people in the crowd commenting on the action glanced over his left shoulder at the woman standing behind him.

Anna stared at the screens, unmoving, her arms still crossed. She was wearing her sunglasses indoors, hiding her eyes. There was no way to know how she felt while watching her friends get shot.

Then the squattest member of the Amazons appeared. It was the one who had let herself die to be a prop for the PTRD-41. She had just returned from the waiting area.

"How's it going, Anna?" the dwarf asked.

"Boss's plan is in motion," the blond woman replied without turning around.

M switched out his magazine and turned the scope to his next target.

It was the silver-haired woman with the Bizon, the fastest of the group. She was about 250 yards off. She zigzagged every three seconds, but it was a very simple and consistent pattern.

"Right…left…right…"

M could easily see the pattern ahead of time. Because she was small, he aimed and fired at her body, rather than her head.

The bullet connected with the midriff of his target, and her body rolled forward and flipped over. He'd inflicted major damage but not instant death. On the ground, she picked up the Bizon she'd dropped and shot it back at him one-handed.

It was no more than pointless resistance. A submachine gun firing pistol bullets was never going to hit him at that distance. In fact, the bullet lines not only weren't hitting M, they couldn't even reach him.

M simply aimed at her head, now a stationary target, and pulled the trigger.

In the brief moment between firing and impact, M saw the delighted smile on her face.

"…"

The eyes in the midst of his fearsome visage were wide in stunned surprise—but the angle of the camera did not show this on the TV screens.

"Good grief, looks like I'm the only one left," grumbled Boss, basing this on the readout of her teammates' HP as she ran with speed unbefitting of her frame.

She looked forward again, just a bit over two hundred yards from her target. The log house was much larger ahead of her now, and she could actually see the man on the second floor pointing his gun at her.

"So how shall I do this now…?" she muttered, when the man's gun shone a red bullet line on her.

"Oh-ho!" She grinned. M was the master of the lineless sniping. This was the first time he had ever shone a bullet line on her. "Ha! Nice one! Good job, M! You figured out what we're thinking already!" she said, praising the man who was trying to kill her.

She came to a stop and leaped to the side to avoid the line. Her large body soared through the air, the bullet passing right where she had been a split second before. She seamlessly landed flat on one hand.

"This is my chance!" she crowed. She held up the Vintorez in a crouch, aimed through the scope, and fired at the man.

The silent sniper rifle spat out the bullet with only the quietest of clicks. The projectile embedded in the railing of the balcony, sending shreds of wood flying.

"Daaa! She just missed!" the crowd shrieked as M fired on the screen.

Just like the other instances, his aim was true, and the bullet landed in the left eye of the braided gorilla with the Vintorez. She lurched, and his second bullet struck in almost exactly the same spot.

The gorilla woman fell onto her back, the impact so spectacular that you could practically feel it. The DEAD tag spelled the end of Team SHINC, the runners-up of the previous final.

More of the crowd mourned their end than complimented M's incredible skill.

"Heh!" Anna snorted.

"That was a bit much, Boss," Sophie opined.

Anna removed her shades and turned to face the shorter Sophie on her left. Her eyes were a brilliant emerald green, which only made her beautiful looks that much more bewitching. Some of the men who'd been sneaking looks at her sighed wistfully.

She paid them absolutely no attention. "How many points would you give Boss for that one?" she asked Sophie.

With the end of Boss, M had eliminated all the threats on his side of the building.

"I wiped out SHINC," he told Pitohui. "How about you?"

While he was shooting, Pitohui had fired twice.

The .338 Lapua Magnums she fired were twice as strong as M's 7.62 × 51 mm rounds. The powerful blast of the Savage 110 BA spread to the sides due to muzzle brake, reverberating down the hallway. It was a gunshot that would make much more noise inside the building than outside it.

He had only asked for confirmation, assuming she had finished off her target, too.

"Actually, I'm not getting anything."

Since she didn't specify a subject, M wasn't sure what she meant. "I'm heading over there."

"Over."

M stood, lifting his gun. The four-foot hole was a bit cramped, so he stepped through the door he'd pumped full of holes instead on his way to the hallway.

First, he deactivated the grand grenade, which was still counting down. Then he stood next to Pitohui, who had the Savage 110 BA resting on the dead body, and held up the M14 EBR to stare through its scope from behind the window.

"Eleven o'clock. Four hundred yards," Pitohui instructed.

"..."

He silently pivoted to the point she indicated and saw a girl who was not Llenn—meaning her partner, instead. She had an MGL-140 hanging from her shoulder on a sling, a large helmet, and a large backpack. She was crawling desperately through the grass, heading right for them.

And the ends of her legs were missing.

It was clear with the magnification on his scope. Moving in concert with her arms, the slender ends of her legs were glowing red, with no feet on them.

"The first shot was a coincidence, okay?" Pitohui explained without looking up. "It hit her cute little foot and ripped it off. So she fell, of course. I waited for a bit, but no one else came out, so I shot her other foot. And even then, she didn't show up. I wonder where Llenn is… Or maybe she just has no intention of saving her little friend?"

She made it sound like they were playing a game of tag.

Injuring a soldier so he wouldn't die but would struggle against pain and the fear of death, then shooting every last comrade who couldn't resist coming to help their fellow was a real-life sniper's technique, as cruel as it was effective.

But *GGO* was a game, after all. So in most cases, it ended up in team conversations like:

"Sorry, pal. Bad luck this round."

"Help me, you heartless bastard!"

"Would putting you out of your misery count as helping?"

"That's not funny!"

In this case, M said, "Just go ahead and finish her off in one. It should be easy. Or did you really run out of bullets?"

"What is that supposed to be?" Pitohui asked. "Kindness? Compassion? Mercy?"

"Those are all the same thing. And they're all wrong. This isn't a real-life battle. Llenn's not going to come save the teammate who was reckless enough to run out into the open. She fought bravely with me last time, all the way to the end. She's got enough smarts to see through this," he replied. "Besides, I'm worried that either Llenn's circling around behind us, or the last remaining team found vehicles and is approaching fast. I cleaned up the south side. That just leaves the north and east. Take her out so we can focus on the perimeter. This isn't time to mess around."

The whole while that M spoke in his measured tones, the enemy girl continued her determined crawl forward. She was about 370 yards off now. It was close enough for her grenade launcher to reach them, and if she managed the difficult feat of landing one through the window, it would be a very dangerous situation for them.

But she still wasn't even pointing it at them, so Pitohui asked lazily, "Can't we wait a bit longer?"

"No. Forget it—I'll do it."

M slid the windowpane up to open it, fixed it in place, then aimed the M14 EBR again.

"Fine, geez."

Pitohui fired.

With a roar, the bullet hit the crawling girl's left wrist. A little gloved hand flew into the air, glowing red with the damage effect.

Out of shock and simulated pain, the girl writhed and turned onto her side, clutching her empty wrist with the other hand. It looked just like she had actually lost her hand and was trying to stop the loss of blood from the stump.

"Oops, sorry. I was aiming for the head, but I missed. I'm not used to this gun," Pitohui said without a care in the world as she loaded the next bullet and fired it.

The second shot also "missed," hitting the girl's right wrist this time. Like the left one, her hand ripped off and flew away.

"Pito…," M muttered darkly, but he did not fire.

She didn't bother to load the next shot. "With that much damage, she should be dead in just a few moments… Wait, what?"

To her surprise, the girl lying still on her side—technically, she couldn't move even if she wanted to—did not feature a DEAD marker.

So even after suffering enough damage to blow all her limbs off, her hit points were still more than zero. You couldn't see an opponent's HP in Squad Jam, so there was no way to know how much health she had left.

"She's so tough! No wonder Llenn picked her for a partner! I wonder where she found her… I don't remember any tiny girls that tough in *GGO*…," Pitohui said, both impressed and skeptical.

Lastly, she said, "But she can't do anything for at least two minutes now, right? You can't shoot without hands!"

In the bar, Fukaziroh's terrible predicament was aired live.

"Whoa! That's messed up!"

"This footage should be restricted to age eighteen and up…"

"Does she think it's fun to torture a little girl like that? Yeah, I know it's just an avatar," ranted those who were outraged.

"She's been blowing off heads and chopping them off this whole time. What's the difference now?"

"That was the same little girl who turned several people to mincemeat at the train station, right?"

"Besides, they're both women…," argued more sensible minds.

Lastly, someone capped off the debate with a truly dull platitude: "Look, it might seem nasty, but a game's just a game. Let's all remember that this isn't real life, okay?"

But moments before all this, Llenn was trying and failing yet again to undo the knot ("Come on! Darn you!") when she heard a gunshot. It was most definitely from this side of the building this time.

Then she heard Fukaziroh say, "Yeesh, the bullet grazed my helmet! Yikes! But lucky me!"

"Are you taking fire? Get down!"

"No thank you!" said her partner. She could also hear the muffled sounds of a vicious gunfight on the far side of the building. The rattling fire of a sniper rifle was something she specifically recognized: M's M14 EBR.

SHINC was charging the building, and M was firing back at them. It was his training that helped her understand all that from the evidence her ears provided.

That meant it was Pitohui who was shooting at Fukaziroh.

What should she do?

For one thing, she had to get the shackle off. She attempted to undo the sling yet again and got nowhere with it.

"Dammiiiiit!" she roared, cursing the entire world.

"Wait, are you still working on that, Alexander the Great?"

"Huh?" Llenn gaped. Then she recalled that Fukaziroh had said something weird when she first ran off.

Whosoever succeeds in undoing the knot shall become the rightful king of the entire world!

And then there was the mention of Alexander the Great.

The two hints melded in her mind, and a half second later, she stopped trying to untie the knot. "Oh, crap!" She reached behind her back. "I should have just done this from the start!"

Just as Alexander the Great "solved" the puzzle of the unsolvable Gordian knot by slicing it in two, she pulled out her combat knife and simply cut through the sling tied around her ankle.

Free at last, Llenn put away the knife and wore her gloves once more. Then she heard more gunshots.

"Yeek! I got shot!" yelled Fukaziroh, rather lackadaisically.

"Whoa! You okay?" Llenn asked, then realized that she could just look at the gauge in the corner of her vision.

Fukaziroh's HP had dropped a bit more than 10 percent; it wasn't that bad, fortunately. The bullet must have missed her head and chest.

"Fuka! Just hide, okay? I'm going to rush to back you up!"

"Nope, can't do that."

"Why not?"

"My foot got shot off. Again. I don't know why youngsters these days are so on edge."

"Huhhhh?"

Llenn searched for Fukaziroh with her monocular. She found her 425 feet away, sprawled on the grass, the end of her left leg glowing red.

The next moment, there was another boom. This time, she actually saw Fukaziroh's other foot get blown off.

"Bwah! Yikes... *Et tu*, right foot?! Man, I could go for a Caesar salad right about now," Fukaziroh chattered, out of either confidence or complete confusion. Her health dropped further, down to about 70 percent.

Llenn looked for the shooter. She had a hunch where she would find her, and it didn't take long.

In the wall of the second-floor hallway, right around the middle, was a small hole that hadn't been there before. At maximum magnification, she could just make out the muzzle. The distant sound of the M14 EBR could still be heard periodically, so this one had to be Pitohui.

She reeled in the nearby P-chan, figuring that if she could see her, she could shoot her.

"..."

But then she stopped. There was no way to aim nearly a third of a mile with a P90. She could probably get a bullet to fly that far, but it would never strike her target, and more importantly, the bullet line would give away her location.

At least with a sniper rifle, she could aim directly at the hole, whether she was skillful enough to shoot it or not.

Oh, if only I'd actually attempted the sniping course during that very first tutorial...

But it was far too late for that. Besides, if she hadn't chosen the submachine gun at the beginning, she would never have gotten this far in the game.

"Well…Llenn…partner… You may want to sit down for this," Fukaziroh said. "I think I've just realized that I can't really move anymore, so I'm prolly a goner."

"I knew that from the start! It was a crazy idea to rush them!"

"But I haven't regretted or learned a thing!"

"You ought to! This is what happens when you act without thinking!"

"Hey, it's better than what you were doing, moping and stuff. Don't you know that famous saying, 'A soldier values speed above all else'? Didn't you cover that in science class in elementary school?"

"No, we didn't!"

As Llenn watched, Fukaziroh continued crawling forward— "Hup-ho, hup-ho. And a one, and a two"—using primarily her elbows and knees.

"Forget about it! Just shoot your grenades from there! It doesn't matter if they don't reach! You don't have to hit her! I'll just jump out when they explode! Okay?"

"Hey, that's not such a bad idea, but—"

Another boom.

"Ahyoo?" screamed Fukaziroh—if that was what it was.

Through the monocular, Llenn saw the bullet-wound effect—and her partner's left hand flying off. That was another 20 percent of her health down.

"Gyaaa! My left hand! Now I can't even wear my engagement ring!" yelled Fukaziroh, who was not engaged.

"…"

All Llenn could do was watch in silence.

With the next gunshot, even her right hand, which was holding her severed left wrist, was sliced clean off to hurtle through the air.

"Uh-oh… This isn't good… Man, it's just not fair that they can shoot without a line…," Fukaziroh grumbled weakly as she lay on her side. She stopped moving. Her hit points went down to the yellow area, about 30 percent left.

"D...d...d..."

Llenn pounded the earth.

"...dammit!"

At some point, she stopped hearing the M14 EBR firing. The world of *GGO* was silent, as though all the raucous battling had never happened.

"Dammit..."

Llenn was alone in the middle of the field, lying on the ground with her camo poncho on.

"Dammit..."

All the days and hours ran through her mind like her life flashing before her eyes.

Nothing in SJ2 had gone the way it was planned.

All she had needed to do was find Pitohui as quickly as possible and beat her somehow. But they'd started out placed on opposite sides of the map, forcing her to travel a very long distance and fight a variety of teams in her way.

"Dammit..."

Llenn had used up a ton of ammo, and while she had gotten a lot more with a magical kiss, Fukaziroh had run short on pink smoke grenades.

"Dammit..."

When they had finally put together a plan to use the last ones at just the right moment, there was a ridiculous bit of interference when everything counted the most.

"Dammit..."

And just when they had regrouped to put together a new plan, a powerful team of rivals came riding up in a vehicle to interrupt.

"Dammit..."

They were beaten in the end, but it caused her opponent to exhibit some monstrous, demonic abilities in battle.

"Dammit..."

And when she had tried to come up with yet another new plan, the best plan of all, every last one of her friends rushed up without her and got thrashed just as badly as she'd feared.

"Dammit…"

Now she was trembling and alone, without any moves left to make.

"Aaaah! Enough!" shouted Llenn to the cloudy sky. "I don't care about Pito anymore! Let her win this damn thing already! If she's that freakishly powerful, then she's not going to die anyway!"

Heh-heh…

Fukaziroh grinned to herself as she listened to the cry of Llenn's soul.

"Like I care about killing Pito anymore! I don't need to bother! Then I wouldn't have had to go through all this trouble! I don't care if she dies!"

"Then what shall be thy plan?" Fukaziroh asked, like a question from God.

"Kill!" Llenn replied.

"Whom?"

"Pito!"

"How?"

"I dunno!"

Bwoosh! Llenn literally leaped to her feet and threw off the camo poncho surrounding her.

"I don't care—I'm just going to shoot her! Or knife her! Or use some other means!"

The sudden appearance of pink in the middle of the field was certainly an attention grabber. It was a girl with a nasty look in her eyes.

"I'm gonna kill Pito!"

She bounced off the ground with both feet.

"Nice! Then I'll help you, Llenn!" said the excited voice of her gun, P-chan, from below.

"Okay! Let's go, P-chan!" she replied, beginning to sprint at top speed.

When she heard that shout, Fukaziroh mentally burst into laughter. *Bwa-ha-ha-ha-ha-ha-ha!*

And then it occurred to her: *So that's what she's like when she goes crazy.*

CHAPTER 19

Save the Last Battle for Me

SECT.19

CHAPTER 19
Save the Last Battle for Me

On the screen in the bar, the pink shrimp tore off her disguise and stood up, exposing her presence in heroic fashion.

"There she is! The defending champion!"

"So that's where she was!"

"Yeah! Go!" cheered her fans.

"You dummy! Why would you pop up there?!"

"You took off the poncho too early!"

"Oh no, she's gonna die…," groaned those who felt despair.

In response to both categories of spectators, the little player in pink began to sprint, making full use of her prodigious agility stat…straight to the northwest.

"Huh?"

In other words, directly away from the log house.

"Theeeerrrrre!" shrieked Pitohui with delight.

Her scope was zoomed in for better searching, and she was now using it to follow the pink blur among the grass.

"I spotted her, too. That's Llenn," said M, M14 EBR at the ready in the window.

"Well, she's mine! If you kill her, I'll kill *you*!" she warned him. "Now come to me!" She glared through the scope, all thoughts on battle, until she saw Llenn in full flight mode. "Huh?"

The girl's tiny back was growing even tinier.

"Hey! What?! She's running away! I don't believe it! I don't believe it!"

Llenn was fleeing so quickly, she was no longer visible from the hole in the building. Pitohui pulled away from the Savage 110 BA and stood up. Then she grabbed the KTR-09 assault rifle nearby, her actual gun, and ordered the dumbfounded M, "Let's follow! Come with me!"

"Er, right... What about her partner?"

"We can worry about that later!"

"But once she gets her limbs back, those grenades will be a pain."

"Shut up!"

Pitohui swung a black boot directly up into M's crotch.

"*Frngk!*" he exclaimed, falling to his knees.

"Come on! Let's go!" she demanded, a request that was now impossible.

"Grrrng... B-but...," M grunted, out of either pain or delight, elbows and knees on the floor. "If she's running away... There's no way...we'll catch up...," he pointed out.

"I know that. She runs like she's a car."

M's pain-or-pleasure had worn off, and he lifted his head. "Well?"

"We're going to chase her down in a car, obviously!"

Llenn's desperate escape from the final battle was entirely caught on camera, of course. The floating eye followed her back as she whipped through the grass at tremendous speed.

"Bwa-ha-ha-ha-ha-ha-ha-ha-ha-ha-ha!" Boss bellowed in the waiting area, just a dark space without a ceiling or walls, only a monitor before her.

Next to her, Tanya said, "Not bad!"

Tohma cheered, "You got this, Llenn!"

And Rosa declared, "We're all counting on you!"

They sat around on the black floor, watching the proceedings with excitement.

A grin rested across Boss's menacing face. She muttered, "Right. That's the Llenn I wanted to beat."

Llenn paused in her dash across the plains and turned back. She tucked the P90 on its sling against her body with her left hand and put the monocular she'd been holding on the right up to her eye.

In no time at all, she was nearly two-thirds of a mile from the log house. At its western edge, she could see the three four-wheel-drive vehicles. Two figures were getting into one of them now. Soon it began to move.

"Heh-heh-heh-heh." She grinned evilly. "Now follow me!"

She changed direction—and headed east.

"There! She's running to the east!" cried M from the driver's seat of the Humvee, clutching the thin wheel and driving it through the grass of the plain.

"I can see herrrr!" Pitohui was standing in the middle of the vehicle's four seats, sticking her face out of the protected sunroof area. She had one hand on a rail and the other on her KTR-09.

"Hang on!" M called out as he turned the Humvee to the right. The shift in momentum pressed Pitohui against the edge of the sunroof area.

"Kya-ha-ha-ha-ha-ha-ha!"

She seemed to be having fun.

"Taaaaaaa!"

Llenn ran and ran and ran for all she was worth. She was making the absolute most of her character's abilities.

Because it was a grassy field, she couldn't actually see where she was stepping. If there happened to be a large rock on the ground, she would immediately trip over it and roll for a good distance.

But she didn't let up at all. She ran pell-mell, checking behind her to see that the brown car was coming closer, and continued on her way. "You won't catch me! Not yet!"

She was running straight east at this point, but the log house was no longer visible on her right; it was well over her shoulder by then. The only thing in front of her was the valley between the snowy mountain and the rocky one—field, ponds, and rivers.

A tiny pink person sped through the plains like a ferocious horse. About five hundred yards behind her was a Humvee giving chase.

"C'mon, M! Pedal to the metal! I can't get a good enough shot!"

Llenn was not as fast as the automobile. They'd been slowly closing the gap, but with the rocking of the car, even Pitohui couldn't land a shot at this distance one-handed.

Behind the wheel, M protested, "I can if you want, but the extra turbulence is going to buck you off! I don't know how rough the terrain will be ahead of us."

"Like I give a shit! Just do it!" she yelled, swinging her leg forward to kick the back of his head.

"Gfhk! Fine… Suit yourself!" M jammed his heavy foot on the gas.

The 6.5-liter V6 diesel turbo engine roared, and a moment later, the Humvee jolted harder. It hurtled Pitohui backward, and it took her considerable arm strength to keep her upright.

"Hi-yo, Silverrrr!" she shouted, like some televised cowboy hero, ponytail whipping, eyes sparkling above the roof of the Humvee. "Let's go, Llenn! Show me how you want to fight!"

The audience in the bar got chills watching Llenn run with the car chasing after her.

"I wonder what Llenn has planned!"

"She's got to have something up her sleeve. I can't wait!"

"Llenn has no ideas," said Tanya in the waiting area.

"Yeah. She's just winging it on a prayer," replied Boss. "But that's the best part."

On the north side of the log house, Fukaziroh was waiting for her hands and feet to reappear, but she did manage to successfully administer a healing kit with just her arms and mouth.

As her hit points slowly filled up, she noted that Llenn's gauge was still in perfect green condition.

Hang in there, she silently prayed. *If you keep trying, you never know what will happen.*

What do I do, what do I do, what do I do, what do I do?!

It was like a mantra, repeating over and over in Llenn's head as she ran.

She rushed off with all the momentum of anger and frustration, but there hadn't been a plan behind it. At the very least, she had avoided the impossible task of trying to rush a building where incredible snipers waited to shoot her, but that was it.

She turned back for a peek.

Ugh.

The boxy vehicle was much closer than before, perhaps three hundred to four hundred yards away now. She could even spot a smile on Pitohui, who had her top half leaning out of the vehicle's roof. In her hand was a long black rod. She didn't know what it was, except that it definitely wasn't a rug beater.

Shit! she swore to herself again, out of however many times it had been that day. *You know, ever since I started GGO, I've been swearing like a sailor.*

But now was the time for coming up with a plan. Should she turn and fire back with the P90? She'd landed a hit from this distance earlier, so maybe she could hope for another stroke of luck.

"No way! At that distance, they'll be shooting at us, too! As soon as we stop moving, we'll get shot!" P-chan argued.

It was true. That was probably an assault rifle in Pitohui's hands. She was certain to win in a shoot-out.

So Llenn kept running.

Ahead on the left, about a hundred yards away, was something that looked like a pond. It was a circle of standing water at least thirty yards across. The surface reflected the dull-gray sky, and there was no way to tell its depth from there.

"..."

Llenn decided to head toward it.

On the screen, the audience at the bar saw Llenn changing course.

"Hang on! That's toward the pond!"

"Is she gonna jump in and swim away?"

"It might not be the worst plan. Even a Humvee isn't going to do much good submerged in water."

"What if it's shallow? It might just be a puddle in a marsh! If it's only eighteen inches deep, it'll drive right across!"

"But they're not gonna be able to tell unless they get really close, right?"

They enjoyed speculating over the various possibilities.

Llenn ran and ran toward the pond, praying the whole while, *Please don't let Pito shoot me!*

She glanced back. The car's distance was just over two hundred yards now.

She looked forward. Thirty yards to the pond.

Okay! Here we gooooo!

Her brain gave the signal to stop. Those machine legs, pumping like pistons, instantly came to a halt. The soles of her boots slid and scraped the soil of the field, slowing her progress.

It was a preposterous way to stop, but she held her weight backward, bearing the deceleration, keeping her legs perfectly balanced, until she came to a full stop without falling over.

It took her just five yards of space to perform this feat.

*   *   *

"What was that?!"

"That was wild," the audience in the bar marveled.

"Hyaaa! What in the—? How did she do that?!" said Tanya.

"*Khorosho!* If Llenn did virtual gymnastics, she would be very good at it!" exclaimed Tohma.

Now that she had stopped and turned herself around, Llenn ignored P-chan, saying, "*I get it, we're gonna shoot back from here!*" and pushing the gun on the sling to hang over her back instead.

"*Huh? Aren't you going to shoot me? Aren't you going to shoot me? Aren't you going to shoot me?*" her gun prattled. She ignored it and put her hand behind her waist.

"Hmph!"

She drew a dark, gleaming combat knife backhanded, then held it up before her eyes like some kind of gladiator.

"Come, Pitohui!"

"Fweh?" Pitohui squawked.

They'd been gunning it so hard to catch tiny pink Llenn, and she'd just screeched to a halt like a jet landing on an aircraft carrier at sea. Then she turned around to face their car with nothing but a knife in her hand.

Pitohui's expression of shock quickly turned to a smile of wild joy.

"Hyaaa! This is lovely!" she screamed from the top of the Humvee.

Rather than continuing to take aim with the KTR-09 rifle, she tossed it into the back seat of the Humvee with a dull thud.

One hundred and sixty yards to go.

"Press on, my noble steed! It's a joust!" Pitohui commanded M. "Hya-hoo!" She drew a different weapon and created a beam of light.

Pitohui made a quick rotation with the Muramasa F9 photon

sword held out level. The glowing sword severed clean the protective material that surrounded the rooftop perch of the Humvee. The parts toppled off the vehicle to either side.

Now there was no structure above the sunroof of the Humvee, just Pitohui's upper half and a blade in her hand.

She held the sword high overhead.

"I shall be thy opponent!" she barked, like a samurai of the past.

M did not ease off the gas.

Yes!

Llenn grinned. The Humvee was just a hundred yards off now, racing straight toward her, with Pitohui and her glowing sword on top.

"Hey, c'mon! You can shoot the lady on the top of the car now! This is your big chance, Llenn! Lift me up and shoot me!"

"Shut up, or I'll pawn you off," she silently threatened her gun. She glared over the black blade before her at the enemy knight on her giant steed, bearing down.

"It's a duel! The shrimp's gonna jump up and slash at her!"

"What's gonna happen?!" the bar roared.

"Awesome!"

"Get 'er!"

"Stab her!"

The waiting area boomed with voices. Llenn could hear none of them.

On the monitors, the pink shrimp stood and waited while the Humvee closed in, engine roaring.

Fifty yards.

Forty yards.

Thirty yards.

"Raaaah!"

Llenn started running. Twenty yards.

The woman atop the car pulled her right arm back, holding the photon sword, preparing herself for a thrust with perfect form. She put her left arm in front of her, a defensive move meant to sacrifice her own limb.

Everyone watching the video understood.

This fight would last all of an instant, leaving no time to blink.

In just two or three seconds, Llenn would use her running start and incredible agility to leap into the air at her target, and the woman would strike back with the photon sword.

So whose head was going to fly off?

The distance between the charging vehicle and the accelerating girl was just ten yards.

And then the spectators had to doubt their very own eyes.

Splat.

She dropped to the ground.

The tiny girl in pink just flopped to the grass. One moment she'd been racing at the Humvee, and then she had stopped and dropped.

She was so flat against the ground that the Humvee's sets of tires passed right over and around her, the chassis easily clearing her head and body.

"Whaaaaaat?!" screeched Pitohui, who saw her opponent flatten herself under the vehicle. "Llenn, you little bastard!"

She spun around atop the Humvee. A pink figure emerged from behind the car and stood up, P90 in her hand, aiming at Pitohui.

"And you call yourself a samuraaaaai?!" yelled Pitohui.

The gunfire was her way of answering, *No, I do not.*

"Llenn! Was this the plan the whole time?" P-chan wondered as it spat fire.

Inside her head, Llenn replied, *"Who would get into a physical fight with a person riding a car?! I'm not Pito!"*

Her aim wasn't particularly steady with just one hand holding the gun, but this moment, when the target was so close, would be her best chance. She held the trigger, intending to empty all fifty shots.

"How dare youuuuu!" roared Pitohui.

Red bullet lines surrounded her, fanning out in great number. Realizing that Llenn had completely tricked her put such a ferocious look on Pitohui's face, any child would have burst into tears upon seeing it.

"Raaaah!"

She blocked one of the lines that pointed to her face with the pale light of the photon sword. All around the car, bullets pinged and thwacked against the body. *Fzhk!* Something evaporated.

Llenn's P90 magazine had fifty rounds. Her onslaught continued.

Pitohui gave up on striking back. She clicked the photon sword off right as she kicked both legs forward, so she fell with a thump back inside the Humvee. A few more bullets nearly grazed her head in the process.

"The pond! I'm braking!" M warned from the driver's seat.

"We're fine! Keep going!" Pitohui commanded.

As she fired one-handed, Llenn thought, *This is going to work!*

The car that passed over her plunged into the tiny lake without dropping in speed. At the rate it was going, they wouldn't be able to stop it from submerging. It might look tough, but it couldn't possibly be an amphibious vehicle.

She used the opportunity to switch out the P90's magazine and approached the edge of the water. This time, she brought up her right hand to aim properly. When the two of them came gasping to the surface, she would slaughter them without mercy.

With all the heavy gear they wore, they'd have to struggle mightily to keep from sinking, so they wouldn't be able to fight back. Of course, if they just drowned all on their own, that would be even better. That way, she could conserve ammo, and all she'd need to do was wait and watch, wondering whether they had drowned yet.

"This is some really grotesque stuff to think about, Llenn!"

"Shut up! As long as I win, that's all that matters!" she told her gun. Meanwhile, she'd run through another fifty-round magazine already. She put the knife in her other hand back into its sheath and switched the P90 to the empty hand so she could pull out the empty magazine.

Sploooosh!

There was a tremendous impact in the water.

"Go, M! Keep it moving!"

"You got it!"

The Humvee hit the pond and kept going.

"Whaaaaat?"

Llenn froze in the act of attaching a new magazine to the gun.

The vehicle was riding across the top of the pond just ahead of her. The large tires were churning up gobs of water, and while it was much, much slower now, it was still moving.

It looked like a water strider.

At first, Llenn wondered whether the tires were somehow outfitted with some special capabilities. Then she realized that the answer was much more mundane.

Holy crap! The water's shallow!

She clicked the new magazine into the P90 and pulled the loading lever.

The car driving across the pond—no, the large puddle—turned briefly to the right, then swung around to the left. It was clearly making a U-turn to come back for her.

"What now, Llenn?" asked P-chan. She began to sprint again, straight for the vehicle.

"It's shallow here! You just can't tell by looking at it!" Pitohui said, reaching over for her gun inside the Humvee as it roared across the huge puddle.

"How did you know?" M asked, pulling the Humvee into a big left turn.

Pitohui popped up with the KTR-09 in her hand and said, "There was that poster about eruption times and places on the wall of the room! Didn't you bother to read it?"

The Humvee completed its 180-degree turn, kicking up buckets of water. It got a bit slower again.

The windshield wipers busily cleaned off the wet glass, hanging from the top of the frame rather than the bottom as was typical. Through the motion, M saw Llenn standing at the edge of the pond, P90 at the ready. She was about fifty yards away.

"What now?"

Pitohui leaned her face up from the back. "Do you need to ask?! We're charging her again. But this time, yank on the wheel right before we get there! Crush her under the tires!"

"..."

M grimaced briefly, but Pitohui was very much enjoying herself. "So far, I've killed by beating, shooting, grenades, and swords, but not running anyone over yet. This is the perfect opportunity to do so. Now get her!"

She smacked M on the shoulder, and he slammed on the gas.

Llenn lifted her P90 to point at the boxy brown beast that came charging at her again. She aimed above the roof—if Pitohui popped her face out, she would be ready to blast her with the highest possible rate of fire.

The tires sloshed and tossed the water as the vehicle pushed forward.

Pitohui did not appear.

"..."

Llenn backed up, still holding the P90 at the ready.

"All right! Go!"

Pitohui stared at Llenn through the windshield, keeping herself low and most decidedly not popping her head out of the sunroof.

When Llenn took a few steps back, she commanded, "Crush her! Even if she starts running away!"

M said nothing, but he maintained his pressure on the accelerator.

Three seconds before she was going to get squished, Llenn started running.

Forward.

She leaped. Her superhuman agility gave her air beyond the ability of any mortal, and she pointed the P90 down into the gaping hole in the roof of the Humvee.

Ka-ka-ka-kang!

The bullets caused sparks as they hit various metal features within the chassis, right as Pitohui shouted, "Gah!"

Llenn leaped into the air, rather than dropping to the ground again, and fired into the roof of the car as it passed beneath her. She had an afterimage of Pitohui's face turning toward her and a few glowing bits of damage, but they had all been on her legs.

Shit! I missed!

She swung her legs forward to prepare for her landing in the water.

"What now? What's the next plan?" her gun asked.

This time, Llenn's answer was *"No choice but to run!"*

M kept the Humvee going to put distance between them and Llenn. "You okay?" he asked, looking over his right shoulder.

"Wow, she's done it! Oh, she's done it now!" snarled Pitohui happily, flipping over the back seat. "You've gone and done it now, Llenn!"

There were two bullet effects on her right thigh, but she still had 80 percent of her HP. M looked forward and spun the Humvee into another U-turn.

Llenn splashed her way across the shallow water, taking

distance from the vehicle. While it was slower than on the grass, her speed was still tremendous.

"Stop! Fine, I'll just shoot her!" Pitohui popped her head out of the Humvee's roof as it scraped to a halt, set the KTR-09 against her shoulder, and flipped the selector to full auto. She was aiming at Llenn as she ran across the puddle. The distance was about eighty yards and growing.

"This…should…do it."

The KTR-09 barked rapidly. A number of large jets of water appeared from the surface of the pond. They rose around Llenn, gushing nearly six feet into the air, as she ran, almost like spontaneous fountains. It was actually kind of beautiful.

The line of jets caught up to Llenn, obscuring her from view, but the bright-red glow of damage indication shone through them.

Just gotta run just gotta run just gotta run!

It was the only thought on Llenn's mind as she raced unsteadily across the puddle, until water seemed to block her vision. By the time she realized it was a plume of water from a bullet, she was surrounded by them, too late to drop down. A dull pain ran through her right knee.

Ah…

She spun as she fell, and she landed on her back in the water.

The cloudy sky was overhead, and much closer, the rising plumes of water, and closer still, the glimmering bullet lines.

I think…maybe…this is…it.

She could see her hit points dropping rapidly—but only to about halfway, when the rapid drop from being shot came to a stop. But since almost her entire body was submerged in water, she was still losing a little trickle of continuous health, as was the custom in *GGO*.

If she stayed here, she would eventually die.

But if she stood up and took a single good shot, she would also die.

It was at the exact moment of that thought that the gunshots and water jets came to an abrupt halt.

"Did I get her?" Pitohui wondered, pausing her fire so the splashes of water could subside. She spotted the bit of pink bobbing in the water. There was no DEAD tag floating over her.

"Not yet, huh? Did I only hit her with one shot? Damn, she's so lucky! Or is it just because she's tiny? Or is it both?"

"Shall I bring us closer, Pito?" M asked.

"Huh? Why should you? I'll hit her the next time."

"No, I just thought you might want to see your target's face when she dies."

"Ooooh… Now you're starting to get it."

"So what's the call?"

"Y'know what? Never mind. Llenn creeps me out enough. I'm afraid she might pop up and kill me if I get too close."

"Ahhh… So you *can* feel fear…"

"Don't look at me like I'm some kind of monster. It's scary. This is fun precisely because I'm scared of dying! I think I need to have a talk with you about this. Have a seat."

"I am sitting."

As Llenn floated faceup, she had to wonder, *Why isn't she shooting at me?*

Her body was above the surface just enough that she could still breathe, perhaps because her gear was so light. It didn't feel so bad, just floating there like that.

She wasn't completely helpless to shoot back, but if she stood up, she'd get shot right away. "Almost zero" was barely any different from "zero."

She had decided to blow off steam and had gotten this far on sheer willpower, but it seemed like this was going to be the end of things. A sudden idea caused her to lift her arm and check her watch.

2:27. The last event had ended on the twenty-eighth minute of the hour, at around this exact time.

"Llenn! Don't give up now!"

"Shut up, P-chan. I don't care."

"Llenn! There's still a chance!"

"It's not zero, but it might as well be."

"Hey, Llenn! You still alive? I'm on my way over!"

"You don't have to bother."

"Llenn! I know you're alive! Where are you?"

"Oh!"

She was so shocked that her jaw dropped, allowing muddy water to flood into her mouth and nose.

"Gblarkh!"

"Uh-oh. Is Llenn suffering? Is she drowning?" wondered Pitohui, who was peering from the sunroof of the Humvee.

"She might be. You lose hit points in the water, so if we ignore her long enough, she'll die."

"Yeah, that wouldn't be bad, either...," Pitohui said, conflicted. M took his foot off the brake pedal and hit the acceleration instead. The diesel engine's pitch rose, and the Humvee began to slowly move forward.

"Um, excuse me?"

"I'm not going to get right up next to her. I'm just moving us about thirty feet closer."

"Hmph... Well, fine. I'm going to shoot her. I don't like the idea of letting her drown."

Pitohui took aim with the KTR-09 at the small pink target floating on the water. The Humvee slowly inched closer, up to the lip of the puddle, then stopped.

Then she and M witnessed Llenn's right hand thrust toward the sky, holding the P90.

"Oh?"

Pitohui crouched, but the muzzle of the gun was not pointed toward them. It started firing right into the air.

"Pardon?"

Pa-ra-ra-ra-ra-ra-ra, it rattled, to Pitohui's confusion. "What is that? Some kind of ritual?"

"Beats me."

Pa-ra-ra-ra-ra-ra-ra. The long string of fifty consecutive shots came to an abrupt end.

"Maybe that was her just making sure she left no feelings behind? In that case…"

Pitohui raised the KTR-09 and took aim, straight at Llenn.

She inhaled, exhaled a bit, and held her breath.

Right as she was about to fire—

Kaboom!

A geyser of water about five yards across erupted in the pond between her and Llenn.

CHAPTER 20
Final Showdown

SECT.20

CHAPTER 20
Final Showdown

"She did really, really great, but it looks like this is the end...," someone in the pub said sadly.

From the moment Llenn started her mad dash, nearly everyone watching had been on her side. From her brilliant trick under the Humvee to her flying leap over it that succeeded in wounding the enemy, each and every maneuver brought a rousing cheer from the audience.

So when the merciless bullets struck her and she sent up plumes of water as she collapsed into the puddle, screams broke out around the pub.

At last, the final moment had come.

On the screen, the Humvee rolled closer to Llenn. Standing in the sunroof's opening was her opponent, aiming right at her. She couldn't miss from this distance.

When Llenn started firing the P90 into the air, public opinion was split between those who thought she was doing it out of terror and those who thought it was a symbol of her last regrets.

When the woman took aim again and put her finger on the trigger, someone jumped the gun a bit and said, "Rest in peace."

So when the explosion caused an enormous pillar of water to appear—*kaboom!*—a number of people screamed.

"Yeep!" "Hyaaa!" "Dwoah!"

However, Anna and Sophie instantly understood what had happened, simultaneously muttering "Ooooh" and "Uh-huh…"

"I see… So the firing into the sky was meant to cover up the sound of her partner's grenades," Sophie said.

"And coincidentally, their car was moving at the time, so the other engine sound was covered up," Anna concluded.

But Sophie smirked and said, "Are you sure that was a coincidence?"

Different things happened all at once on different screens.

On one screen, as the shock wave of the water geyser passed over Llenn, she leaped to her feet, used an emergency med kit on herself, and clicked in a fresh P90 magazine.

On a different screen, Pitohui did a one-eighty and pointed the KTR-09 directly behind the car.

And on the final screen, another Humvee was racing across the plain. It was close to two hundred yards from the pond and closing in fast. The light angled through the cabin, revealing that the driver behind the wheel was a little girl, her hands and feet intact again.

"Tch! We played around a bit too much!" spat Pitohui, blasting away with the KTR-09. The bullets seemed to home in on Fukaziroh's Humvee, but naturally, they all bounced off it.

After ten shots, Pitohui gave up on that. "Aaargh, forget it!"

The enemy Humvee was coming straight at them.

"It's gonna smash into us! Grab something—I'm gonna gun it!" M shouted, stomping on the pedal. Pitohui pressed her butt into the back seat.

"Yaaaaaah!"

Fukaziroh had her tiny foot jammed against the gas pedal as hard as she could. Her hands clung to the big steering wheel. Through the windshield was another vehicle of the same type.

"Outta the waaaay!"

On the video stream, the newly arrived Humvee plunged toward M and Pitohui's vehicle. The new one still had armor around its sunroof, so it was easy to tell the two apart. The armored Humvee's rush brought some life to the crowd that had until recently been funereal for Llenn.

"Ooh! It's gonna slam 'em!"

"That's the best way to destroy the chassis, for sure."

"But…isn't it gonna hurt the girl driving it, too?"

"Who cares? One of us for two of them? Bring it on!"

M turned the Humvee to face directly toward the oncoming arrival. Once he knew that the other car was going to ram him, there was no point in turning sideways to flee. It would just be that much easier for the other car to get an angle to upturn his. At that point, it was inevitable that he'd roll. They'd get thrown about the interior and hurt badly. If the program calculated that you broke your neck, that could mean instant death.

The best option, of course, would be to turn tail and escape. That would be the effective way to minimize any collision damage. But when that wasn't possible, facing directly forward offered the highest chances of escape. The driver could spin the wheel left or right at the last possible moment and hopefully clear out of the way.

The two vehicles rushed across the grassy plain toward a headlong collision—until one of them abruptly changed course.

"Whoa!" "Huh?"

The audience was taken aback—and for good reason. It was the truck with the armor plating still on it that moved.

The two cars passed by each other at breathtaking velocity. The one heading toward the pond plunged straight into the water. It sloshed through it and promptly arrived at the side of the running girl in pink, then turned and slid to a stop to its right to shield her from any incoming gunfire.

*   *   *

Through the bulletproof glass, Fukaziroh leered and said, "Hey, baby! How'd you get so drenched? Why don't you take a tour with me in my sweet ride?"

"Yes, yes! Take me with you!" Llenn clamored, covered in filthy water.

Fukaziroh smirked. "I like a girl who's honest about her desires! You're not goin' home tonight, sweetheart!"

"It's so heavy!" Llenn yanked on the rear side door, which was like a bank-vault door with all the armor plating it featured. She did get it open, though, and got inside before slamming it shut.

Inside, she made her way to the middle of the vehicle and popped her head out of the sunroof to look behind them.

"Hyaa!"

Naturally, M's Humvee was bearing down on them, descending from the plain into the water. It was just forty yards away.

"Just drive, Fuka! Anywhere!"

"You got it! Are there sleazy motels in this world?" Fukaziroh slammed on the acceleration pedal.

And thus, the first—and no doubt the last—car chase of SJ2 began.

The floating camera captured the image of the vehicles, one fleeing and one pursuing. They crossed the pond and got back onto dry land.

In one Humvee, Pitohui yelled, "M! Take out all the grenades you've got!"

He complied with her command. With his right hand on the wheel, he opened his menu with the left and selected everything with the word *grenade* in its name, plasma or not, then materialized them all.

When the light had coalesced into matter, a variety of explosives landed and rolled on the front passenger seat.

In the other Humvee, Llenn asked, "Your shots will blow up even if you throw them?"

Fukaziroh's MGL-140s and backpack were resting on the passenger seat. The owner replied, "Nope, doesn't work. Gotta shoot 'em."

"Damn!"

"Wanna drive for a sec?"

"I can't do it! And...when did you get your license, Fuka?" Llenn asked, unable to resist her sense of curiosity.

"I started going to driving school not too long ago. It's just too inconvenient not having a car. If anything, I shoulda gotten it earlier! Forget studying for tests! Huh...? Wait, didn't I tell you about that?"

"No, you didn't! But that's awesome! No wonder you can drive this thing so well!"

"All I did was finish the entrance ceremony at the school. If anything, I've been too busy with all this to practice driving."

"Huh? Then...how can you drive it?"

There were little streams along the plain, and each time they crossed one, the tires lost a bit of traction and destabilized the car, but Fukaziroh's fine handling kept it under control so that they maintained a direct path over the empty plain. It was excellent driving.

"Oh, simple. I play some driving games on a different account."

"With all the time you spend in *GGO*?! How much gaming do you do?!"

"Hey, it came in handy, right?"

"Huh? I guess so," Llenn said, right as the back seat rocked to the right. There was an explosive boom.

"Whoo!"

Fukaziroh swerved sideways, straightening out the vehicle to counteract the sudden shift in momentum. She did an admirable job.

Llenn poked her head out of the armored sunroof. Through the bulletproof glass, she examined M's car pacing them about twenty yards back and to the left.

Pitohui's hand appeared from the round hole in the roof and tossed something. It arced through the air toward them—a plasma grenade.

"Eep!"

It hit the rear of the vehicle with a thud, and Llenn ducked her head back into the chassis. But the projectile did not explode on impact. It rolled off the rear slope of the car body and onto the ground, where it blew up about five yards behind them.

Apparently, the timer on the fuse had been set too long, which saved them. But the shock wave of the blast rattled the vehicle, and it killed much of their speed.

"Dammit!" Llenn popped her head out of the sunroof again, aiming her P90 at the rear Humvee. Because the car was rocking and rumbling, she couldn't get a good aim, even at this close distance. But that didn't matter; she shot about ten bullets, full auto.

Sparks burst off the vehicle's hood and roof, but nothing hit Pitohui inside the Humvee. As evidence of that, she tossed another explosive.

This time, her aim was perfect. The plasma grenade hurtled exactly toward Llenn.

Uh-oh, that's going to land inside the car. If it blows up in here, both Fuka and I will die, she understood, everything playing out in slow motion.

Llenn had two options.

The first was for her to jump out. In midair, she could turn around and manage to slide with her feet without taking fall damage.

But Llenn chose the second option instead.

She lifted the P90 with both hands. "Hi-yah!"

Gonk!

With the side of the gun, she struck the plasma grenade back before it could land inside the car. The orb fell outside the vehicle instead and exploded on the ground far behind the two Humvees.

"Whew!" She exhaled.

"That was so mean, Llenn! How could you use me as a bat?" P-chan whined, but she ignored it.

She readied herself for the next projectile, but this time, M's car was slowing down, putting distance between the two of them.

Did they give up? she wondered for a brief moment.

"Llenn! Up ahead!" Fukaziroh nearly screamed. Llenn spun around and could scarcely believe what she saw there.

About a hundred feet ahead, there was another small puddle-ish pond, from which rose a geyser over thirty feet tall. This was not the plume of some projectile landing in the water. It was an actual geyser of water from the earth, like a fountain. It had not been there when she looked earlier.

"What the hell is thiiiis?!"

"I don't knoooooow!"

The car carrying the screaming Fukaziroh and Llenn plunged toward the fountain. Fukaziroh was just barely able to adjust their path to the right to avoid completely crashing headlong into it. The giant fountain passed just feet to the left of the vehicle instead.

The falling water thundered into the Humvee's sunroof.

"Bwah! Owww!" Llenn howled, startled at the virtual pain signals the water was sending. In fact, her skin was actually glowing with the signs of damage effects. Her hit points were definitely going down, if not as much as when she got shot. She was at about 50 percent.

"It's boiling water!"

"Huh?"

"This whole area is a hot spring! All those pools are just geysers waiting to erupt! I can't believe what we wandered into!"

Llenn connected the dots. They had wandered into a deadly trap set by none other than Mother Nature herself.

"My goodness!" Fukaziroh exclaimed. "So we've got all the hot water we can use? Just the thing when you've got a cup of instant noodles to heat up!"

"Really? That's what you're concerned about?"

The audience in the bar was equally stunned by what they saw on the screen, but they'd seen a geyser eruption on the screen earlier, so that wasn't what surprised them.

"How did M know to avoid it?"

The Humvee had altered course right before the eruption, as if M and Pitohui were aware that it was just about to happen. No one could answer how they'd done it.

Except for Pitohui, who had completely memorized the chart of the valley, the locations of the geysers, and their stated eruption times, as they were listed on the wall of the log house room. She sat in the back seat of the Humvee, checking her watch.

"Down to the second. Gotta love the virtual world."

"Fuka! This is a bad place to be! We need to move!" Llenn urged, watching M's Humvee to her left.

"Yeah, that sounds nice, but it's not gonna happen" was the response she received.

"Huh? Why not?"

"Because this car's about to stop."

"Why?"

"Lack of gas. There's a light blaring at me on the dash. And it even includes a readout that helpfully indicates how far it can go."

"And what does it say?"

"About a thousand feet."

"What—?!"

That would happen in just moments. Apparently, the vehicle hadn't contained much gas to begin with. She recalled that the hovercraft from the last Squad Jam had run out of gas very quickly, too.

"What now, Llenn?" asked her partner.

"Well, I guess that leaves us no choice," Llenn said, glancing at the car containing M and Pitohui. "Ram 'em!"

"Pito, we don't have any fuel. Maybe fifteen hundred feet."

"Oh, that's sad," said Pitohui without a trace of sadness, fixing a thirty-round magazine to her KTR-09. "Run into them, then."

*   *   *

To the overhead cameras, two Humvees were running in parallel over a grassy field dotted with pools and streams here and there—only now the cars were rushing closer together.

A muddy little girl in pink popped her head out of the car on the right.

A woman with a navy-blue bodysuit popped her head out of the car on the left.

Llenn stared at Pitohui as she approached.

Pitohui stared at Llenn as she approached.

The two vehicles were going to collide, nose to nose, right there on the plain—except that just before it happened, they both leaped out through the sunroofs.

Rather than attempting to withstand the impact of landing and maintain balance, they both accepted the momentum and rolled on the grass instead.

Llenn clutched the P90 tight, making herself even smaller. Pitohui adopted a similar stance, but to her detriment, her gun was much longer. The KTR-09 caught the grass of the field and was ripped from her hands.

"Tch!"

"Hyaaaa!"

"Gaaah!"

While the women were rolling, the two Humvees flipped upward with the momentum of their impact and rolled over in opposite directions.

"Bwaahhh!"

"Hrrrgh!"

As the massive vehicles spun and rolled, their drivers, Fuka-ziroh and M, experienced a roller-coaster ride of centrifugal force. They gripped their steering wheels for dear life, pushing with all the muscle of their legs and arms to keep their backs against the seats and stay put.

If either got thrown from the driver's seat, they'd either slam around the interior or get tossed right out of the open sunroof.

Each Humvee did five full rotations and ended up on its roof, stopping about sixty yards from the other.

"Gweeih…"

"Phew…"

Both Fukaziroh and M possessed a tremendous amount of strength. They had managed to survive their theme-park rides without safety belts and without being thrown around.

Fukaziroh's chin strap was digging painfully into her neck.

"If this was real life, I'd be dead… Once I get my license, I'm definitely going to wear my seat belt and drive safely…"

Llenn leaped from a moving vehicle, did several somersaults, and still bounded swiftly to her feet.

Where is she?!

She spun around, P90 at her waist, looking for Pitohui. She'd seen her jump out. She must be close by.

Then she spotted her target, just over thirty feet away.

Pitohui, not yet completely on her feet, was without a gun in her hands.

"Aaaaah!"

She blasted the P90. A horizontal spray three feet off the ground, like shooting a hose sideways. If she tried to jump side to side, she would get hit.

Pitohui did not stand.

Instead, she fell straight onto her back, pulling XDM pistols from her thigh holsters and firing them.

The shot from her right gun grazed Llenn's left shoulder, while the one from her left gun did the same to the right shoulder, leaving bullet effects like knife scars. Llenn took her finger off the P90's trigger.

In that case—!

She turned her right shoulder toward Pitohui and held the P90 out in her right hand alone like a pistol, keeping a slim profile.

Pitohui's next bullets passed around Llenn's stomach and back. In combination with how quickly Llenn moved, it was like she had dodged the shots with sheer reaction speed.

I can do this! I'll close in and finish her off! Llenn thought, placing her finger on the trigger again. *"It's your final job, P-chan!"*

"You got it!"

The gun burst into motion. The rattle of automatic gunfire echoed across the grassy field, as did Pitohui's shriek.

"Hyaaa!"

The P90 was tilted upward in Llenn's hand. It pointed into the sky—and the bullets it was firing vanished there as well, naturally.

Pitohui's third pair of bullets from dual pistols had landed just below the muzzle of the P90, deflecting it upward with force.

Llenn saw her, flat on her back with only her face lifted up, pointing two guns, smiling wildly. The pair of bullet lines extending from the XDMs spread just enough to jab at Llenn's eyes individually.

And with nothing but red in her sight, Llenn thought, *"I'm sorry, P-chan."*

P-chan replied, *"Nah, it's cool."*

Pitohui fired her fourth pair of bullets.

The two .40-caliber bullets emerged from their guns at the exact same moment, heading straight for Llenn's face—until they struck the body of the P90 she held up to guard herself, breaking through the reinforced plastic.

"Taaa!"

Llenn started running, right at Pitohui. Holding up a shield twenty inches long and eight inches wide before her eyes.

"Haah!"

Pitohui fired for the fifth time. These bullets, too, struck the

P90, hitting the body and barrel of the gun with a shower of sparks.

The sixth shots knocked the P90's magazine loose, hurling its remaining bullets into the air with the internal springs.

The seventh shots—never came. Llenn's speed already had her upon Pitohui.

"Taaa!"

"Gnnf!"

She planted her little foot directly into Pitohui's face as she launched into a jump. She flipped in the air, removing the P90's sling from her shoulder as she landed.

In that moment, Pitohui twisted herself up, face glowing as though she'd been given a nosebleed, pointing the heavily stocked XDMs at Llenn.

But before she could shoot them, the pistols themselves shot from Pitohui's hands.

"Wha—?!"

Llenn had taken advantage of her agility to sneak closer and swung the P90 around by the sling. Even a plastic gun body full of holes, lightened without a magazine of bullets, could be an effective twenty-inch weapon.

"Nice move!" she heard Pitohui say gleefully.

They froze then—a ten-foot standoff.

Llenn let go of the sling, freeing up both her hands. The P90 could probably still shoot, but she didn't have time to load a new magazine. Pitohui was also empty-handed, now that Llenn had knocked her pistols away.

"Llenn," Pitohui said, smiling like she had when they'd quested together.

"What is it, Pito?" Llenn asked, smiling back. Her hand slowly crept behind her back.

"Thanks so much for coming out to SJ2. My back's against the wall because of you! I'm so happy I get to have such a thrilling fight."

"You're welcome. But to be honest, this whole thing is giving me an ulcer!"

Slowly, very slowly, Llenn's fingers crept for the hilt of the knife.

"Really? But you're going to get a nice third-place prize for your trouble. Winner last time—third place this time. That's very impressive! Of course, if I'd taken part last year, I would've won!"

"No, Pito, you can have third," Llenn insisted, looking for any of Pitohui's remaining weapons. As far as she could tell, there was nothing that looked like a gun.

All she could see was a thin knife on the outside of her boot. That made it easy to pull free, but it wouldn't have enough attack power. Unless she hit a very vital point, like the eyes, Llenn had enough hit points to withstand an attack.

More dangerous was the photon sword. It was three feet long and could slice through a knife. Llenn didn't stand a chance against it.

Where is it now?

Since she couldn't see it, that meant it was likely behind Pitohui's back, but could she draw it quickly enough? Was it placed somewhere that would allow her to draw and swing in one motion, like the famous *iai* katana move?

No, it's not, she decided. Pitohui's main weapon was the gun. She would prioritize firearms and choose to use them first, just as she did with the pistols earlier.

"Hmm, I'd rather not. I only need first place. In fact, I don't even need that. All I want is to survive the battle royale. The top prize is just a side effect of that. But I will take what is mine."

They were ten feet apart. Close enough that she could draw her knife and close the gap in an instant.

But if Pitohui went on the defensive, her attacks would essentially be useless. If she closed her legs, for example, or guarded her neck and face.

If she had any chance of winning at all, it would be when

Pitohui launched a fierce attack of her own. It would be better if Pitohui's photon sword was difficult to draw.

As she continued searching for a potential weapon, Llenn said, "Look, it's just a game. Who cares if you die, right? It's not like you're actually dying."

"Maybe for you, Llenn. But for me…it's a little bit different."

Pitohui's voice was harder now, heavier. So Llenn intentionally lightened her tone. "Oh? What do you mean? Could you tell me, right before the end? You won't be able to say after I kill you."

All she needed was a moment of opportunity when the other woman attacked. But it had to be a very big window.

There was one thing she could do about that.

"Well, I don't know that you'd understand if I told you. But if I had to describe it, it's more like…I'm really risking my life in the game, maybe?"

Pitohui's tone was casual, but Llenn saw a seriousness in her eyes that she'd never seen before. Her smile was conveyed with her mouth and nothing else.

Maybe it's time to finally anger the demon. Scary as it might be…

Llenn inhaled slowly and prayed.

Please, AmuSphere. Just don't auto–shut down on me.

"Risking your life for a game? You mean like that game that was all over the news, *Sword Art Online*? Isn't that—?"

"'Isn't that' what?" Pitohui asked, her eyes like gun barrels.

Llenn felt her pulse racing, but there was no backing out now. She put on the biggest smile she could possibly make. "Isn't that incredibly *stupid*? I'm so glad you didn't have to play that legendarily shitty game!"

But Llenn did not anticipate that Pitohui would look so…

…sad.

So ready for tears.

So hurt.

She reached her right hand around her back—the arrival of the moment Llenn had been waiting for.

Llenn leaped.

Her hand was on the knife before her first step landed.

She was in range of the taller woman, pulling out the blade backhanded, on the second.

She passed through her legs, slicing open the inside of the left thigh on the third.

She jumped hard to the right, twisting her hand on the fourth.

The blade slashed the left side of Pitohui's throat, adding a new marking to her facial tattoos.

"Gafhk!"

Pitohui toppled to her right, red damage light streaming from her neck—and when her hand hit the ground, she bounced back upward like on springs.

"Huh?"

It was the sort of physics-defying maneuver you expected to see from a break-dancer. Pitohui caught her fall and not only supported herself with just her right arm, she pushed herself back to her feet.

Then her arm continued, shooting toward Llenn's face with tremendous speed.

All Llenn saw was a gray cylinder.

Gonk!

There was a strange sound in the middle of her face. She shot back a good ten feet, then slid another fifteen over the grass, until she finally splashed into one of the pools of water.

It all took just an instant to happen, but Llenn was cognizant of the entire string of events in frightening detail.

Pitohui had drawn the photon sword and struck her with it. The only silver lining was that she hadn't had the time to hit the switch and activate the actual blade of light.

Her hit points dropped to about 40 percent. It was practically a miracle she still had the knife in her hand.

Then Llenn looked at Pitohui. Her left femoral artery was cut clean through, as was the carotid artery on the left side of the neck.

That ought to be enough to kill your average character.

Oh, right. Pito's anything but normal.

It was a bit late to be remembering that now.

"Whew! You got me good." Pitohui looked up to the sky wistfully. "I've only got twenty percent health left."

You've still got twenty?! Monster! Zombie! Llenn thought but did not say. She was at the lip of the thirty-foot pool, mind racing for what she could do in this situation.

She was a good twenty-five feet from Pitohui. If she attacked with the knife, she'd either be rebuffed or be sliced in two by the photon sword.

So what do I do what do I do what do I do what do I do?

There was nothing she could do. Llenn didn't have the throwing skill to hit her target with the knife from a distance.

I'm stumped. I'm screwed.

She was going to die in moments.

Speaking of which, how was Fukaziroh doing now? She still had plenty of HP remaining. Good old hardy Fukaziroh.

But that didn't mean anything now. It was completely beside the point for Fukaziroh to kill Pitohui.

It just wasn't going to work out.

She couldn't think of an idea, so she gave up.

Then Pitohui engaged in a most puzzling course of action. She picked up the P90 Llenn had used to bat her pistols away. The magazine had blown out when it got hit by the bullets, but there should still be one in the chamber. One bullet left to fire.

Pitohui carefully pulled the loading handle halfway to confirm that the bullet was indeed there. Then she set the gun against her shoulder.

"Is this P-chan Number Two?" she asked, making it sound like some kind of weird home address. Llenn nodded. "Then I'll at least let you die by your own gun. Don't move."

Pitohui put her finger against the trigger.

She had used just about any and every gun in the game, so of course she had experience with a P90. There was no way she'd miss at this distance.

The only thought in Llenn's mind was that she would die by her favorite gun, P-chan. She wasn't thinking about winning SJ2 or killing Pitohui or anything else like that.

"*Why, P-chan? That's so mean,*" she pleaded to it.

Immediately, it replied, "*Don't give up! Look closer!*"

"*Huh?*"

"*Look closer!*"

"*Pardon?*"

"*Look closer!*"

The orders were getting so annoying that Llenn did as she was told. Pitohui with the P90. Her finger resting against the trigger. The muzzle pointed at her.

"*It's not there!*

"*I don't see it!*

"*I don't see the bullet line!*

"*There's no red line that should be pointing from the end of the gun straight to my forehead!*

"*Why? How come?*"

There was only one possible answer.

Splosh. Llenn got to her feet in the water.

"Taaaa!"

She clenched the knife and began running. Right for Pitohui, who smiled at her.

"Time to die, Llenn."

Pitohui's finger pulled the trigger.

"*I'll keep you safe, Llenn!*"

There was a muffled burst.

Pitohui shrieked. "Aagh!"

P-chan made its last act of resistance in her arms. The barrel had burst. All the pressure of the bullet and the gunpowder explosion erupted not from the end of the muzzle, but somewhere inside the gun, rupturing the metal and cracking the body from within.

It was already in tatters from when Pitohui shot it, and now the gun was truly destroyed.

Llenn foresaw all this happening.

There was only one reason she could imagine that there would be no bullet line coming from the gun in that situation: It was that the gun couldn't fire.

No bullet lines appeared for guns whose ammo had all been fired or never loaded in the first place. And neither did they appear for damaged guns.

That was why Llenn noticed. But Pitohui did not. And this was because regardless of the circumstances, a helpful bullet circle always appeared for the shooter.

Llenn banked on this to launch into her final charge. And her bet was a winner.

Not only was it a dud shot, it was more than that. At the very, very end, P-chan had protected her.

"Thank you, P-chan!" she exulted, racing toward Pitohui, who was momentarily blinded by the shards of plastic and metal that assaulted her eyes.

Llenn added her left hand to steady the backhand grip on the knife and held it in front of her chest. It was almost like she was praying to God.

Water burst from the pool at the exact moment that she leaped out of it. It was a geyser eruption, and if she'd been in there, the scalding water would likely have killed her instantly.

Against the backdrop of the towering fountain and the roar of its eruption, Llenn closed the gap to Pitohui in an instant. She leaped at the end, raising the tip of the knife to the level of Pitohui's face and swinging.

She lunged for Pitohui's eyes, which were still glowing with the damage effect.

*   *   *

"Yaaah!"

Despite the fact that she couldn't see, Pitohui's hands closed over Llenn's wrists.

It was just inches before the tip of the knife stabbed her eye. She couldn't have seen it coming, but she had a steady, accurate grip now. She either sensed the incoming attack or just had a hunch.

Pitohui toppled backward, pulling Llenn with her and planting her foot on the girl's midriff—and launching the judo throw known as a *tomoe nage*.

The world flipped upside down in Llenn's eyes, and she landed hard on her back in the grass.

"Gre-gok!" It was the sound of a frog being squashed. Because it was grass, she didn't suffer any numerical damage.

"Haaa!" But the very next moment, Pitohui stood and lifted her by the arms, causing Llenn to dangle in the air. Pitohui had her hanging, both hands around the knife completely trapped in just her right hand. There was a huge gap between her toes and the ground.

"Whewwwwww!"

The demon queen exhaled a huge breath, her eyes flashing.

"Verrrry interesting. Even your precious gun tries to keep you safe, eh?"

Dammit! Leggo!

Llenn flailed and kicked, but there was nothing for her legs to do except attempt to knee and kick Pitohui's stomach—and it had absolutely no effect on the much stronger woman.

She tried and tried, to no avail. Llenn's physical-combat ability simply wasn't good enough to do any damage to other players.

The geyser eruption behind her was waning now. Once it had stopped entirely, Llenn gave up her fruitless struggling.

The knife, then?

If she let go of the knife she was still holding, wouldn't it hit Pitohui in the face? It took willpower to let go of her actual, honest-to-goodness final weapon, but she didn't have any other option.

Llenn opened her hands, praying for a miracle, and dropped the knife toward Pitohui's face.

"Haah!" the other woman snarled.

Chonk. She caught it in her teeth.

"Huh?"

Yes, the eight-inch knife blade, sharp edge inward, was trapped right between her teeth. Pitohui suffered no damage at all.

"Ahhhh." Worst of all, she had given her enemy another weapon. Pitohui grabbed the hilt with her free hand and continued, "This is a pretty sweet knife. Are you giving it to me? Or are you indicating you want me to kill you with it?"

"Neither!" yelled Llenn, somewhat childishly.

"Then let's just throw this away," Pitohui said like a nursery school teacher, and with a flip of her hand, she tossed the knife into the grass.

Now Llenn was truly trapped.

"This is incredible, Llenn. I ought to learn by your example—the way you never give up, all the way to the end," Pitohui said. It was hard to tell whether it was meant to be serious or a joke.

Then she called out, "M! Come over here."

Belatedly, Llenn remembered that M was around, too. He'd been completely outside of her thoughts. If M had had his gun trained on her, too, she would've been dead already.

"Yeah, I'm coming," said a voice from over Llenn's right shoulder. She craned her head, still dangling, and saw the large man approach, carrying his M14 EBR. And to her surprise—

"Fuka!"

He was also escorting her partner, Fukaziroh.

Fukaziroh's helmet was gone, exposing her braided blond hair. There was duct tape around her wrists—and one more piece over her mouth for good measure.

She'd known from the HP readout that Fukaziroh was still alive, and she'd considered it strange she never heard the girl's voice. This would explain the combination.

And with herself trapped, too, that meant Team LF were PM4's captives.

M marched Fukaziroh up to about five yards behind them and ordered her to sit. Her legs were free, but without the use of her hands, there was little point in trying to run. She sat down cross-legged without complaint.

Pitohui ordered, "Find me the XDMs. Just one of them will do—they're lying around here somewhere."

M looked around the grass and found one of the pistols right away. He brought it back to Pitohui.

"Thanks."

She grabbed it from him with her free hand and shooed him back to Fukaziroh's side. Llenn tried her best to kick the pistol away, but Pitohui just extended the arm she was using to hold her, putting her out of range. "We're just going to keep you over here for a bit."

Llenn knew she was light, but the way that Pitohui could keep her under control with just one arm—and extended at that—was nothing short of frightening.

Pitohui then reached over with her gun hand and pointed the XDM toward the other two.

Bang. She fired it.

Bang. Another shot.

Llenn had seen a number of shocking, unexpected things in SJ2—but this was easily the biggest shock of all.

"Rrgh…"

It was M who was groaning from the pain of being shot, glowing damage effects on his large cheeks.

He fell heavily to his knees. There was no DEAD tag over him, so he was still alive, but he'd been shot twice in the face. That had to mean huge damage.

Next to him, Fukaziroh was definitely just as shocked. Her eyes were so bugged out, it actually looked kind of comical.

"Wh-what are you doing, Pito?!" Llenn demanded, dangling from her other arm. "That is a no-no! I thought he was your pal-pal! Was that okay-kay?" she said, so bewildered by the event that had just transpired that she started babbling.

Pitohui glanced at her. "Was that a haiku?"

"N-no! Why would you shoot M? I can't believe this! He's your teammate!"

"I have my reasons. He shot you, too, last time. Didn't he?"

"Oof... W-well, yes, but..."

"I'll tell you why. Because that little M over there betrayed me."

"Wh-whaaa—?"

The familiarity of the situation caused Llenn's voice to crack. But that wasn't what Pitohui wanted to say, apparently.

"Earlier, when your little partner drove the other Humvee up, he moved our vehicle just before she arrived. He said it would make it 'easier to aim,' but that was a lie," she claimed.

"..."

Llenn was lost. She could only listen. For his part, M knelt in silence, light glowing on his cheeks.

"In the side mirrors, he could see the other vehicle approaching. And in order to keep me from finding out, he ran the engine and moved us when he didn't need to. So what was it for? To allow your partner to arrive and keep me from killing you at that point. Of course, before that, I also allowed him to wipe out the Amazon team you were working with, just to isolate you, I guess. I can forgive him for that."

So M—who had sworn up and down that he would not bring personal emotion into the game and would act only for Pitohui's sake—had acted out of some kind of sentiment...

Llenn recalled how Goushi had looked back then. The handsome man who pushed her back against the wall and spoke of the strength of his love.

Pitohui asked the silent man, "Does the accused have a rebuttal?"

"No," he said.

She pointed the XDM at him. "Any last words?"

"I love you."

"I know that. But you're not allowed to bring love into the game."

Bang.

Just one shot at the end.

M slowly slumped forward from his knees, bullet between his eyes.

"Aaaah!"

He collapsed onto the grass, and this time the sign said DEAD.

"H-hey! Why would you do that, Pito?! I can't believe this! You monster! You devil! You demon king!"

"Ooh, demon king. I like that." Pitohui smiled. And then, still holding Llenn in one hand and her pistol in the other, she improbably began to sing.

"Mein Vater, mein Vater, jetzt faßt er mich an! Erlkönig hat mir ein Leids getan!" (My father, my father, he seizes me fast, for sorely the demon king has hurt me at last!)

Llenn recognized that song. It was "Erlkönig," the piece of music written by Franz Schubert that was titled "Demon King" in Japan.

Her singing voice was shockingly clean and beautiful. There was nothing demonic about it in the least.

"Hey, Pito! Let go of my hands so I can applaud!"

"Ha-ha, very funny. I'm not falling for that one."

When Pitohui looked at Llenn, thus pulling her eyes away, Fukaziroh lifted her duct-taped hands behind her head. She wriggled her wrists, and the heavy, tough tape split right in half, giving her free use of her hands again.

Then she spun her right arm over the back of her head, grabbed a handle there, and pulled it out. Her long blond hair came undone and fell toward the ground, but not before she began to run. With her open hand, she ripped off the tape over her mouth.

"Owww!"

In her right hand was the "hairpin" that had held her hair in place. Her final weapon, which she had fashioned from a knife ground down to a thin point.

* * *

Pitohui noticed before Llenn did.

She fired—*bang-bang-bang.* The XDM's bullets hit Fukaziroh's shoulders and thigh but did not stop her charge.

"Haah!" Pitohui exhaled, impressed at Fukaziroh's toughness, then swept back her leg and held out Llenn right before her face.

"Ah!" Fukaziroh hit the brakes suddenly, unable to stab her own teammate.

Llenn grasped the situation and shouted "Cut! Kick!" so quickly, it must have sounded like one word.

But Fukaziroh understood her meaning. "Roger that!"

She jumped toward Pitohui, who was holding up Llenn as a shield. "Haaaah!"

The blade sliced sideways, a line of light.

Fukaziroh had swung a sword just about every day in *ALO*. "Missing her mark" was not in her dictionary any longer.

Even the stunted little knife hit its target perfectly: the arm.

Llenn's thin arms. Both of them.

The blade perfectly severed her arms just below where Pitohui had them held.

And as Fukaziroh landed on one foot, she kicked out powerfully with the other.

It hit Llenn right in the back as she fell, propelling her forward.

At the cost of most of her remaining hit points, and her forearms and hands, Llenn gained her freedom. She also got the push on the back she needed.

"Gaaaaaah!!"

She opened her mouth wide and snapped down on the right side of Pitohui's neck.

"Wha—?!"

Gla-jhurk!

There was a hideous noise, something she had never heard before, as her teeth sank into Pitohui's neck. Red light shone.

"Aaagh!" Pitohui dropped Llenn's hands and writhed in agony.

Hrrrrrnnnnnggg!

Llenn put all the effort into her jaw that she could, clinging for dear life.

Her only thought: *Must kill Pitohui.*

Pitohui was aware that her hit points were steadily dropping, with teeth in her throat that would not dislodge.

"L-Llenn…," she murmured.

The girl answered with a tremendous burst of air from her mouth and nose. *Frrrnt!*

"Llenn… You really…will be…the…death of…me…"

Hurrrrrr!

It wasn't clear whether that exhalation was meant to be affirmative or negative.

"I see… So I'm going…to die here…," Pitohui mumbled, slowly toppling backward. She fell, and with her went Llenn, who was still clinging to her neck.

"Pwah!" Llenn finally let go.

She looked at Pitohui, who had the eyes of a dying person. "You're not going to die, Pito! I mean, I won't let you! Er, I mean, yeah, I'm going to kill you here and now, but I mean in real life!"

"Wh…at…?"

"M told me! He told me how you were going to die for real if you died in SJ2!"

"Oh…shit… That clown…," Pitohui murmured, grinning.

"You and I made a promise that day, Pito! That one day, we'd have a real fight, and if you lost, we'd meet in real life. A promise between women!" Llenn bonked her with the severed end of her arm. "A ritual toast!"

"…" Pitohui stared at her with dying eyes, then erupted. "Pfft!"

"Keep the promise!" Llenn said at the same time, smiling. She opened her mouth wide and bit down hard on Pitohui's windpipe, squeezing with all her strength to crush it.

The last remaining bit of Pitohui's health vanished.

* * *

At the moment that Llenn ripped Pitohui's throat out with her teeth, the bar was as silent as if it were empty.

In fact, it was essentially at capacity, between the audience and the various players who had returned already after dying, including the members of Team SHINC.

But at this moment, it was silent.

Then gunshots broke that silence.

"Huh?" "Whoa!" "What?!"

The pair of girls on the screen were riddled with bullets.

Damage effects glowed all over them, and they toppled over instantly, DEAD tags floating over their bodies. It was incredibly sudden and anticlimactic.

The camera angle switched to a grassy plain about a quarter of a mile away, where smoke rose from the guns of futuristic super-soldiers outfitted in huge armor.

In the sky behind them, a message said, *Congratulations!! Winner: T-S!*

"Oh…"

So Team T-S, which had spent the entire game running away from trouble, had snuck in and scooped up the biggest prize at the very, very end.

The storm of angry roars and boos couldn't possibly have been audible in the event map, wherever that was, but regardless, the six members of T-S wisely did not return to the bar.

Time of match: one hour, thirty-five minutes.
The second Squad Jam was over.
Winning team: T-S.
Total shots fired: 79,408.

CHAPTER 21
Applause

SECT.21

CHAPTER 21
Applause

Sunday, April 19th, 2026.

The forecast for Tokyo's high that day was getting up to eighty degrees, taking it from warm into hot.

At 1:07 PM, a car sidled up to the street in front of a high-rise apartment building in the city. It was a deluxe German SUV, polished to a sparkle.

"Damn, that looks nice! I wish I could cruise around in one of these!"

"You don't have your license yet, Miyu."

"I could cruise in the back seat."

On the wide sidewalk, Miyu and Karen had their jackets draped over their arms as they waited, chatting about the fancy car. Miyu still had the same hairstyle and glasses as when they met during spring vacation; apparently, she liked this look. Karen hadn't changed her style since cutting her hair.

They were dressed in loose, comfortable clothing—simple slacks and shirts—but Karen did have a cute little necklace over her collarbone.

"So is M going to show up or what?" Miyu asked.

"It's Goushi. His name is Goushi Asougi," Karen replied, looking around.

"I'm sorry about that. I got held up by traffic," said a voice from a parked car, drawing their attention closer again.

Opening the driver's door was a handsome man in a navy-blue suit, sharp and crisp, his hair neatly done.

"Whoo!" Miyu grunted.

Oh... He's still alive. I'm so glad, thought Karen.

✳ ✳ ✳

Fifteen days earlier had been April 4th, the day of the event.

After the distant shots unceremoniously killed Fukaziroh and Llenn, they were returned to the waiting area.

SJ2 ended the moment they died, so there was no need to wait out the ten minutes. In that dark space, Llenn saw the same message prompting her to choose between returning to the bar or logging out. It also said that she was a runner-up.

There were two MGL-140s on the floor in front of Fukaziroh, whose long hair was still undone. All Llenn had was a knife and a machine gun.

She chose to return to the bar, rather than sit back and mourn the loss of P-chan the Second. The moment she and Fukaziroh materialized on the little stage in the pub, they were surrounded by raucous cheering. A crowd of people were congratulating them on their valiant effort. Among them were Team SHINC and MMTM.

Llenn had only one question: Are Pitohui and M, the third-place team, here?

The audience at the bar asked one another and searched around the room, but they were not present. Llenn apologized and promised she would be right back, before logging out.

Karen didn't even take the AmuSphere off when she woke up in her own room again. She sent a message straight to Goushi's address. PLEASE, OH, PLEASE!

The cell phone buzzed in her hands as soon as she grabbed it. The message was very brief.

I'M TALKING WITH HER NOW. ABOUT OUR FUTURE.

✳   ✳   ✳

"Goushi, this is Miyu. Miyu Shinohara. She's my best friend and my VR teacher, Fukaziroh."

"Hey! Thanks for all the help! I haven't forgotten about the tape you slapped over my mouth," Miyu said with a huge thumbs-up.

"Wow, you really are incredibly hot. Are you kidding me? Did you walk out of a manga or something? I wouldn't mind getting married. You doing anything after this?"

She was as unfiltered as she was regularly in *GGO*. Goushi looked her straight in the eyes, neither smiling nor faltering, and said, "Thank you for the compliment. But I cannot do that for you. My heart is already promised to another."

"Dah!" Miyu made a show of looking disappointed. Then she asked the obvious. "Would that be Pitohui's player?"

"Yes."

"Dang it. So much for that, I guess."

Goushi bowed his head to her. Then he said, "I have no words to express my thanks to you two. I've caused you a great amount of trouble. So I would like to attempt to make up for this today. Pito's player agrees and is very much looking forward to meeting you."

Karen narrowed her eyes with a grin. "Same for me!"

Goushi's follow-up message came on the previous Monday, April 13th, over a week after SJ2.

The new school year had begun at college for Karen. She was studying hard every single day and had not logged in to *GGO* once since the big event.

Miyu was going to both college and driving school in Hokkaido and was back in *ALO*, enjoying herself as much as ever.

Fukaziroh's *GGO* gear was now at rest in a locker Llenn was renting. Whether those MGL-140s would ever shoot grenades from their gaping muzzles again was anyone's guess.

Goushi's actual message was simple: PITOHUI SAYS SHE WANTS

TO MEET YOU. DO YOU HAVE TIME IN THE AFTERNOON AND EVE-
NING NEXT SUNDAY?

Karen accepted the offer, of course, and asked him where she
should go and when.

Goushi replied, I'LL TAKE A CAR TO YOUR APARTMENT BUILD-
ING AT ONE O'CLOCK. GIVEN THE TRAFFIC, PLEASE HAVE EATEN
AND USED THE RESTROOM BEFORE I GET THERE.

That was the whole message. Pitohui prevented him from saying
anything more. Worried, Karen called Miyu for advice. She said,
"Oh yeah, she's gonna murder you. Revenge for the game." That
was rather scary. "So I'm gonna tag along. Just tell M, 'That cute little grenadier I was fighting with wants to meet you guys, too.' And
then add, 'You can even pay for her trip to Tokyo, if you want.'"

Karen e-mailed this message to Goushi, assuming he would
blow off the bit about the travel expenses, but he accepted right
away and sent the confirmation number for a round-trip flight.

So on Friday evening, Miyu touched down at Haneda Airport.
She would be staying at Karen's apartment.

Yesterday, on the 18th, Saki and the other gymnastics team
members at the high school visited Karen, too. It was the tea
party they'd agreed upon.

They had chosen to help out with the plan to kill Pitohui, when
they'd been looking forward to winning the event so badly, so
Karen knew she owed them a show of appreciation. She and
Miyu went out to get groceries and returned with an appalling
amount of snacks and junk food.

April 20th would be Karen's twentieth birthday. The younger
girls remembered that fact.

"I know it's a bit early, but happy birthday, Karen!"

They had brought a present for her, pooling their allowance
money together to get her a delicate necklace of tiny metal links
with a little decorative item.

"We know it'll look great on you!"

It was exactly the sort of thing she would never buy for herself
but always wished she could wear.

"Oh! Thank you..."

Her eyes welled up with tears, and though it took several tries to get it right, she put the necklace on. The six gymnasts cheered.

"Nice! And this is from me!"

Miyu gave her an entire box of special instant yakisoba noodles that could be bought only in Hokkaido.

And then, the 19th.

Goushi started driving the SUV with Karen and Miyu in the back seat. They made their way through the Sunday traffic, nice and slow and safe.

"Wow, the interior is swanky, too! You can barely hear any of the outside noise. And these leather seats aren't too soft or too tough! If only this could be my practice vehicle!" Miyu exclaimed, enraptured.

Karen leaned forward and asked, "Where are we going, Goushi?"

Miyu added, "Yeah! That's a big question! And if you think you're gonna abduct two sweet young ladies, you're sorely mistaken! I bet you're trying to take us to the port to load us on a ship and sell us overseas! Well, I already set everything up: If I don't touch base tonight, my folks are gonna call the police!"

She was either excited or angry, or possibly both. Karen hadn't heard that stuff about calling home, but she knew Miyu was capable of doing something like that. She made a mental note to remind her friend to call tonight.

Goushi replied, "Oh, don't worry. We're not planning to ride any boats today."

"Well, that doesn't tell us a whole lot! Listen, we're both minors! Even if Kohi's reaching the legal age tomorrow!"

"Oh... I didn't realize that. Happy birthday."

"That's better. Don't you have a present for her?" Miyu demanded. The car stopped at a light, so Goushi looked over his shoulder at them.

"I don't have anything arranged, but I bet the president will."

"Ahhh... And is this 'president' Pitohui's real-life identity?"

Miyu asked. Goushi nodded. "Then the mystery is solved! So what's she like?"

"She said she wanted to reveal that for herself. I cannot say."

The light turned green, and he resumed driving.

With safe and practiced ease, he took them from the main road onto the highway. When they crested the hill to reach the elevated highway, it was jammed shut. The car joined the queue, but it was practically walking speed now.

Goushi turned the car to automated follow mode and took his hands and feet off the controls. The vehicle would take it from here.

"That's Tokyo for ya! Is this going to mess up your plans, Goushi?" Miyu asked from the back seat.

"I allowed for plenty of time, so we should be fine."

"Oh! So…I guess we'll just hang out and chat! Or do you have something for us?" she prompted.

"Well, let's see," Goushi said. "I can tell you how Pito and I came to meet."

"Ooooh! I wanna hear that!" Miyu said, eyes sparkling.

"Huh…?" Karen's eyes widened. "Are you sure…?" She just couldn't imagine why he would suddenly offer that kind of information.

"The truth is…Pito told me to tell you. It's easier than explaining it later, and we're going to have time in traffic anyway. If she hadn't said that, I would probably have kept it hidden my entire life," Goushi explained.

"Ohhh, I see." "Oh, I see…," the girls said in unison.

"However… It's kind of an intense story, so you might feel a bit unpleasant as I tell you," he warned.

"Well, I've certainly experienced the sweet and bitter sides of life in equal measure at my age, but I don't know about Kohi. What do you say?"

"I'll listen," Karen said immediately.

"You're sure? You might not be able to sleep tonight."

"Well, I've already come this far. Plus..."

"Plus?"

"I would imagine that Pito asked him to tell me because she wanted me to hear it."

"Mmm," Miyu murmured, actually looking serious for once. She patted the leather shoulder of the driver's seat. "Well, go ahead, Goushi."

"All right. First, take a look at this," he said, passing back his smartphone. Karen saw that there was a photo on the screen.

"Hmmm?" "...?"

It was of a pudgy young man.

There were people cut off on either side of the image, which made it look like a section of a group photo. The background looked like a college campus; it was probably some sort of school club or class picture.

He was quite overweight, fat hanging from his face and belly. His slack face looked young still, but the body type also made him look much older. His hair was long but not in a fashionable way. He wore a dirty sweatshirt and baggy jeans in a rather unflattering combination.

In short: "Yeah, he is not doing anything for me," said Miyu, rather sharply. "So who is this? It's not a headshot for a marriage service, is it?" she guessed. "Because I'm sorry, but I cannot marry anyone who looks like this. What about you, Kohi?"

Karen didn't believe it was for a marriage-arrangement service, but she considered who it might be and why Goushi would show them something like this.

"You don't mean to say...?"

She stared at the smartphone again and spread her fingers on the screen to zoom in on the man's face. Since it was already clipped out of a larger group photo, the resolution got very blurry at once. The finer contours around his eyes weren't clear at all, but Karen had an idea.

"Is this...you, Goushi...?" she asked.

"What?! No way!" Miyu said on her right.

"Yes, it's true," Goushi replied at the same time.

"Bwah—!"

"That's me, around the time I first met Pito."

"No way!" squawked Miyu, unable to hide her shock. She snatched the phone from Karen's hands and squinted at it. "You know... Now that I get a better look at it, there's a lot of handsome under there. This is a guy who'll be quite the looker if he loses some weight! And at that point, I might just be in the right mood to marry him!"

She wouldn't be Miyu if she had any shame. Karen grimaced uncomfortably, but Goushi seemed to find this quite funny.

Karen examined the smartphone again before returning it to the front seat. Goushi himself briefly looked at the image before turning off the screen and putting it in his pocket. The car was driving itself, but it was still against the law for drivers to stare at their phones.

"For as long as I could remember, I was fat," Goushi explained. "I couldn't imagine ever being as skinny as other people. I hated having my picture taken. I think that's the only one I have from that period."

Karen was going to sit back and listen, but it occurred to her that it might be a difficult thing for Goushi to talk about. And he was the driver, so he needed to pay attention to the road. She just wasn't sure how she should respond to keep the conversation flowing.

Fortunately, Miyu did. "Yeah, everybody's got a past, huh? So what then?"

I'm so glad she's here, Karen thought. She sat back and listened.

"I never had any kind of self-confidence. It seemed like my life was never going to turn around, until one day, I met a woman."

"Eek!" Miyu gasped. All of a sudden, his story was getting sentimental.

"So I started stalking her."

"Eek?" she repeated, less certain this time. All of a sudden, his story was getting weird.

And yet...

Well, knowing those two...

Karen was surprised at how unsurprised she was. Perhaps all her time in *GGO* and around them had given her a sterner spirit than she realized.

"This is a very ugly, pathetic story about me. As a college student, I was having difficulty lining up a future job, and it was like my heart and mind were being scraped with sandpaper every day."

"But you didn't lose weight?"

"It was the stress that made me eat..."

"Then how did you lose—? Sorry. Please continue."

"One evening on the way home, I was overwhelmingly hungry, and because I didn't have any other options, I went into a really fancy, fashionable coffee shop, the kind I would never visit otherwise. When I saw the waitress who brought me water, it felt like someone had just shot a .45-caliber round into my brain."

There was a creeping element of happiness in his voice as he spoke, Karen couldn't help but notice.

Miyu asked, "And that...was Pito's player?"

"Yes. She was like a goddess. I had never seen a more beautiful woman in my life."

"Uh, have you looked over your shoulder?"

"You two are very pretty as well, but you simply don't compare to her. At least, not in my opinion."

"I'm going to sue you for defamation! Anyway... Please continue."

"By listening to her and the manager speak, I learned that she was working there full-time, as well as striving for her own dream career. She went to a night school for business and was studying like mad."

"Mmm. So what's up with the stalker part? I mean, if you just show up at the coffee shop all the time, that only makes you a 'regular.'"

"Well, I was so taken by her beauty that..."

"You asked her out?"

"No, I followed her home."

"Him, officer. That's the guy, right there."

"No, really, I don't know what I was thinking at the time... I certainly could have been arrested. Just about every day, I followed her after she left the café to her school or apartment, always from a safe distance."

"And you didn't get caught? Nobody notices that in Tokyo, then?"

"I was very careful not to be spotted. I knew that if I followed her all the time, I would stand out, so I memorized her routes and studied the area so I knew which alleys I could go down at which times to naturally wind up behind her again. At some point, I just built up a natural skill for having a map in my head."

"Yuck! Creepy!"

"Yes, it was very creepy of me."

But all Karen could think was *Of course! That's how he developed that insane spatial awareness!* She had just solved one of M's many mysteries.

"But eventually, that period of activity came to an end...," Goushi said sadly.

Miyu asked, "Um... Is this safe for a minor to hear? Kohi's still nineteen as of today."

"And your birthday is months away still, Miyu!" snapped Karen, breaking her silence at last.

"Oh, we don't need to worry about that. Please continue, Goushi."

"Okay. One evening, I was following her, gazing at her beautiful back and imagining myself being side by side with it..."

"Creepy! ...And?"

"I realized that a man was following her."

"What, like...you looked in a mirror?"

"No. This was definitely another man, one who had been at the coffee shop a few times as a customer. A handsome businessman in a suit."

"And?"

"Like always, I changed my route several times, always winding up back behind her, and by that time, it was clear—he was a stalker. I mean, *also* a stalker."

"And?"

At this point, Miyu's interjections were just minimal prompts to continue. Like her, Karen was ravenous for the juicy details.

"There was a point where her route passed by a little natural park. It was the quietest, loneliest part of her trip. Then the businessman jumped on her, holding her arms behind her and covering her mouth, dragging her into the park. At first, I was taken aback, then I felt a surge of absolute fury within me, and I remember rushing toward the spot where they vanished."

"A-and what happened?"

"The next thing I knew, I was lying down in the park, and she was tending to me."

"Ooooh!"

"Her beautiful face was right next to mine, and she was softly saying, 'Are you all right?' I thought I had died. I had to be in Heaven. But I was wrong. According to her, I suddenly rushed in screaming and started fighting with him—kind of. It wasn't real combat, just childish struggling. In the end, I just fell over; the man kicked me once, then ran off. I hurt all over, but none of it was really that bad, so I think I was lucky."

"Nice one! I mean, no, it wasn't! What happened next?"

"She said, 'You're the gentleman who comes to the café quite a lot, aren't you? My apartment is nearby, so come there with me. I need to tend to your injuries.'"

"Yowza! And?"

"My mind couldn't work properly at that point, so I followed her, believing it was all a dream. When I got inside her beautifully organized apartment, it smelled so nice, I could have died happy on the spot."

"That's so romantic," Miyu said dreamily. "And after that is when you two became…"

"After that was a total nightmare," Goushi said in the same matter-of-fact tone he'd been using all along. "The next thing I knew, my hands and feet were tied. My memory is a bit foggy, so I don't remember how things got there. It's all as vague as a movie I saw in my childhood at this point."

"..." "..."

"After that, she scolded me, insulted me, and struck me. She said things like 'You stalker!' and 'I knew you were doing this all along!' and 'I wish you and that other creep were dead!'"

"..." "..."

"I learned that she wasn't some sweet-hearted angel, but a horrifying demon harboring violent and destructive urges deep within her psyche. I was helpless. I bawled and wept all night. When she released me in the morning, she took embarrassing photos and said, 'If you tell the cops about any of this, I'll reveal all of your stalking behavior.'"

"..." "..."

"After that, I became her 'boyfriend.' If she called, I had to go to her, no matter how busy I was. I couldn't focus on getting a job, and I couldn't really take college classes, either. Eventually, I grew to love that life. What better calling could there be for a man than being at the side of a beautiful woman and serving her needs?"

"Um, have you sold the movie rights yet? Because I could direct this," said Miyu. Her talent for cracking a joke about anything was tremendous.

So this is how Pito and M came to be. I guess this means the M definitely doesn't stand for map, Karen thought, adopting the expression of some wise detective who'd just cracked the case.

"Wow, that's love for ya!" Miyu said happily.

"Yes. At the very least, there was love between us. And there still is."

"Eee! So did you lose all that weight for her?"

"Actually, I didn't really do anything by design... It just happened while I was working as the demon lord's henchman. When she called, I had to run to her side. She would force me to do stuff all night without any time for meals. Once I had lost a certain amount of weight, I tried to be mindful of my appearance so that I didn't embarrass her when we walked around together in public."

"We should write a book about this—*The Henchman Diet*! It'd be a bestseller!"

"Maybe…someday. At any rate, she and I lived together happily, if unconventionally. She made her dream come true, and I helped root her on. They were very fulfilling and successful times—until that day just over three years ago."

Karen finally spoke up. "You mean November 6th, 2022?"

"That's right."

Miyu glanced at Karen. "Ummm, what day was that?"

She answered, "The launch day for *Sword Art Online*."

"That's right!" In order to explain the situation, Karen had told Miyu that Pitohui had been an *SAO* beta tester and what had happened after that. "Ah yes, I see… I understand very well… It was a really fascinating story, in fact…," she said, nodding repeatedly.

Karen asked Goushi, "And did Pito want us to hear all about that stuff, too? That wasn't your decision?"

"This is by her request. She said, 'No secrets from Llenn!'"

"Okay…"

After they passed through a major junction, the traffic on the highway cleared up, and the car began to travel smoothly again. Goushi took the wheel and resumed driving the SUV himself. Through the windows, the forest of high-rises rushed past.

It took only a brief period of silence for Miyu to say "Sorry, napping" and promptly conk out, so Karen just watched the scenery out the window.

The car exited the highway and went back onto empty surface streets. Karen continued gazing out the window, deep in thought.

"…"

From time to time, Goushi looked at her profile through the rearview mirror.

"We'll be arriving soon. Please wake Miyu up," he requested. Karen prodded her accordingly.

It was 1:57 now. They'd been driving for nearly an hour, which seemed like a lot, even in this traffic.

"Oof. Where are we? Osaka? Kyoto?"

"No, we're still in Tokyo," Goushi replied. Indeed, they were smack in the middle of the capital, surrounded on all sides by towering buildings.

"Ugh, this is the problem with Tokyo! You go, like, one mile an hour!"

They were crawling through a packed shopping district, mingling with taxis.

"We're almost there. It's the building ahead on the right," he said. They craned their necks forward to look through the front windshield at a building about the size of a school gym, black and square, with almost no windows. It was very strange.

Miyu said, "There's two things that place could be—and only two: either the hideout of some shady organization or a music venue."

"Correct. You're very sharp, Miyu."

"Yes! So...it's a hideout?"

"No, a music venue."

"D'aww! That sucks, because I was hoping to go to this Elza Kanzaki concert today!" Miyu complained, flailing around in chagrin.

Elza Kanzaki's concert was today, somewhere in the city, and they had failed to win one of the exclusive tickets in the online lottery. And these were explicitly smartphone tickets attached to your ID, so there was no way to buy them secondhand, even if you had all the money in the world.

"That's perfect, then," Goushi said as he drove into the parking garage around the back. "This is where the Elza Kanzaki event is happening."

"Huh?" squawked Miyu.

"Goushi, are you saying…?" Karen started to ask.

He looked back at her. "That's right. Pito is the owner of this venue. She found Elza Kanzaki before anyone else and gave her the stage that made her famous."

"It's going to start at two o'clock. I'll have an employee escort you to the VIP area, where you can enjoy the show. There's no time right now, so you can meet with the president after that," Goushi said, then relayed his orders to a man in a suit who approached the car.

The man quietly ushered them into the employee entrance and gave them stickers to put on their clothes that marked them as guests. He sat them in the center of the front row in the upstairs part of the venue. They could see the entire stage perfectly without having to get up. It was literally the best seat in the house.

They commanded a view over nearly a thousand people below and sat between some very fancy men and women who clearly seemed to be big players in show business. Miyu was in a daze.

"Ummm… Okay, you've paid me back for the help," she murmured to Karen.

Karen smiled back, just before the lights went down.

The concert she'd been dreaming of was…well, like a dream.

Elza Kanzaki, the petite and demure black-haired beauty, was far, far more beautiful and delicate than the pictures and videos made her look. Her voice was more pleasant to listen to than anything she'd heard from her MP3 player.

* * *

When the show was over and the crowd started leaving, Goushi approached their seats.

"Please wait here for a little while. When the crowd has died down, I'll take you backstage. The president would like to meet you there. She says she'll introduce you to Elza Kanzaki, too," he added.

Miyu sank into her chair, eyes watery. "Kohi... I think I might just die from happiness..."

"I would agree with you—but there's still an important mission remaining, so it'll have to wait," Karen said firmly.

"Oh, right... We can't die until we meet Elza Kanzaki and declare our undying love for her..."

"That's your mission?"

"Was there something else?"

"Ha-ha-ha." Karen laughed. She turned an eagle eye to the stage below. Where the crew was now breaking down the instrument setup, there was practically an afterimage of the woman who'd just been singing there.

The crowd thinned out, and the people in the VIP area left for the lobby. When the girls were alone, Goushi told them, "They're gathering for a little meet and greet down there, but they'll have to wait. We're going straight backstage." He beckoned them on.

Miyu made a face that Karen had never seen on her before and said, "Okay, t-time to go... Just don't get...nervous... Okay?"

They followed Goushi down to the ground floor and past a sign that said NO GENERAL ADMITTANCE! There was a scary-looking fellow there who let Goushi pass once he recognized him.

"Perks of being the president's...," Miyu muttered, unsure whether to use the word *boyfriend* or *slave*, but in any case, he had weight around here.

After ten endless seconds down the hallway, the trio came to a stop before a dressing room door that said ELZA KANZAKI.

"This is it."

Before they had time to compose themselves, Goushi knocked.

"Come in!" said a woman's voice from inside, cheery and bold. Goushi pushed it open and motioned the girls inside.

"Excuse us," Karen said, bowing her head as she entered.

And then she saw the dressing room, about one hundred and fifty square feet, had only two women in it.

Seated about fifteen feet ahead of them, in the same simple skirt and T-shirt she wore for the encore, was Elza Kanzaki.

The other woman stood next to her. She looked to be in her mid to late thirties. She was tall for a Japanese woman, at five foot six, though not as tall as Karen, and her figure was full, with an ample chest and tight waist. Her long hair was dyed brown and tied in the back, and she wore accentuating makeup and a dazzling red suit-and-skirt combo. She looked bold and powerful, the instant image of a woman executive.

Goushi closed the door and introduced them to her. "This is the owner of the company that manages this music venue, Rei Satou."

The kanji for her given name meant *beautiful*, and it seemed appropriate. She turned to them, looking slightly tense, and in a voice clear and energetic, she said, "It's a pleasure to meet you! Now, which of you is Llenn and which of you is the grenadier? Wait—don't tell me! I want to guess."

She put a hand to her chin.

"…" "…"

Karen and Miyu looked at each other in silence.

"Hmm," Rei murmured.

Miyu just stared back. "…"

Karen glanced at Elza Kanzaki instead, who was being ignored. She took two steps toward the chair. Then…

Clap, clap, clap-clap-clap-clap-clap-clap-clap-clap-clap-clap.

She gave the little woman who stared up at her a round of applause.

"……"

Elza Kanzaki's gaze was a mixture of suspicion and possibly even fear as she received the enthusiastic greeting.

Clap-clap-clap-clap-clap-clap-clap-clap…

Miyu, Goushi, and Rei all watched her with deep concern.

"Your singing was absolutely incredible! I've been waiting for so, so long to give you the applause you deserve!" she practically shouted, she was so rapturous.

Clap-clap-clap-clap-clap-clap-clap...

"Um… Excuse me…," Elza Kanzaki stammered, overwhelmed by the six-foot-tall girl towering over her. She pulled back, but the table blocked her way.

Over all the applause, Miyu spoke up. "I'm sorry… My partner here kind of loses sight of what her priorities should be when she gets overly nervous…" She walked up to Karen, who was still excitedly clapping, and said, "C'mon, Kohi, you can do that later! You're doing this in the wrong order! First, you need to introduce yourself to Pito!"

She tried to pull her friend's arm. The applause abruptly stopped, and the dressing room was quiet until Karen's voice broke the silence.

"It was wonderful, just wonderful. Truly a wonderful rendition of 'Demon King'!"

This time, the resulting silence was broken by a woman's snort.

"*Bwah!* Bwa-ha-ha-haaaa-ha-ha-ha-ha-ha-ha-ha-ha-ha-ha-ha!"

Gales of laughter continued.

"Bwa-ha-ha-ha-haaa-ha-ha-ha-ha-ha-ha-ha-ha! Hee-hee-hee-ha-ha-ha-haaa-ha-ha-ha!"

Elza Kanzaki laughed and brayed with such force that you wondered where her little body stored this much power. She clutched her belly as she rocked in the chair, eyes filling with tears.

"Huh?" Miyu turned back to Goushi and Rei, looking for answers.

"Tee-hee?" said Rei, sticking out her tongue.

"…" Goushi just stared up at the ceiling.

And then she figured it out.

"Whaaat?!"

It was Elza Kanzaki, laughing at the top of her lungs, who was Pitohui.

* * *

"Bwa-ha-ha-ha-ha-ha-ha! Hee-heeee! Ah-ha-ha-haaa-ha-ha!" Elza cackled, kicking her feet in the air, like she'd eaten some kind of forbidden mushroom. If others could see her, she might have left the building in a straitjacket, the way she was carrying on.

"Ah-ha-ha-ha-ha-ha-ha-ha! Phew…"

After a full twenty seconds of laughing, she finally stopped.

"Your reason!" she demanded, without moving from her seat. She was speaking to the woman a foot taller than her: Karen.

"For a long time now, and also on the trip to get here, I've found one thing to be a bit strange," Karen answered.

"Oh? How so?"

"Well, as for what seemed weird today…"

"Yes?"

"I wondered why Goushi would have chosen to go on such a detour."

"Oh?" Elza said, craning her neck. "What do you mean?"

"It took nearly an hour to drive from my apartment to this venue. With the traffic, we made it just in time, so that the performance started just after we were shown to our seats."

"I'm glad you made it in time!"

"Yeah. But it seemed like it was intentional."

"How come?"

"Once Goushi took us off the highway, we went down a number of surface streets. We didn't repeat any of them, but I was watching the scenery out the window the whole time, so I could tell that he was making several unnecessary turns to eat up time. I could figure that out because of learning to read maps in *GGO*," Karen said.

Miyu snuck a look at Goushi, but he avoided her gaze. "Holy crap," she muttered.

Elza said, "Ahhh… And why do you think he got you here right in the nick of time?"

"I think it was to avoid getting here early and giving up the surprise. If we had time, we might've struck up a conversation with the special guests seated around us. It wasn't a guarantee, only a possibility, but he manipulated the time to ensure it couldn't happen. And then he told us we'd meet you backstage and introduced Rei to us as a dummy. So that you—Pito—could enjoy watching our reaction."

"Uh-huh… Is that all?"

"One more thing. There was something big that always weighed on my mind."

"And that is?"

"Goushi knew my address, real name, and my appearance. That was impossible."

"So I hear. He went straight to you to beg you to be in SJ2, correct?"

"I wondered for a long time how he could do such a thing… I never told him my name, address, or my height. I didn't tell you, or anyone in *GGO*. So it was very mysterious that Goushi would have access to that information. He didn't tell me why when I asked him, either."

"Mm-hmm. But why did that become a clue that helped you figure it out?"

"I finally recalled what the only possible reason could be. Because I wrote a postmarked letter to someone explaining that my name was Karen Kohiruimaki, and about my height complex, and how I was playing *GGO* with a shrimpy avatar to get over it."

"Oh?"

"I wrote it to you, Elza Kanzaki. I've never written a fan letter to anyone aside from you. And even if you didn't read it yourself, Goushi worked for your company and could have read it on his own. You're the president of the Elza Kanzaki Agency! If you had said Rei was the president of the agency, and not the live venue, I might have actually believed it."

"Dahhh! I got a bit lazy on that one…," Elza said, smacking her forehead.

Behind her, Rei added, "I was so ready to play along, too! Darn!"

"Sorry about that. I'll make it up to you later. Mentally speaking."

"As long as you keep singing at my place, I won't complain. And now I'll leave you young folks to it!" Rei waved a hand and turned to leave the room. Right before she shut the door, she added, "Oh, and your other guests are waiting, so don't be too long."

The door clicked shut, and Elza got to her feet.

"Well, I meant it to be one last gesture of resistance, but since you blew right through my cover, I guess there's no point hiding it." She met Karen's gaze with her own. "I kept my promise, Karen."

The next moment, Karen rushed for little Elza.

"Hrgh!" Buffeted and squished by the much larger girl, Elza briefly held her breath.

"I'm so glaaaaad! I'm so glad you didn't dieeeee!" wailed Karen.

"Because you killed me, that's why! Let go—you're hurting me. I'm dying over here."

"Oh! I'm sorry!" Karen said, pulling back in alarm.

Elza told her, "Hunch down—I can't see your face."

"Huh? Okay…"

Karen got down on a knee and lowered her tear-stained face to the same level as Eliza's. Elza put her hands up to it. "Yep, you're cute in real life, too! I like you!"

Then she put her lips on Karen's.

"Mmgh?!" Karen blinked again and again for the two seconds Elza stayed there before pulling away. "Mwaaah?"

Her face was as red as boiled octopus, and she tried to protest, but Elza just laughed.

"C'mon, it's not hurting anyone. Besides, I watched the SJ2 replay, and you totally kissed the guy who gave you the ammo

on the cheek! This is way more wholesome than that sordid transaction!"

"Th-that was a woman! And I was thanking her for giving me the ammo I needed to beat a c-c-certain someone!"

"Oh, so it's true? I thought those hips moved in a feminine way. I wonder why no one else noticed? Well, in that case, kisses with girls don't count, so you shouldn't mind it at all, right?" Elza said, kissing Karen again.

"Wha—?"

Over her shoulder, Goushi added, "I forgot to mention: She's a heartless vixen who will put the moves on men and women alike. You should be careful not to get too close to her."

"It's a little late for that, Goushi. Make that very late. Now my poor friend is eternally stained!" chirped Miyu.

"Fwah…" Karen gasped and fell to two knees this time. She swayed, her face feverishly red. Elza leaned in, her face angelic, and right next to Karen's ear whispered, "Oh, Karen… Do you mind if I come visit you next? We could even have a sleepover."

"No!" shouted Karen, red-faced. It was an instant response. "I'm not meeting you anywhere outside of *GGO* anymore!"

On an unspecified day of an unspecified month, two characters sat beside each other under the red sky of *GGO*, backs against a boulder in the midst of the burned, sandy wilderness.

One was dressed all in pink and was very short. Resting on her knees was a P90 painted pink.

The other was a pretty woman in a navy-blue bodysuit who had a figure like a cyborg. At her side was a KTR-09 assault rifle with a drum magazine attached.

"No kissing! If you do, you'll get a harassment warning, and I'll shoot you!"

"Fine, fine, no kissing. Why would I kiss anyone in *GGO* anyway? C'mon, let's just meet up IRL!"

"No thanks! Goushi was angry that you're playing around when you should be busy with your next show."

"What? Are you two e-mailing now? Tell you what, you can have him!"

"I don't want him! Take better care of your partner!"

"Oh, but I do. However, to use a well-known literary saying, 'This is this, and that is that.'"

"And *this* is the end of *that* topic!"

"Tch! Fine, then. I'm good with just spending time in *GGO* with you again, Llenn. Video games sure are fun, huh?"

"That's right. Games are meant to be enjoyed! They're not where you go to risk your life!"

"I said I was sorry. And I promise I won't do anything that stupid again. As long as I live, I'll enjoy myself in other ways."

"That's good to hear! On another topic…"

"Hmm?"

"You really are merciless when you fight, Pito. You're truly dedicated to doing whatever it takes to win."

"I guess so. But I didn't think that anyone would be better than me at that."

"Wow… Who's the fearsome opponent who would make you say something like that?"

"Huh?" Pitohui stared at her, eyes wide.

"Huh?" Llenn echoed back.

"…"

Pitohui appeared to be thinking of what to say when there was a muffled explosion on the other side of the rock.

"Got 'em!" "Got 'em!"

They leaped out from behind their cover, guns in hand.

The End

SPECIAL TEARJERKER EPIC II
I Fight with My Pride on the Line! II
~Let the Gunshot of My Soul Ring
Across the Town~

It was about ten minutes after the start of the second Squad Jam.

"Huff...huff..."

In the town on the west side of the windy map, a player heaved and panted, lying in the bed of an overturned truck. He had an unremarkable avatar with an unremarkable face and figure. He wore very typical woodland-camo fatigues beneath a vest with a number of pouches for ammo magazines.

Only his gun was nice, the expensive Swiss SIG SG 550 Sniper rifle. This was a custom sniper version of the SG 550 assault rifle. It had the best specs and highest price of any 5.56 mm gun.

"Huff...huff... Dammit... All my allies...have been wiped out..."

Up in the left corner of his vision, all five of his teammates were down to zero HP. And his was only at about 5 percent left, as the glowing bullet marks around his body made visually obvious. The next bullet that so much as grazed his skin would kill him.

The truck was in the middle of a large intersection, surrounded by similar abandoned vehicles. There were a whole lot of bodies behind this wreck. Over twenty, in fact.

"Ugh, why did this have to happen...?" he murmured, staring up at the cloudy sky.

Those who saw the previous Squad Jam probably remembered him.

He was the man who was shot by SHINC's sniper in the desert. In real life, he was a novelist in his fifties who spent all day writing books about gunfighting, and as some people knew, he was also the financial sponsor of the tournament.

Yes, he had sneakily entered his own sponsored event, and yet, not only did he not win, he didn't even place in the top five.

On top of that, when it was revealed that the *special prize* he sent out to the champions and runners-up was a signed set of his own books, it was...not warmly received online. He made the mistake of self-googling.

"Who wants that?!"

"Straight garbage."

"Nice stealth marketing."

"That doesn't even count as stealth marketing."

"Plus, they're individually addressed, so you can't even sell 'em!"

"It's cyberbullying!"

"Way to slander your heroes..."

The toll these comments had on his mental health was, suffice to say, draining.

But instead, he chose revenge! He abandoned his writing job to work on his *GGO* skills, determined to win the next time around. He was going to show them all. He'd get back at them with an obnoxious "Hey, I run this event, and I also won—with pure skill and no cheating! Whoopsie! Tee-hee!"

So he took up arms with comrades who were aware of this unfortunate personality flaw of his, and he delved into *GGO* like never before. He was so unreachable in real life that his book editor actually had to create a *GGO* account to get in contact and demand his latest manuscript directly—but at least his character was tougher than before.

And just when he had pumped himself up ("Hell yeah, I'm gonna go sponsor the second round!"), some other jerk completely blew up his spot and sponsored it first. Furthermore, the new sponsor offered prizes that were way more popular with the audience.

"Arrrgh! This sucks! This sucks!"

He nearly had an aneurysm. He threw himself on the floor and flopped around. But he was not the kind of cool competitor who could admit defeat and walk away. He decided to enter SJ2 in order to steal the grand prize, and indeed, he did pass through the preliminary round with ease.

Now it was a few dozen minutes into the main event. His team had a strategy. The "Let's run away from danger and then swoop in at the last moment to snatch victory away!" strategy. It was a pathetic strategy, but at least it was a strategy.

So they headed into the first Satellite Scan intending to flee from trouble, but...

Why did this have to happen?

Instead, other teams fled toward them into the neighborhood area to escape the powerful LF and SHINC. It turned into a giant, chaotic fracas with many squads involved.

Bullets assaulted them from behind vehicles and buildings, giving no indication of who was friend or foe. Grenades clattered past. In just minutes, the battle was over, and silence returned abruptly.

He had shot a number of enemies but suffered great damage himself. He was lucky to be alive, in fact.

Rustle, rustle, thump.

Something moved on the other side of the truck. Without any of his teammates alive, anything that was moving in this world was inevitably an enemy on one team or another.

Awww... Guess I'm not...getting that prize...

He closed his eyes and reflected on his life.

In the span of two seconds, he thought of the very first BB gun he ever had, the sensation of the first time he shot a real gun overseas, the shotgun he bought with his book royalties, and the fun he had playing *GGO*. Lastly, he remembered the look on the faces of the girls in his eighth-grade homeroom when he brought an air gun in and showed it off—a look that said, *Ew, what's wrong with him? Is he a kid? Grow up.*

Rustle, rustle. Thump.

The sound of something scraping on the ground was closer and louder now. Whatever it was, it was probably approaching from the other side of the truck. At this point, even his fancy sniper rifle wasn't much use. He'd dropped his pistol when it was hit by a stray bullet in the big battle, and he didn't know where it was now.

Guess I'll just give up and die!

There was no point in struggling any longer. He might as well go out with a bang. Was there any reason to do otherwise? No, there wasn't.

With that thought, he laid the SG 550 Sniper on the ground. Then he removed two plasma grenades, the only other weapons he had left, and held them in each hand.

Farewell, he said in silence to his favorite gun.

Click.

"Yaaaaaaah!"

He hit the buttons for both plasma grenades and emerged from behind the truck, bellowing with his last breath.

Then he saw the battlefield littered with corpses and someone's gun dangling from the side of the truck, scraping the ground as the breeze blew it.

Oh! There are no enemies! I'm the only one who survived! Yahoo! I'm still in it! I might even be able to set up from a distance and snipe my way to victory! he thought to himself in triumph.

He celebrated right up until the moment the plasma grenades, which he had forgotten about, exploded, enveloping him in the blast.

The End

WARNING
Important notice from the author:
The commentary starting on the next
page contains spoilers about
the firearms in this book.

Sword Art Online Alternative GUN GALE ONLINE

A GUN PRIMER

An explanation from *Sword Art Online Alternative Gun Gale Online* author Keiichi Sigsawa about the guns that play a major role in the story, accompanied by profile illustrations of each one!

Illustrations: Kouji Akimoto

PROFILE

I had the pleasure of drawing the design for "The Flute," one of Kino's guns in Keiichi Sigsawa's *Kino's Journey* series. I love drawing finely detailed mechanical designs with an analog G-pen. I also draw manga sometimes and build bicycles.

COMMENT

I'm very happy and grateful to get the chance to take part in this book with Kawahara, Sigsawa, and Kuroboshi. This was a lot of fun to do. Please keep in mind that all the guns depicted here are as they exist in the Sigsawa World, so save your complaints about the fine details, please. (*sweats*)

P90

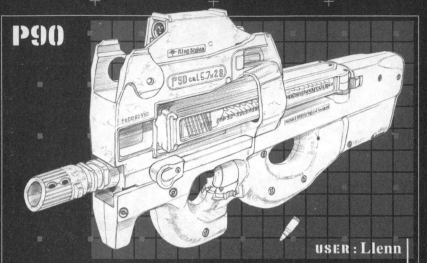

USER : Llenn

At first, this creatively designed gun looks like a spaceship, but once you get a little closer, it really looks like a spaceship. The bullets are contained in the magazine in parallel and turn ninety degrees as they enter the chamber. Sadly, our main character's gun seems to get trashed consistently.

MGL-140

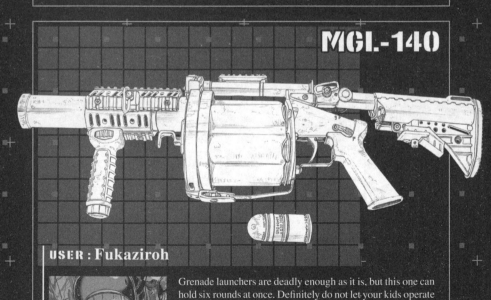

USER : Fukaziroh

Grenade launchers are deadly enough as it is, but this one can hold six rounds at once. Definitely do not let your kids operate this gun. The beauty of its design is in the eye of the beholder. Needless to say, this behemoth is not the kind of gun you dual-wield with one in each hand.

GUN EXPLANATIONS by KEIICHI SIGSAWA

M14 EBR

A gun customized so far from its M14 base that it's like one of those people who get so much plastic surgery, they turn into someone else entirely. Given that it's the result of focusing on sheer function and performance, I think you could call it a kind of beauty all on its own.

KTR-09

An American custom model of the AK series. It still uses the same basic frame but with the stock of the rival M16—a kind of melding of East and West. Perhaps this gun itself is a message that the Cold War was long in the past.

VINTOREZ

USER : Boss (Eva)

A silent sniper rifle that can also fire on full auto, if the user wishes. This Russian transformer will give you a real scare. It looks like the Dragunov, but there's also a kind of lamely comical air about it. But it's scary. It doesn't make any sound, and that's terrifying.

DRAGUNOV

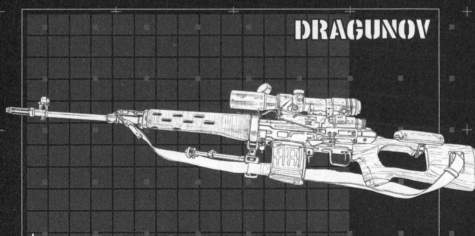

USERS : Tohma and Anna

It's the Russian repeating sniper rifle that every gun-obsessed teenage nerd dreams of at that stage of their life. The thin barrel is stylish, and so is the name. How much cooler would my life have been if I'd carried this to school on my back? What do you mean, I'd get arrested?

GUN EXPLANATIONS by **KEIICHI SIGSAWA**

PKM

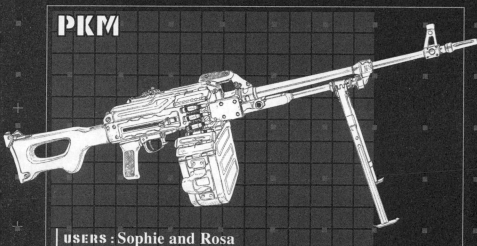

USERS : Sophie and Rosa

A masterpiece machine gun designed by Kalashnikov, creator of the AK. I think it's awesome, and it never gets used in stories, so I put it in mine. Just in case you find one in the street, remember that the ammo belt feeds into the right side, rather than the left side like usual.

BIZON

USER : Tanya

A Russian submachine gun with a distinctive cylindrical magazine that loads bullets like a spiral staircase. Are all Russian guns freakish or what? I can't get enough of the ugly, sluggish design. It's better with the silencer.

M107A1

USERS : Pitohui and M

Barrett's masterpiece gun, which is practically synonymous with antimateriel rifles. Size matters! The enlarged tube at the end of the barrel is a silencer, but apparently, the gun makes a ton of noise even with it on. It's in all the movies. Pitohui's a star!

PTRD-41

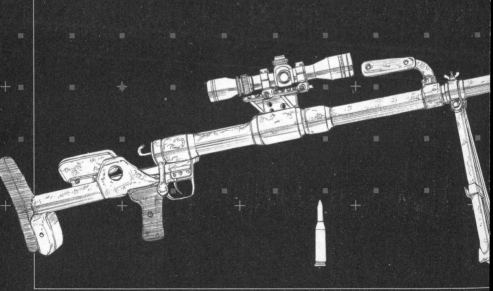

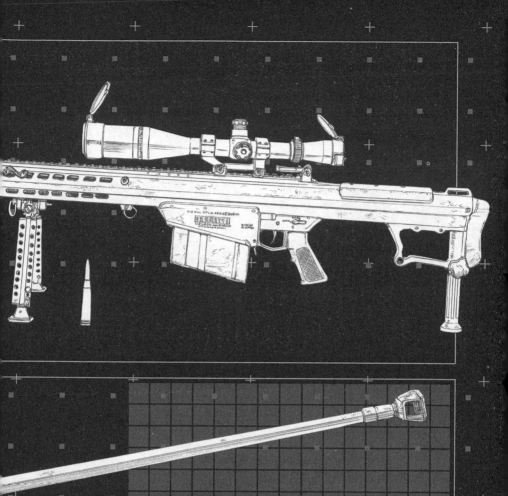

USER : Tohma

A long, long, very long gun. When you see pictures of infantry marching with these things, they look like medieval lancers. You could probably fight pretty well just spearing enemies with it. It's a World War II gun, but the ammunition is still made to specification for heavy guns today, so you could potentially fire one of them.

AR-57

USER : Clarence

A real freak of a gun that uses the P90 system, with the popular American AR-15 (i.e., M16) lower part attached. Why did they think of this? Why did they do it? You can't get hung up on the little questions. The empty cartridges fall out of the original magazine slot.

TYPE 89

USER : Commentary Player

No Image

It's a local Japanese gun and one that you cannot use unless you're a professional, like a member of the Self-Defense Force or Maritime SDF. If only they'd export it so I could shoot it in America! This one has a folding stock, which makes it easier to transport. It might even fit inside your book bag.

R93 TACTICAL. 2

USER : Shirley

A high-powered German sniper rifle. The basic construction is the same as the hunting rifle model, but the sniper edition has a very angular stock design. The grip goes vertical, and the user can adjust where to position their shoulder and cheek. If you used this to shoot deer, you might stick out.

ITHACA M37

USER : Player Who Fought Llenn

A very excellent shotgun. Ithaca is the name of a city in New York State, though writing it out in Japanese makes it look like the gun might've been created by a guy named Isaka. This will appear on the exam. By the way, the upper tube is the barrel, and the lower tube is the magazine.

No Image

Hello! This is Kouhaku Kuroboshi.

I tackled this book's illustrations hoping to keep up with Llenn and her high-speed battle style. I feel like I'm in good physical condition when I draw GGO. I guess it's because I draw with a lot of momentum. Even if it gives me that forty-something shoulder pain...